HOT FOR TEACHER

EXTRA CREDIT
BOOK 2

GRAE BRYAN

Content warnings: age gap; imbalanced power dynamic (student x professor); elements of consensual BDSM (dom/sub dynamics, forced orgasms, spanking, praise kink); parental neglect (past/childhood and present)

PROLOGUE

Chase

Chase sat on the stiff leather couch, hunched uncomfortably over his test paper, trying to will his brain to concentrate for just another five minutes.

He'd been offered a spot at the desk, but that would have been ... too much. Too close.

The uncomfortable couch was safer.

Or at least, Chase had thought so. He'd almost finished his makeup exam—had managed to focus in the small, contained space of Professor Burke's office, had managed to block his brain off to the pheromones so overpowering that even he, as a beta, sometimes found them distracting—but then Professor Burke had taken a call, and it had all gone out the window.

He had a really nice voice.

It was this sort of smooth, deep rumble. Chase liked it. He liked the way Professor Burke used it even more. He was always giving these clear, concise instructions and letting all his students know, just as clearly, whether he was pleased or displeased with how they'd chosen to follow them.

Some students hated it. They thought he was too intimidating, and when they slacked off and faced the consequences, they found his displeasure too intense, especially when his pheromones came into play. His student reviews always mentioned how scary he was, more so than the average alpha.

But Chase liked him. He liked Professor Burke and his voice the same way he liked math, the same way he liked Professor Burke's statistics class. So much of life had too much ambiguity. There was always some amount of guesswork, always ways to do better, to work harder. With Chase's old lacrosse coaches, it had always been, "That's a good play, *but—*"

Always a "but." Always room for Chase to be faster, stronger, better coordinated. Always a way he was letting someone down.

But with math ... with statistics ... There was always a right answer, wasn't there? No guesswork, no ambiguity. Only red marks on a page, with a score at the end. Good or bad, it was easy to figure out.

Chase peered out from under his lashes as he finally filled out his last answer. Professor Burke was at his desk—a massive oak thing that they had to have built inside the room, since there was no way it had fit through the door—murmuring quietly into his phone. He was facing the wall, his stern profile made sterner by his furrowed brow, a lock of dark hair falling over one eye.

He was handsome, wasn't he? In an unapproachable sort of way. His student reviews liked to mention that too. Hot but too imposing for it to matter.

He looks like he'd talk you through it, but you wouldn't like what he had to say, one particularly inappropriate review had said.

It took Chase a second longer than it should have to realize they were now sitting in silence. Professor Burke was no longer speaking into his phone, and his dark-blue gaze was focused right on Chase.

Chase moved his eyes back to his paper immediately.

Professor Burke cleared his throat. Not like he was nervous—never that—but more like a warning. Like he was preparing Chase for that smooth voice, maybe. "Apologies, Mr. Adler. I'm afraid I had to take that. Should I extend your time?"

Chase shook his head, rising from his seat with his exam paper in hand. "No, sir. I'm finished."

"Hand it here."

Chase walked over to the desk, handing his paper to Professor Burke. He widened his eyes in surprise when Professor Burke took out one of his red pens, scanning the paper.

He's going to grade it right this second?

Chase had been just as surprised when Professor Burke had told Chase he'd be taking his makeup final in Professor Burke's office, during his office hours. He'd said he didn't have a TA to spare, and that his hours would be free. He'd claimed no students would be coming to see him so soon after the final exam.

Maybe Chase made some sort of noise, because Burke paused, cocking a brow. "Somewhere to be, Mr. Adler?"

Chase shook his head. "No, sir."

It always paid to be polite with Burke. He didn't insist upon formalities, but he clearly preferred them.

Chase had been paying attention. Possibly too close attention.

"Good." The word of approval was clipped and short, but that didn't stop it from sending a little tingle of warmth through Chase.

Good.

Burke marked Chase's exam quickly—as skilled at speed-reading as he was at everything else—and then handed it over.

Ninety-two percent.

"Nice work, Mr. Adler."

Another tingle of warmth went through Chase, and he grabbed his paper, his cheeks hot. "Thank you, sir."

Burke held on to the test for a moment, leaving both their hands suspended over the desk, their fingers a hairbreadth away from touching. "You've been one of my top students this semester, did you know that?"

Chase shook his head.

"Even though you never once raised your hand."

Chase didn't know what to say to that, so he said nothing.

Burke released his hold on the exam.

Chase tucked it against his chest, and then they were both silent. Chase should thank him again, tuck his paper away, and leave. But he stood here, waiting. He didn't even know what he was waiting for. Something more, maybe. Something like that clipped "good" only ... better.

He was standing, and Burke—*Professor* Burke—was seated. It should make him less intimidating, but it didn't. Not at all. Chase was hyperaware of the size of him. His height. The breadth of his shoulders. All Chase's own muscles, hard-earned from years of sports, seemed somehow inconsequential in comparison.

After a long moment, Professor Burke's gaze ... changed. His lids lowered, and his eyes darkened. They were already a deep sort of blue, and now they looked practically black. The heavy pheromones in the room deepened—sweetened—and Chase's heartbeat sped up.

Professor Burke knew what Chase was waiting for, didn't he?

It relaxed something in Chase, even as his heart raced like crazy in his chest. Professor Burke would tell Chase what he was waiting for. Chase only had to wait a little longer.

But in the next breath, the moment passed. Professor Burke sat back in his chair, letting out a slow exhale. The pheromones in the room went back to normal—maybe Chase had imagined that they'd changed at all. "You're free to go, Mr. Adler."

It wasn't a suggestion.

Chase nodded his thanks, unable to muster the words. He walked out of the office, test still in hand, not sure why he felt so strangely bereft. Whatever he'd been waiting for from Burke, he wasn't going to get it. That was their final exam he'd just completed. The class was over.

It was time to push the imposing alpha professor firmly out of his mind.

But still, as he made his way out of the mathematics building, Chase couldn't help sniffing at his sweatshirt.

He smelled like leather. Leather and sweet cherries.

1

Chase

Hair still damp from his shower, Chase came out of his bedroom to hear his roommates arguing in the kitchen.

Or more like Spencer was nagging and Noah wasn't being quite as forgiving as usual.

It wasn't totally unheard of—stick two alphas and a beta in close quarters for the school year and sometimes tempers were going to rise, no matter how much they loved one another—but it was rare for it to be at this level before the semester even began.

Chase reached up to adjust a baseball cap he wasn't wearing, then dropped his arm. Time to play peacekeeper, he supposed.

"C'mon," he could hear Spencer saying. "You make 'em the best."

"Dude. They're scrambled fucking eggs. How do I make them better than anyone else?"

Chase shuffled into the kitchen of their three-bedroom apartment—paid for oh so generously by his parents, not that they'd ever set foot inside the place—and found the two alphas in question facing off over a frying pan. They were dressed similarly, in sweats and T-shirts, but otherwise they were as different as two alphas could be, other than them both being annoyingly hot.

Spencer, tall and lean, had his dark hair artfully tousled in a way that was pretending to be haphazard but most definitely wasn't (Chase knew for a fact the guy used at least three different hair products). He was making an outraged face that just barely flashed his tongue piercing.

Noah, just as tall as Spencer but built more broadly, with loose blond curls that actually *were* haphazard and a surfer's tan to match (not that he got any surfing done in Arizona), was scowling, which was rare for the upbeat alpha, but he'd been in a pissy mood since he'd been blown off by the mystery omega he'd lost his virginity to over winter break.

"Chase!" Spencer greeted with more enthusiasm than the moment warranted, waving the frying pan in the air. "Tell Noah he should make us eggs. It's the first day of the semester. We have to eat breakfast together."

"You don't have to make them," Chase told Noah, ignoring Spence's squawk of outrage.

He had to have known Chase wasn't going to join in on the peer pressure party.

Noah's scowl dropped in an instant, and he sighed, taking the pan from Spencer. "I'll do it." He bumped shoulders with the other alpha. "Sorry, man. Woke up on the wrong side of the bed."

Pathologically incapable of holding a grudge, Spencer just shrugged, coming over to Chase and throwing an arm around his shoulder, casually scent marking him as he did.

Spencer was always doing that—scent marking them—something to do with never getting enough of it from his family growing up. Neither Noah nor Chase minded. Noah probably because he came from a big-ass family and missed getting scent marked by his siblings. And Chase because he understood the urge—and where it came from—all too well. Better than he'd ever told either of his roommates, that was for sure.

So Chase just tilted his head, giving Spencer better access to his scent glands as Noah took out eggs from their communal fridge.

"Chase, you want toast?" Noah asked. They both knew Spencer wouldn't—he kept himself on a strict regimen to keep his physique exactly the way he wanted it. More hang-ups from a scrawny, underfed childhood, and neither of them pushed him on it.

"If you're having some."

Noah nodded, tossing some slices of bread into the toaster. He wasn't scowling anymore, but he didn't exactly look happy either. Which was a shame because Noah had the kind of wide, face-changing smile that could cut through anyone's defenses. When the three of them had met during freshmen orientation, almost three years ago now, Chase had harbored a little bit of a crush on him. He was pretty sure Spencer had too. It was hard not to with Noah. He was confident, kind, and gorgeous.

They'd both gotten over it a long time ago though. It was just a rite of passage everyone had to go through, having an unrequited crush on Noah Teller.

And the one he's finally fallen for won't even text him. Figures.

Chase could only hope Spencer wouldn't poke the bear any more than he already had this morning. Chase wasn't, like, super-stitious or anything, but he figured it didn't hurt to start the new semester on the right foot. Make sure things started off calm and cool and with everyone happy with everybody else.

But that was just the way he was, liking things even-keeled. Of the three of them, Noah was effortlessly charming, Spencer was alluring almost in spite of himself, and Chase ...

Chase wasn't sure what he offered, actually. A little bit of quiet, maybe. A willingness to hang in the middle and not pick sides. He'd used to blame his more subdued nature on being busy with sports, but he'd quit lacrosse last year and he wasn't any rowdier now.

Chase wasn't insecure about it or anything—he knew their friendship was legit. But he wasn't loud and out there like his friends could be. He was aware he was decent-looking, but he didn't catch the eye in an instant the way Noah or Spencer did. He didn't make as much sense in their trio, at least on a surface level.

It worked, though, the three of them. The other two seemed to like that Chase was chill. They didn't ignore him just because he wasn't always the life of the party. Hell, Spencer could barely leave either Chase or Noah alone on a good day.

At least, having gotten his scrambled-egg wish, Spencer seemed to have mellowed now. He'd given up taunting Noah and was just resting his head on Chase's shoulder, watching Noah comply with his request.

Chase gave him a pat and then shrugged out of his friend's hold, heading to the fridge and pouring out two glasses of orange juice for him and Noah and a glass of milk for Spencer, which Spencer immediately started adding a hideous amount of protein powder to.

It wasn't long before Noah started dishing out eggs. Spencer dragged Chase to the table, yelling out, "Extra cheese on mine!"

Chase had no idea why Spencer could have cheese but not bread, but Noah didn't bat an eye, tossing some more shredded cheese on Spencer's plate of eggs, his initial reluctance to make them breakfast clearly long gone.

This was what the three of them did, ever since they'd started living together last year. Ever since they'd met, really. They took care of each other in little ways. It was nice, kind of pack-like in a way that was soothing to their instincts. Initial crush aside, Chase loved these two like brothers now. He was grateful to have met them.

So after cheersing their drinks, Chase dug into his eggs with gusto, ignoring that little nagging feeling that asked, *Then why doesn't it feel like enough?*

———

AN HOUR LATER, Chase and Noah had said goodbye to Spencer (or their version of it, wherein Spencer had pinched Chase's cheek like he was a little baby and Chase had unsuccessfully attempted to punch him for it) and were on their way to Omega Studies.

It was a fucking gorgeous morning, sunny and mild in the way only Arizona could be in the beginning of January. The winter weather almost made up for the summer heat. Not that Chase would know the full scope of that—he'd been going to his parents' lake house in Minnesota every summer since he was a baby. But apparently he was about to have his knowledge of Phoenix in the summer drastically expanded, as his parents had informed him over Christmas that they'd be traveling this year, and he was expected to stay where he was.

"We can't be paying for a fully staffed house just so you can run around underfoot and get in their way all summer," his mother had told him. "You understand, hm?"

So, anyway, Chase supposed he'd find out the extent of his heat tolerance real quick. Luckily, Noah and Spencer were sticking around this year too. They could suffer together, and they had a whole glorious semester to anticipate the pain.

As they walked across the quad toward their lecture hall, Chase caught Noah looking at his phone for the hundredth time. "Still no text?" Chase asked.

"Maybe—maybe I wasn't any good," Noah mumbled, morose as shit.

His night with the mysterious omega had been Noah's first time. Crushes on him may have abounded, but he'd never reciprocated—not until now. Still, Chase highly fucking doubted that bad sex was the issue. Lack of skill was one thing, but truly bad sex usually required either malice or obliviousness, and Noah didn't have much of either.

What he did have, however, was the power to emit some world-class horny pheromones.

As a beta, pheromones were more muted to Chase than to an alpha or an omega, but he could still smell them. And he could *really* smell these.

"Dude," he warned.

"What?" Noah asked, still staring at his phone.

Maybe he *was* a little oblivious. Sometimes.

"Are you—" *Looking to fuck the next passing omega*, Chase almost said, then coughed, wrinkling his nose. "Your pheromones, man."

"Oh fuck." In an instant, the rich, salty scent that had been screaming, *Sex now, please!* settled down into a more neutral aroma. "Sorry."

"No worries." Chase coughed again before he could help it. "I can barely smell it," he lied. "Just thought you might not want to rock up to the lecture hall putting out sex signals for all to scent."

Noah shoved his phone back into his pocket, clearly annoyed with himself. "What's *wrong* with me?"

Chase shrugged. "You've got a crush." He switched the brim of his cap backward, wanting the full force of the morning sun on his face. He was suddenly feeling pretty good. He may have been drifting a bit this year (or possibly ever since he'd quit lacrosse the year before), but at least he wasn't dealing with unrequited love. Or lust, as it may be. "Happens to the best of us."

"Doesn't happen to you."

Fully smug now, Chase just grinned, looking over his shoulder at Noah as they walked. "That's because I'm—*oof!*"

He'd hit a wall. A brick wall. That was what it felt like, at least.

What it *looked* like, though, was that Professor Burke was standing in front of him, all tall and broad and imposing, and Chase had run straight into him like a complete asshole, knocking half the professor's printed handouts onto the ground.

That was what it looked like.

Chase stood there, frozen. He should be apologizing already, shouldn't he? Apologizing *profusely*. But he was stuck in place.

He'd succeeded, more or less, in putting Burke out of his mind over the break. Mostly. Sort of.

Chase *might* have paid a little too close attention to certain rumors about a bar Burke frequented and its proximity to a certain kink club. He might have wondered about why *that* bar next to *that* specific club. He might have thought a little bit about who Burke went home to—or home with.

But that was just ... random speculation. An ear to the ground sort of thing. The guy was interesting. And ... here. Right now. In front of Chase.

He looked fucking good, too, which was supremely unfair. Burke was wearing dark slacks and a tightly fitted button-down, the sleeves rolled up to show strong forearms, all tanned and olive-skinned. He kept his dark hair longer on top, and it fell forward in a way that was unexpectedly rakish for such a strait-laced professor.

Not that Chase usually went around calling people "rakish" on the daily, but he'd taken a class on Regency-era literature last semester, and some things had stuck.

So fuck it. Burke's hair was ... rakish.

And also he was staring at Chase. *Glaring.*

Luckily for Chase's untimely paralysis, Noah stepped forward just then, leaning over to grab the lost papers. "Sorry, man. I'll grab—"

Leather. Dark and rich, without even a hint of sweet cherry.

Noah stopped mid-motion, halfway bent over, frozen in place by the power of Professor Burke's pheromones.

For some reason, that broke Chase's own immobility. Burke's pheromones were intense, but Chase didn't have Noah's reaction to them. He liked them. They smelled ... good. Masculine and rich and kind of comforting in their intensity.

Sexy as fuck.

Chase pushed the unwelcome thought aside and knelt, grabbing the papers he'd knocked out of Burke's hands. "Here you are, sir."

A dark-blue gaze locked onto his, and Chase had a new appreciation for the term *steely-eyed*. "There's a good boy," Burke murmured, so softly Chase almost missed it.

And just like that, Chase went hot. All fucking over. His throat dried up, and his heart started racing like he'd sprinted halfway around the quad in the last five seconds.

There's a good boy.

Fuck. Why did Chase like that so much? It was kind of condescending, wasn't it? He was fully grown—he wasn't a boy at all, no matter how much older Burke was.

But Chase did like it. A whole fucking lot.

Whether Burke knew the effect his words had just had on Chase, it was impossible to say. He only nodded, not a hint of emotion in his expression. "Carry on, then."

And then he walked away.

"Who the fuck was that?"

Noah's question knocked Chase out of his fog, although he couldn't tear his eyes away from Burke's retreating back. Chase was no delicate flower, but he wasn't built like *that*.

"Professor Burke," he managed to say. "He teaches statistics. I had him last semester."

"How the fuck did you survive?" Noah gave an exaggerated shiver. "He's terrifying."

Chase shrugged. *Terrifying* wasn't the word he'd use—unless terror made Noah's dick hard—but he kept that to himself. "If you're polite, he's actually pretty chill."

"His pheromones are ..." Noah let out a slow, deliberate exhale. "Just be glad you're a beta."

"Yeah." Chase laughed, although the sound came out a little off. Because the thing was, if he'd been an omega, he would have been fucking *soaked*. The whole quad would have been able to smell his slick.

Probably not what Noah meant.

Chase tugged Noah's arm, leading him in the direction of their class, hoping his face wasn't as red as it felt. "Sure."

If nothing else, being a beta let Chase keep his secrets close.

Even if he wasn't exactly sure what those secrets were.

But as they walked into class, Professor Burke's quiet words kept playing in Chase's head.

There's a good boy.

2

Killian

"All right, Killian. I have a question, and you need to answer with complete honesty."

Killian took a sip of his whiskey, arching a brow at Devon, a hopelessly arrogant blond alpha and one of the few people Killian would call a close friend. "I'm listening."

"Did the bartender piss in your whiskey?"

Killian took another sip of his drink, letting the smoky flavor roll across his tongue. He pretended to think it over. "Not to my knowledge."

"Then what, exactly, is your problem? Your face is scaring away all the pretty omegas. And betas. And alphas, for that matter."

Killian looked pointedly around the mostly deserted bar. It was still early on a Thursday night, and they were some of only a few patrons. Only one was someone Killian recognized from the club he and Devon both frequented, and he knew for a fact that Devon wasn't interested in that particular omega.

Devon sighed, leaning back in his chair and loosening his tie.

He had a penchant for dressing up in suits and then mussing himself up in a way that made him seem more approachable than he actually was. It was his way of luring his omega subs into a false sense of security before he pulled the rug out from under them. "Let's go across the street."

"I told you I'm not interested tonight."

"You're always interested."

Killian shrugged, running a hand through his hair. That was usually true enough. He had a high sex drive, even for an alpha, and the club across the street had always catered to his ... specific interests well enough. Until recently, at least.

"What's the deal?" Devon asked, echoing Killian's thoughts. "Tired of taking control in the bedroom?" His face screwed up in a look of false sympathy. "Need to be under someone else's strong hand for a change?"

Killian scoffed, flicking his coaster at his annoying friend. "Hardly."

"Well, I hate hunting alone. Should I be looking for someone else to drag here on my free nights?"

It felt like defeat to admit it, but Killian wasn't interested in being whined at by Devon every evening either. So perhaps he *would* take a break. From the club, at least—not from going out altogether.

Killian refused to become one of those shut-in professors who only ever shuttled between their homes and the university.

"Maybe you should start with calling Prince for a bit," Killian told Devon after a moment, naming the absent third of their trio.

Devon nodded, not pressing any further. Perhaps Killian should be grateful—if it had been any of Devon's subs, he would have been relentless. He didn't like not being in the know.

Not that there was anything to know. The scene here had just gotten ... small. Killian had dallied already with most of the suitable omegas who'd caught his eye, and none of them had held his interest long enough to consider a more permanent arrangement. And he wasn't interested in participating in scenes at the club otherwise. He was into more ... private scenarios. Killian wasn't flashy like Devon, or even the way Prince could be when he got his hackles up.

Devon tossed back the rest of his drink and pushed away from the bar. "You won't mind if I desert you, then?"

Killian waved a hand. "By all means."

Devon started to turn away, then stopped. "I'd be careful, you know," he told Killian, slapping a hand on his shoulder. "You're already a cold fish. I'm afraid without certain outlets, you might become a frozen one."

Killian smirked, brushing Devon's hand away. "Have you been keeping that little comment in your pocket just for me?"

"I have. How did you like it?"

"Tame to the point of ineffectual," Killian surmised.

Devon pointed a finger. "See? Cold. You could at least have gotten angry."

Except Killian didn't *get* angry. Annoyed, sometimes. Angry, almost never. He didn't find most things worth the energy it required. He supposed there was some irony there, seeing as how the student review sites always commented on how frightening he was. But Killian never raised his voice, never lost his temper.

He simply had heavy pheromones and a resting asshole face.

"Anyway, tootles," Devon said, turning on his heel with a mocking salute. "Maybe you'll get lucky and find what you're looking for here."

"Doubtful," Killian murmured when his friend was too far off to hear.

Mostly because Killian wasn't looking for anything. That was the problem, wasn't it? That nothing and no one was catching his eye.

Green eyes. Pink lips. A cap pulled low over an absurdly pretty face.

Killian slammed back the rest of his whiskey, signaling the bartender for another. *That* image was something he shouldn't be thinking of at all, and definitely not in this context.

The beta.

Killian had indulged in that weakness too many times already. Twice too many, to be exact.

The first mistake had been holding the makeup exam in his private office.

Killian didn't hold makeup exams himself. He had TAs for that sort of thing. And he certainly didn't grade them right there on the spot.

But he hadn't meant anything by it at the time. His TAs had been busy with the end of the semester, and he'd had his required office hours free and open. And Killian had been ... mildly curious. He'd noticed the close way his beta student watched him during lectures—not warily, like the other students, but with some sort of inscrutable intent—and Killian had wanted to see what his star student of the semester would do in a closed room with Killian's pheromones.

Sadistic of him? Possibly. He'd known what the likely outcome was—other than the occasional omega, most people were uncomfortable with his scent in close quarters, even betas.

If Mr. Adler had balked, Killian would have been all understanding smiles and words of encouragement, scheduling the beta's exam for an alternate time with a TA. That would have been that. Curiosity assuaged, with the added bonus of reminding Mr. Adler that Killian was not a suitable professor for any sort of undergraduate crush.

But Mr. Adler had instead settled on Killian's office couch with a quiet, contented sigh, getting to his work right away, as if Killian's pheromones were soothing rather than suffocating. He'd completed his test with focused efficiency. And when Killian had graded that test on the spot—curious to see if Mr. Adler's scores matched Killian's standards—and handed it back to him, Chase Adler had stood there, staring. Waiting for ... something.

The odd moment had stuck in Killian's mind. Like a pebble in his shoe, setting him off-kilter when he least suspected it. Forming the tiniest crack in his rock-solid foundation.

Which was the only way to explain this past Monday, when Killian had slipped and called Chase—Mr. Adler—a good boy. And the beta student had looked at him like Killian had just opened a portal to another world.

If the smallest little phrase could do that to him, what would it be like to—

No. Fuck no.

Killian did *not* lust after undergrad students. Not even former ones. He may not have reached forty yet, but they had still always seemed like toddlers to him. Rowdy and undisciplined and more interested in smearing each other with pheromones than solving a simple statistics problem.

Except the beta hadn't been like that at all. He was ever so polite. Ever so punctual. Always saying "sir," even now, when he was no longer Killian's student. It wasn't even Killian's preferred title—not in the bedroom—but it still did something to him. His cock was starting to fill just thinking about it.

Fuck that. Time to go home.

Killian left the rest of his drink on the bar, along with his payment and a large tip. He mentally reversed his decision for momentary abstinence.

Killian would come back tomorrow, in a better state of mind, and find himself someone, no matter whether they were in the scene or not. He'd take that someone home, and he'd fuck Chase Adler's sweet, polite, "Here you are, sir," right out of his mind.

Chase Adler would not be a problem.

Killian would make sure of it.

THAT HAD BEEN THE PLAN, anyway.

A plan that had gone completely awry just about a minute ago, when Killian had shown up to his favorite bar to find Chase Adler sitting at the end of it.

Now Killian was standing just inside the doorway. He'd clocked the boy immediately—recognized him from the back of his goddamn head. Chase was wearing his ever-present baseball cap, but Killian already knew that underneath it he'd find straight dirty-blond hair—the kind that couldn't decide if it was blond or brunet—parted in the middle and just long enough to tuck behind his ears. He knew that hair covered a face that looked like if a nineties heartthrob and a Disney prince had a baby. He knew he'd find full lips, striking green eyes, and a young man who was handsome bordering on pretty.

Chase Adler was dressed in his usual informal athleisure wear, but Killian also knew he wouldn't smell at all like sweat. He'd smell clean, almost minty. He always did. Chase might not have had pheromones to emit, but scenting him wasn't a hardship by any means. The one drawback was that, covering his natural scent, Chase always smelled of two strange alphas. Brothers or room-mates, Killian would guess, judging by the light touch of those pheromones. Presumably a lover would be more heavy-handed.

Killian would fucking smother him in his scent, if that boy were his.

Well, that was an unwelcome thought.

Fuck. Killian could leave. *Should* leave. If he'd seen any other student he recognized this close to his usual hunting grounds, he would have.

But now that Chase was here, Killian couldn't help his curiosity. This wasn't a popular undergrad location for a casual night out. It was too far from campus, and the drinks were much too expensive for the college crowd.

And Chase was here alone.

He should have looked out of place, there among the expensive suits and high heels of the other patrons, but he had a quiet confidence that seemed to allow him to fit in anywhere. He wasn't fidgeting or glancing around. He was sipping calmly at his cocktail, something clear in a tall glass.

He wasn't even staring at a phone.

There was, however, another destination this bar was conveniently adjacent to. Was Chase perhaps gearing up to cross the street? If he was ...

Some unnameable emotion surged in Killian, and he forced it back down with a quiet curse.

But no, Killian wasn't leaving.

He wasn't going to *do* anything—he hadn't lost his senses completely—but he was nothing if not an academic. He had an academic question now—namely, what the fuck was one of his former students doing at this bar?

And observation was the only way to get his answers.

Killian took a moment, making sure his pheromones were under wraps as he folded his shirt cuffs up to his elbow and then strode more fully into the bar.

He took a seat at one of the high-top tables within Chase's line of sight, nodding to the bartender, who started pouring Killian's preferred whiskey without a word before coming out from behind the bar to drop it off at his table.

When the bartender made to leave, Killian stopped him with a gesture. "The kid at the end," he said, surprised at the gravelly edge to his own voice. "What's he drinking?"

The bartender answered immediately, seemingly without having to think, "Gin and tonic with lime."

Interesting. It was a country-club type drink. Not the watered-down beer or obnoxious shooter combination one might expect of an undergraduate student.

Or maybe Killian was just being a judgmental, pretentious asshole.

It wouldn't be the first time.

"You want to get his next one?" the bartender asked, familiar with Killian's usual methods. Really, Killian should learn the man's name one of these days.

"No." Killian tugged his whiskey closer, handing the bartender his card. "Close me out, will you?"

Killian sat with his drink, watching the side profile of a certain Chase Adler. Student. Beta. Polite young man.

Killian sat and watched and waited.

3

Chase

Professor Burke was here. At the bar. Here at the bar where Chase had come expressly to catch sight of him.

Chase just hadn't thought it would actually work.

He had maybe been in a weird mental state since he'd realized the omega Noah was so twisted up about was actually Professor Miller, their Omega Studies teacher. And then Chase had caught Noah just the other day researching their university's policy on student-teacher relationships—mainly that there wasn't one, at least not in writing. Chase was pretty sure that had something to do with the campus heat services, but that wasn't the point.

The point was Noah had fucked a teacher. They were *allowed* to fuck their teachers.

Well, actually, they probably weren't—and Noah and Professor Miller would probably get into a fuckton of trouble if someone found out—but it wasn't *officially* forbidden.

And just knowing that was all it had taken for Chase to start wondering: Had Professor Burke ever fucked a student?

It was maybe even a reasonable question to ask, because how else would the student body know about the bar Burke haunted—and the club it was adjacent to—if someone hadn't seen him there in the flesh?

So now Chase was here. And also Burke was here. Professor Burke.

Chase had sensed him the moment he'd come through the door, with his leather-rich pheromones wafting in like the world's most unfair temptation. The professor had taken a seat at a table where Chase only had to turn his head the slightest bit to the side to see him.

Did Burke remember Chase? Did he even know who Chase was? Theirs wasn't a small university, and Burke probably taught way too many students to keep track of. And a new semester had already started. Maybe he'd said that thing he'd said to Chase only because he couldn't remember Chase's actual name.

Or maybe Chase had imagined it. Wouldn't Noah have said something, if Burke had really said ... the thing?

Chase hadn't told his roommates he was coming here. He loved them, but Noah was struggling enough with his feelings for the omega professor, and Spencer couldn't keep a secret if someone sewed his lips together. So Chase was flying solo.

Having a drink on his own was kind of nice, even, other than the jittery nerves dancing in his stomach like asshole butterflies. The bar was quiet and softly lit, with dark, jewel-toned upholstery on the chairs and booths that made everything feel a little ... forbidden.

Or maybe that was Chase projecting.

He finished his drink, squishing his lime down with his straw, and the attentive bartender meandered over. "Another?"

Chase nodded. "Please." And then, because it would be far too tempting to keep slamming drinks until he had some sort of liquid courage in his veins, "And I'll close out."

The scent of leather hit Chase's nose again, faint but tantalizing, and just like that, Chase held out a hand. "Or, wait. Keep it open. Sorry. Thank you."

The bartender shrugged like he didn't care either way, pouring Chase another gin and tonic, adding a lime, and sliding it over.

Chase stood from his barstool, drink in hand. This was it. He'd decided he was allowed one stupid, embarrassing moment, and then he would put it behind him. No one would know, anyway. No one but him and Burke.

He walked over to the professor's table. The alpha was sprawled back in his chair, surprisingly thick thighs spread wide, with none of the rigid posture he showed in his classroom. He had on another button-down with the sleeves rolled up, and Chase had to keep his eyes off those damned forearms in order to keep his cool.

Burke was watching Chase approach over a tumbler of what looked like whiskey, his expression unreadable.

"Professor Burke?" Chase asked when he was standing across the table from him, gratified that his voice came out steady. "I, um, had you last semester?"

Burke nodded. "I remember."

Some of the butterflies roiling in Chase's stomach settled. He was memorable, then, at the very least. Not just another random student in a sea of faces.

He steeled his nerves. *Go big or go fucking home.* "Can I buy you another drink?"

Something flashed across Burke's face—surprise, maybe?—and then he shook his head slowly. "I'm only having the one."

"Oh." Chase's cheeks flamed. There it was, his one embarrassing moment, already gone. "Understood, I—"

The chair next to Chase shot out from under the table. "But you may take a seat. If you like."

Chase stared at the chair dumbly. Burke cocked a brow.

Holy shit, he's asking me to stay.

Chase jumped onto the seat. Too eager by half, but oh the fuck well. He set his drink on the table and placed his hands in his lap.

They watched each other.

"I enjoyed your class last semester," Chase told him.

Another slow shake of Burke's head. "Try again."

Burke didn't want to talk about school. Of course he didn't. He probably came here to get away, to de-stress or whatever.

Chase resisted the urge to clear his throat. "Are you from around here?"

Burke grunted. "Phoenix? No."

He didn't expand on it, didn't offer up his city of origin, so Chase told him, "Me neither."

Burke's lips twitched up at the corners. "And where are you from?"

"Minnesota, sir."

The "sir" just came out, a habit at this point, but Burke didn't seem offended. Instead, something hot gleamed in his eyes. "Ah. The manners make sense."

"Just how I was raised." But Chase bit back the "sir" this time.

"Your parents' influence?"

"Sort of."

"Not close?"

"No."

"I'm surprised." Burke took a sip of his drink, dark-blue gaze dancing over Chase's face. "You seem like you'd be the perfect, dutiful son."

Chase wasn't sure if he was being teased or not. He shrugged anyway. "Dutiful, yeah." At least he had been, once upon a time, when it had seemed worth the effort. "But not—not close."

"Me neither," Burke told him, an echo of Chase's earlier words.

Chase tucked that little tidbit of information away somewhere safe in the back of his mind. Burke didn't seem to be hurting for it, the lack of closeness with his parents. It didn't seem like much *could* hurt him. He was … steady. Solid. Larger than life.

Like his hands. Like the one currently dwarfing that poor tumbler of whiskey in its hold. Chase wanted those big hands on him, wanted to see how far that broad grip would span across his waist.

Fuck. No. Conversation—they were having a *conversation*.

"Siblings?" Chase asked. Had his voice gone all husky, or was that in his head?

"No."

"Same."

They went silent again. Chase was usually better at small talk than this. It should have felt awkward, like the world's worst nondate. But *awkward* wasn't the word Chase would use. He felt … calm. No longer embarrassed by his own presence here. Maybe it was the strength of Burke's pheromones, which were deepening the longer Chase sat there. Sweetening, almost, that cherry note coming out to play again.

Was this what omegas felt like all the time, surrounded by strong alpha pheromones? It was pretty damn nice.

Chase let out a small, contented sigh before he could stop himself.

Burke leaned forward in his chair, the movement almost startling in its suddenness. "What brings you here, Chase Adler?"

Chase suppressed a shiver at the sound of his full name said in that smooth voice. Apparently Burke really did know who he was.

"Did you come here to meet someone?" Burke pressed, his pheromones suddenly thick in the air.

Chase nodded without thinking, then shook his head. "Just … curious."

"About?"

Instead of answering, Chase took a large swallow of his as-yet-untouched drink. "Do you come here a lot, sir?"

"I do." Burke swirled his whiskey, looking into the glass as if considering something. And then his next statement took Chase's breath away. "There's a kink club across the street. Haven. Perhaps you've heard of it?"

Holy shit. Holy shit. Holy shit.

"V-Vaguely," Chase managed to say. And because he didn't want this line of conversation shut down, he hurried to add, "You're a member?"

"I am. Not the most active." Burke's tone was casual, but as he met Chase's eyes, his gaze was anything but. It was heavy, with the weight of a physical caress on Chase's skin. "I don't dom for anyone regularly, and I don't participate in any public scenes."

Chase couldn't believe they were talking about this. He didn't know how it had started, and he didn't know how to keep from messing it up. "What do you do, then?" he asked cautiously.

"I watch. Mingle. Occasionally search for someone ... compatible. Take them home for the night."

Chase set his lips to his straw, then backed off without taking a drink. "How do you decide if they're compatible?"

"How does anyone?" Burke's eyes bore into him. Should Chase blink? He should probably blink. People blinked, didn't they? "A conversation. Chemistry."

Chemistry. Chase had to ask. "Pheromones?"

"Often, yes."

"What if someone doesn't have any?"

Burke cocked his head. "Are you asking me if I ever take home betas?"

"Do you?" It wouldn't be that unusual if Burke didn't. Some alphas preferred to stick with omegas, where they could safely scent compatibility on the surface and be sure of a welcome receptacle for their knot.

Oh fuck. Don't think about Burke's knot.

Except now it was all Chase *could* think about. Burke's knot, thick like his thighs, stretching Chase open. Could Chase take it? He bet he could, with enough prep. He'd fucking make sure of it.

Oblivious to Chase's horny daydreams, Burke swirled his whiskey again, the motion hypnotic. "I'm almost done with my drink," he said, seemingly out of nowhere. "I'll be leaving afterward. So if you have something you'd like to ask me, Chase Adler, now would be the time."

Chase parsed through the words, trying to get at their true meaning. If he was right, it meant maybe Burke was *not* actually oblivious to the horny daydreams.

And even if he was wrong, Chase wasn't going to waste this opportunity.

"Take me home," Chase said quickly. It hadn't been a question, so he tacked on, "Please." And then, for good measure, "Sir."

Burke watched him for a long, long moment. Chase held his gaze steadily, without speaking. He wasn't going to waste his time trying to talk Burke into anything, not when the alpha clearly knew his own mind better than most.

Eventually, Burke pushed his empty glass away. "This will be one time only. And if I find myself the subject of campus gossip afterward, you will regret it. Do you understand?"

The butterflies that had been subdued in Chase's belly exploded into activity. Fuck fucking fuck, he was going home with Burke. "Understood," Chase said quickly. "But, um, you're already the subject of a little gossip, sir. That's how I knew to come here."

That leather-cherry scent flared in the air, sharp as a bite, and Chase realized his mistake a moment too late. He'd just admitted to Burke that he'd come here for *him*.

Burke rose from the table, something unreadable in his gaze again. He nodded toward Chase's drink. "Pay your tab, Chase. I'll be waiting outside. You'll drive with me."

———

THE HOUSE they pulled up to fifteen minutes later was a single-story further from campus than Chase might have expected, with a walled-off yard like most of the houses in these neighborhoods. It no doubt had a pool in back, something small but no less refreshing in the summer heat.

It could have been considered modest, but as Burke led him inside, Chase clocked the furniture immediately—antique, sturdy, expensive as hell. Either the university paid its professors better than Chase had thought or Burke had other means of wealth.

Chase stood on the threshold, the door now locked behind him, as Burke set his keys and wallet neatly on a dark wooden entryway table. They hadn't touched on the car ride—they'd barely spoken—but the lack of contact hadn't done anything to dampen the heat simmering in Chase's belly, or quiet the nervous energy of his anticipation.

Burke turned suddenly, grabbing Chase's hand, and Chase had only a moment to register the zip of electricity at that first touch before his cap was tugged off his head and he was being slammed against the wall, a hot mouth on his.

Fuck. *Fuck*.

Chase had been kissed before. Touched before. Fucked before. But never in his life had he experienced anything like having his mouth claimed by Professor Burke. Burke's kiss wasn't a question, or an offer, or even a seduction. He just … took. Devoured Chase's mouth and grabbed hold of everything he had to offer, those strong hands firm on Chase's waist.

The kiss was confident. Arrogant, even. The scent of cherry-sweetened leather rose in the air, tearing through any remaining shreds of Chase's defenses.

Chase maybe should have met that energy, battled against Burke in turn. Instead, he just … surrendered. Melted against the wall, muscles limp and mouth open, letting Burke tilt his head the way he wanted, lick into him the way he wanted, claim him however the fuck he wanted.

He was rewarded with a deep, primitive growl, and then Burke was nipping Chase's bottom lip sharply before pulling back, those dark-blue eyes of his heavy-lidded.

Chase was gratified to see that Burke was at least just as short of breath as he was, panting as he stared at Chase, his massive erection pressed firmly against Chase's hip.

"I enjoy taking control in the bedroom," Burke said, that smooth voice of his huskier than Chase had ever heard it. "I enjoy when my partners submit to me. I think you'd be very good at that, Chase Adler."

Living with alphas for as long as he had, Chase could have taken that as an insult, but Burke let the words fall from his lips like they were the highest praise.

"But if you don't want that—if you don't want to play those games—we can easily have a satisfying, energetic, vanilla fuck and call it a night."

Chase didn't have to think over his answer. "I want it," he said.

"Do you know about safe words?" At Chase's nod, Burke pressed, "How about the traffic light system?"

"Green for good," Chase said immediately, although he would be keeping the reason he'd done this research in the first place to himself. It was bad enough he'd admitted to Burke why he'd shown up at the bar. "Red for stop. Yellow for ... slow down?"

Burke made a small hum of approval, then pressed his thumb to Chase's lower lip, eyeing his mouth hungrily again.

Chase laid a hand on Burke's wrist. If Burke kissed him again, they weren't going to get much talking done. "Um. You haven't told me *what* you like, exactly. You want to tie me up? Hurt me?"

Burke shook his head, dropping his hands back to Chase's waist. "I'm not particularly sadistic. Nor am I that into bondage.

Although, I may require you to push through some ... discomfort for my pleasure."

At Chase's questioning look, Burke gave him what some might consider a mean smile. "Forced orgasms, sweet boy."

Sweet boy.

Burke's thumbs rubbed against the bare skin above Chase's waistband as he shrugged. "Some submissives find me too vanilla as a dom. If you were looking for whips and chains, you've come to the wrong place."

Chase thought of Burke telling him what to do, calling him "sweet boy," forcing him to come. He swallowed through a dry throat. "I don't think that will be a problem for me."

"Good." All at once, Burke released him, stepping back. "My bedroom is the second door on the left. Undress and wait for me. I'd like you sitting at the edge of the bed when I arrive. I'm going to pour myself another whiskey." He grabbed Chase's chin, tilting his head up to meet his eyes. "I've only had one, and I'm not impaired. I will never *be* impaired when playing with you, do you understand?"

"Yes, sir."

Burke shook his head, clucking his tongue. "Try again."

"Yes ... Professor?"

Nothing. Chase racked his brain, then licked his lips, trying a third time. "Yes, *Alpha.*"

Burke's eyes gleamed. "There it is." He dropped Chase's chin and tilted his head in the direction of the bedroom. "Go."

Chase was supposed to wait naked in a bedroom he'd never set foot in before while Burke poured himself a leisurely drink. A drink he most likely did not intend to finish. It might have been an insulting request, if not for the heat in Burke's eyes, the way he looked like he wanted nothing more than to rip Chase's clothes off right there and fuck him against the door.

It *was* a game, Chase realized. A test of both their willpowers, as well as Chase's obedience.

Well, fuck it. Chase was an athlete. He was good at games, well practiced in self-denial in pursuit of a higher cause.

He slipped past Burke and walked down the hall, listening to Burke's footsteps heading in the opposite direction, presumably to find the kitchen. Or maybe a bar cart—he seemed like the type.

The bedroom Chase found was large but uncluttered, the bed neatly made with a dark-gray comforter and cream sheets. It had more of that heavy, dark antique furniture. A matching set—dresser, bed, bedside table, and wooden chair with a brocade seat.

Burke had elegant taste as well as money. If not for the age gap, the inappropriateness of their respective positions, and the fact that Burke was about to introduce Chase to the world of kink, Chase's parents might even approve.

The room smelled like Burke, too, and Chase inhaled greedily. He was grateful he couldn't catch any underlying omega pheromones. Chase knew what this was—the "one time only" had made it pretty clear—but he didn't need any sensory reminders of it.

He toed off his shoes and stripped, folding each article of clothing neatly and setting it on the bedside table, where the only other occupants were a phone charger and a novel. Chase didn't recognize the title, but it had the look of a spy thriller.

Cute.

Naked, Chase sat on the foot of the neatly made bed. He was almost surprised to find he was still hard. He'd thought maybe his nerves would kill his boner, but if anything, they just seemed to ... enhance it. Was that a thing? Boner-enhancing anxiety?

Any moment now, Burke would be in here with him. He was going to touch Chase, kiss him again, make him come—possibly more than Chase wanted to. He was hopefully going to fuck him with that alarmingly large erection.

Chase's belly tightened, his cock jerking in the air. He wanted to wrap a fist around it, to relieve some of that ache, but he had the feeling that wasn't allowed, even if Burke hadn't expressly forbidden it.

So Chase sat with his hands gripping the edge of the bed, his feet flat on the floor. The air was cool but not cold. He was comfortable and uncomfortable at the same time.

He waited for his alpha.

4

Chase

Burke's steps were heavy in the hall, although it sounded to Chase like he'd removed his dress shoes at some point.

The alpha stopped in the doorway of the bedroom, and Chase's breath caught. The shoes were gone, yes, and Burke had unbuttoned the top three buttons of his shirt, a smattering of dark chest hair now peeking out. He was holding a tumbler of whiskey with one of those single oversize ice cubes.

Definitely a bar cart guy.

Burke stood in the doorway for a long moment, his gaze tracing over Chase's nude form, the weight of it as heavy and heated as his touch had been.

Chase was comfortable with nudity. He liked his body just fine, and he had plenty of experience with the casual nakedness of team locker rooms and a certain roommate with very few boundaries. But he'd never been ... perused like this. So thoroughly, yet with an almost detached air, despite Burke's obvious approval for what he saw.

Chase was hyperaware of every inch of his own skin. Of his cock, which stood heavy and full, aching to be touched.

He had a feeling he'd be waiting for that touch quite a bit longer.

Instead of dampening his desire, the thought made Chase hotter. He had to wait, to prove to Burke that he could be good and obedient. When Burke finally touched him, it wouldn't be some half-sincere fumbling in a dark bedroom at a kegger—it would be a *reward*.

Burkes sipped his whiskey, his gaze now sliding over to Chase's neatly folded clothes, the shoes he'd lined up on the floor. Burke's lips tilted up at the corners, and he walked over, setting his glass next to the pile on the bedside table. "What a polite young man you are, Chase Adler," he murmured.

Chase didn't think a response was required, so he stayed silent.

Burke picked up the wooden chair, carrying it over and setting it in front of Chase. He took a seat, his thighs spread wide again, their knees close to touching. He was hard—the bulge almost alarmingly massive in his dress pants—though he didn't seem particularly bothered by it. He leaned back, setting his chin on his hand. "You have a beautiful body."

Chase's cheeks warmed, and this time he did respond. "Thank you, Alpha."

"You haven't touched yourself."

It was a statement, not a question, but Chase still shook his head. "I didn't think I was supposed to."

Burke hummed his approval. "How right you are. What good instincts you have, sweet boy. A natural."

Chase still couldn't tell if Burke was teasing him when he spoke that way, but it warmed Chase to the tips of his toes regardless. Fuck, was he supposed to be this easy? Burke was pressing buttons he hadn't even known he had, and Chase suddenly felt like they were giant and bright red and obvious to everyone but him.

Burke leaned forward, leather and cherry in the air, and set his hands on Chase's knees, his thumbs caressing the skin there. The touch burned, and Chase's cock jerked.

Since when was his fucking *knee* an erogenous zone?

Burke smiled. "How should I reward you?" Before Chase could even think of a possible answer to that—*touch me, suck me, fuck me*—Burke pressed a hand to Chase's chest, pushing him gently but firmly. "Lean back, hm?"

Chase leaned back until his back hit the mattress, his legs still hanging off the edge of the bed. The change in position took Burke out of his line of sight.

Chase felt more exposed than ever, with Burke no longer visible but undeniably present, seated between Chase's spread knees, his broad hands sliding up Chase's thighs.

Chase could feel him looking. Watching.

Chase's breath caught again as Burke's hands continued to trace his skin. Up to his hips. His stomach. Down again, to the soft, sensitive skin of Chase's pelvis. Down further to Chase's balls. Burke weighed them in his palms, rolled them between his fingers.

Chase let out an embarrassing whimper, covering his face with his hands.

A pinch at his thigh, brief but sharp. "Oh no, sweet boy. Can't have you covering that pretty face. Hands down on the bed."

Chase set his hands down immediately, clawing his fingertips into the covers to keep them there as Burke lifted Chase's painfully full cock and balls out of the way, his thumb tracing down Chase's perineum.

"How quickly do you think you'll come," Burke mused, ignoring another one of Chase's strangled whimpers, "when I finally stroke this poor, pretty cock?"

"Very quickly, sir," Chase admitted. There was no use pretending—Burke had barely touched him and his cock already felt like it was going to explode any minute.

A nip at Chase's hip, a there-and-gone burn.

"Alpha," Chase corrected. "Very quickly, *Alpha*."

"And how quickly can you go again? On average?"

"I—I don't know."

The thumb tracing Chase's taint like a promise stilled. "No one's made you come more than once in one go?"

"No, Alpha."

Burke let out a low rumble of a laugh. "Oh fuck, this is going to be fun. You poor, poor thing."

He continued petting Chase, rubbing not just his fingers but also his wrists against Chase's inner thighs, the creases of his pelvis. Scent marking him.

And since Chase had no pheromones of his own, by the end of all this, he'd smell only of Burke.

He was going to reek of him.

Chase's cock jerked at the thought, precum streaming from it like a fucking fountain now.

"Let me guess," Burke mused, licking a stripe along Chase's hip, ignoring the high-pitched whine Chase let out at the unexpected warmth of his tongue. "You had a high school sweetheart. Lost your virginities together, respectful and romantic."

That was exactly how it had happened.

"Yes, Alpha," Chase confirmed. And then, because he somehow knew Burke would get a kick out of it, "She was head cheerleader."

Becca Summers. She and Chase been friends already through classes, and she'd walked up to him the first day of junior year, saying, "I think we should date." He'd agreed easily—she was beautiful and funny and smart, and he couldn't think of a reason why not. And he'd agreed just as easily when she'd called him a month before graduation, saying she thought they should break it off, free themselves up for college.

He'd later found out she'd told her friends she thought he was "unknowable."

Chase wasn't sure about that. Just because he didn't crack open his chest for public consumption at every opportunity meant he was some sort of teenage sphinx?

All that was beside the point because Chase was rewarded for that bit of honesty with a rush of warm breath over the head of his cock. Burke was *chuckling*, right above Chase's dick.

"Of course she was," Burke murmured, sounding pleased.

Chase wished he could see his face.

Without warning, a lubed finger started circling Chase's hole, and Chase's hips jolted up without permission. Burke held him down with a firm hand, as if expecting it. "And have you ever been fucked?"

"Y-Yes," Chase answered through a gasp, the tender skin around his hole tingling with that teasing touch.

The tip of Burke's finger dipped in, just barely. "By an alpha?"

"N-No. Betas only."

"Ever taken a knot?"

Chase tensed—fuck, was Burke really thinking of knotting him?—and then forced himself to relax, allowing that probing finger to slip in all the way.

Fuck, Burke had thick fingers. "No. Not yet."

That earned him another chuckle, and maybe that was what emboldened Chase to ask, "Is this a seduction or an interview?"

It felt like he'd been teased for hours already, and he wanted more of those thick fingers inside him. He wanted that thick alpha cock pounding into him. *Fuck self-restraint*, he thought desperately. *I want to be fucked. Now.*

Burke's finger withdrew, and suddenly Burke was surging over him. Chase's breath caught in his throat at having that steely gaze suddenly locked with his. "It's whatever the fuck I want it to be," Burke growled. His hand slid up Chase's chest to cup his throat. "You're hiding a bit of a brat behind those good manners." Burke's hold tightened, the slightest hint of a threat. "I'll have to keep a close eye on you."

Then he slid back down, out of Chase's sight, and shoved his hand back down between Chase's legs. He slid his finger back inside, crooking it mercilessly, and Chase bit back a moan, only for the sound to escape him despite his best efforts when a second finger joined the first.

Burke was a liar though. He wouldn't be keeping a close eye on Chase at all. He'd already said this was one time only. But Chase didn't point that out. Partly because he *wasn't* a brat, no matter what Burke said, and partly because maybe if he turned a blind eye, it wouldn't be true. Out of sight, out of mind. It had always worked for his parents.

Don't fucking think about your parents when your professor's fingers are inside you, asshole.

Those fingers started twisting inside him, and then finally a hand wrapped around Chase's cock, stroking confidently. The nefariousness of Burke's teasing came to light when Chase realized he was going to blow his load in the next thirty seconds.

As if reading his mind, Burke taunted him with his smooth, deep voice, "Besides, I don't need to seduce you, Chase Adler. You're fucking gagging for it already."

On the next upward glide of his hand, Burke's thumb dipped into Chase's slit, and Chase groaned, his hips bucking up desperately, more than proving Burke's point.

What followed was an almost brutally efficient hand job, with Burke's fingers scissoring and crooking inside him all the while. Chase came with a hoarse shout, his thighs shaking and his toes curling in the air, but Burke didn't stop.

He didn't even slow down.

He kept stroking Chase's softening cock, Chase's cum easing the glide.

"Oh *fuck*." Chase's hips bucked again, this time in a frantic effort to escape that now painful touch. "Too much," he hissed, although for some reason he didn't try to actually knock Burke's hand off him.

"Oh, I know, sweet boy," Burke crooned, his voice full of false sympathy.

"Fuck. *Fuck*." Chase's hips were twisting in the air now, and Burke used a sharp elbow to hold him in place. Chase keened. "I thought you weren't—weren't a sadist."

"I'm not." There was a hint of a laugh in Burke's low, rough voice. "This isn't about hurting you. It's about bringing you pleasure. On my terms. Because that's what brings *me* pleasure." Burke's voice dropped into something even more soft and intimate. "You can put up with a little discomfort, can't you, to bring me pleasure? Hm, sweet boy?"

Well, when he put it like that ...

Of course Chase could do it. He was no stranger to pushing his body past its limits. He'd run endless drills on shaking legs, finished multiple games after vomiting during the third quarter.

He could handle one fucking torturous hand job.

That didn't mean he didn't whimper like a fucking baby when Burke thumbed at his slit again.

"Color, sweet boy."

"Green."

And then Burke's mouth was on him.

Holy shit. Holy fucking *shit*. Professor Burke was sucking Chase's cock, and it fucking *hurt*. Chase cried out, his fingers clutching the bedspread so hard he thought he might rip it.

Burke popped off, tutting at him. He stroked Chase's hip in big, soothing sweeps of his hand. "Relax, sweet boy. I know you can do it."

Chase forced himself to slow his panting, to take deliberate, deep breaths. *In and out, in and out.* Burke started suckling at the head of his cock again, but Chase didn't let himself tense up this time. Burke's mouth was warm and wet, but he was going easy on Chase. He wasn't sucking too hard—not yet.

Chase could do this.

And then Burke crooked his fingers, rubbing at Chase's prostate, and that hot clench of discomfort in Chase's belly ... shifted.

"There it is," Burke crooned softly. He mouthed at the base of Chase's cock, which was somehow once again filling with blood. He kissed and licked along the sides, lapped at Chase's balls, and when Chase was mostly hard again, hollowed his cheeks and sucked him down.

It was heaven. It was torture. It was some weird spot in between. And Chase was pretty sure if Burke's arm hadn't been holding him down, he'd have shot straight off the bed.

He wasn't usually loud in the bedroom, but as Burke worked him over, Chase couldn't seem to stop moaning and whimpering and letting out frantic "oh gods" and equally desperate "oh *fuck*s."

It almost felt like his second orgasm was sucked out of him against his will, but that didn't stop it from flooding Chase's whole body with overwhelming force. His every muscle was trembling and shaking as he shot his load into Burke's welcoming mouth.

Burke swallowed.

Professor Burke just swallowed my cum.

Before Chase could process the unreality of that, Burke pulled off his cock with a grunt. Chase rose onto his elbows, unable to resist catching a glimpse of him.

Burke looked ... kind of wrecked.

His dark hair was even more mussed than usual, and his lips were red and spit-soaked. He was panting and flushed. But his eyes ...

Those eyes were hungry. Ferocious.

They looked like the eyes of an alpha in rut.

Burke started unbuttoning his pants—how had he given Chase two orgasms already and was still fully clothed?—and then he was pulling out what was definitely an alpha's cock. Thick, long, uncut, the head so red and angry it looked painful. Chase only got a glimpse before Burke was flipping him over.

He heard the telltale sound of a little foil packet tearing.

Burke's voice was hoarse when he told him, "I'm going to fuck you now, Chase Adler. Color?"

Chase had just come once more than he should have. His cock was oversensitive, and his body was limp as a fucking noodle. But he somehow found the strength to raise himself to hands and knees, canting his hips, his head lowered between his trembling arms as he answered without hesitation, "Green. My color's green."

5

Killian

Killian hadn't planned on fucking Chase Adler. He really hadn't.

He'd planned on getting the pretty beta on his knees and feeding him his cock. Planned on defying expectations by being oh so gentle and generous with it. No face-fucking, no choking, no hair-pulling. Just holding steady as he let Chase lick and suck and slobber to his heart's delight.

But Killian hadn't anticipated the effect Chase would have on him. The beta's submission to him was *beautiful*. Deliberate yet generous. Easy without feeling careless. As if, for whatever reason, Chase had chosen Killian and was now willing to give him anything and everything he wanted.

If Killian didn't fuck Chase tonight—if he didn't pull that tight, muscled ass back and plunge his cock into it right this fucking second—he wasn't ever going to get it out of his mind. He'd end up going back for more, and he couldn't do that.

One night had to be enough.

Because Killian didn't fuck students. And he certainly didn't fuck students harboring secret crushes—students who'd come to a bar specifically to find him and seduce him.

And fuck if Chase hadn't even had to try, had he? He'd just sat there with his prissy gin and tonic, barely speaking, and Killian had folded.

And that was the problem. It had to be one night only—goddamn *had* to—because Killian had a feeling that if he fucked Chase Adler more than once, he was never going to get him out from under his skin. He was self-aware enough to know that.

It might already be too late, for that matter. Killian could feel it as he watched Chase arch his back and cant his hips. Presenting for his alpha like the perfect little omega, for all that Chase was a beta.

Fucking hell.

Killian rolled on a condom with trembling fingers, grabbed those tempting hips, and notched the angry, aching head of his cock into that waiting hole.

Tight. Hot. Fucking heaven.

Each inch was tortuously won, never mind that Killian had prepped Chase more than thoroughly with his fingers.

Chase had none of an omega's natural slick, and Killian was a well-proportioned alpha.

Killian had never realized how hot it could be, that fight to gain territory. Like he was claiming Chase's body against its will, and Chase was letting him. *Begging* him.

Chase's beautiful muscles were trembling, worn out from Killian's earlier torture. The kind thing to do would be to get him flat on his stomach with a pillow under his hips and drive into him without the poor kid having to hold himself up.

But Killian didn't feel like being kind. Not when Chase had him twisted into knots without even trying. Not when he was so perfectly willing to put up with discomfort for Killian's filthy sake.

"Look at you," Killian murmured when his hips were flush with Chase's ass, Killian's swollen cock pulsing in time with his heartbeat as Chase's gorgeous form shuddered against him. He slid his hands up Chase's sides, caressing that muscled back. "Taking every inch of me so perfectly."

Chase let out a low whine, his inner muscles clamping around Killian's dick like a vise. Killian wasn't naturally chatty when it came to fucking, but it was worth the extra effort for the way Chase desperately choked on each word of approval.

He took praise so beautifully, this unassuming beta.

Killian slid his hands back down, pulling Chase's cheeks apart with his thumbs in order to watch himself withdraw, his cock dark and ruddy and glistening. He plunged back in, this time in an easy glide.

Chase moaned, long and low.

Fuck. Killian should tease him more. He should show this beta what it was like to be with a skilled and experienced lover and not another bumbling undergrad.

But Killian couldn't. He just ... couldn't. Instead, he started driving into Chase desperately, practically rutting into the poor boy, using his grip on Chase's hips to slam him back with each thrust.

He was rewarded with a desperate, keening, "Oh, fucking *fuck*," followed by the most glorious, punched-out moans. Again and again and again.

Killian threw his head back, groaning his own pleasure. Chase didn't need an omega's slick. He was the perfect fucking cock sleeve just as he was. Killian should tell him that, when he was able to form words again and not just growl like a damned beast.

Pheromones filled the air, rich and thick and probably suffocating. Thank fuck Chase was a beta, or Killian would have been traumatizing him with the strength of them.

When he realized he was too close *way* too fucking soon,

Killian paused with his cock deep inside the beta, stroking his hand up Chase's back, feeling those gorgeous muscles again. The words came out almost angry as he growled, "This body of yours is fucking ridiculous."

When Killian had first caught sight of Chase, nude and waiting prettily on his bed, it had been like a punch to the gut. Underneath his baggy exercise shorts and zip-up sweatshirts, Chase was lean and cut—no showy muscles but still well defined, with tantalizingly pale skin around his groin and buttocks. He'd spent a lot of time shirtless in the sun in tiny shorts, from the look of it. His body was strong, yes, but also pretty. To match his pretty goddamn face.

Some kind of athlete; Killian would swear by it.

Killian let his hands wander over and around Chase's hips, only to find exactly what he'd hoped for. "Fuck," he whispered, almost reverent. "You're hard again."

Even after all that torture, even with Killian fucking into him without a touch to spare for Chase's spent dick.

What a good fucking boy.

Chase gave a piteous whine as Killian thumbed at the head of his cock, and another low growl escaped Killian's chest. "You'll come again," he ordered, deciding it as the words were leaving his mouth. "While I'm fucking you."

"I can't."

Killian smacked Chase's hip. "You'll come again, or I'll stuff my knot into you right now." Chase let out another low moan, and Killian almost laughed. "You'd like that, wouldn't you? So eager to please, you'd take an alpha's knot without any prep."

Here Killian had told himself he wasn't naturally chatty, and he couldn't stop. Fucking. Talking.

"You could do it too," he mused, circling his thumb over and over, liking the way it made Chase writhe against him, his ass choking Killian's dick. "I don't know if anyone's told you, but this tight ass of yours was made to be fucked. I barely had my fingers in you and look how well you're taking me."

Killian spread those pretty pale cheeks again, admiring the way Chase's hole stretched tight around his girth. "Perfect fucking hole," he praised. "Touch yourself for me."

Chase shook his head furiously. "Can't—can't hold myself up."

"You can. You're so strong, sweet boy. You can do it. Lower onto your forearms."

Chase did, the movement deepening the arch of his back. He sneaked one hand down in between his legs, whimpering as he grabbed his own cock.

"Oh, look at you," Killian crooned. "Listening so well. If you manage to come before me, you'll get another kiss."

Killian promised it lightly, as if he weren't dying to give Chase exactly that. Their kiss earlier had been deadly—the way Chase had melted into it, open and sweet and unbelievably perfect.

Fuck. Maybe Killian shouldn't kiss him again after all. What he needed was to get off, to get out of this lustful, worshipful headspace he was in.

No more pauses.

Killian pulled back, slamming into Chase again with a groan. He started up a steady pace again, driving into the beta over and over, using that gorgeous body exactly the way he wanted.

But now Chase seemed desperate to get what Killian had promised. He wasn't passively taking it anymore—he was slamming his ass back to meet Killian's hips, his wrist working furiously even as he whined like he was in pain.

His desperation was beautiful.

It was Chase who came first, with a wrecked and wretched sob, his channel clamping down around Killian.

And that was it. Killian jerked Chase up with an arm around his chest, claiming his mouth as the world went dim around him,

Killian's orgasm barreling through him with more power than it had any right to, given his extensive experience.

Chase whined and whimpered into the kiss. Killian fucked that pleading mouth with his tongue and emptied himself into the condom. He wished he was bare. Wished he was filling Chase with his cum. Wished he wasn't so carefully keeping his half-inflated knot out of that welcoming hole.

But that wasn't what this was. It couldn't be.

So Killian slowed down, pressing sweet kisses to Chase's lips, murmuring, "There it is. You've earned it, hm? You did so well. So well."

He lowered Chase onto the bed. The beta was a vision, all tear-streaked cheeks and glassy eyes, every inch of him shaking. Killian lay down beside him and tugged Chase into his arms, sweeping his hands up and down Chase's sides.

"D-Didn't take you for a cuddler," Chase muttered eventually.

Killian pinched him lightly. "I don't shirk aftercare, sweet boy."

Chase let out a soft, weary laugh that tugged on something strange in Killian's chest. "How long does it last?"

All fucking night. "However long you need."

"What if I need a long time?"

"Then that's what you get."

"For being—being such a good boy?" The way Chase said it, so shy, like he was trying out the words for the very first time, tugged again on that place inside Killian, deep and tender.

"Even if you were a very naughty boy, I'd still give you what you need afterward." Killian pressed a kiss to Chase's nose—*what the fuck was that?* He cleared his throat. "But yes, Chase Adler. You were a very, very good boy for me."

Chase let out a little sigh and wrapped his arm around Killian's waist, tucking himself in close. He nuzzled his head into Killian's neck and lay there, unashamedly breathing in Killian's pheromones like they smelled of light, fluffy cotton candy and not the overpowering leather scent Killian had so often been told was extremely off-putting.

Killian had already scent marked Chase to an absurd degree, unable to help himself when he'd had Chase lying sweet and pliant in front of him. And the thing about Chase being a beta, without any powerful pheromones of his own, was that Chase now smelled *only* of Killian. He was absolutely saturated in Killian's scent, his natural mint covered completely by cherry and leather.

It was more satisfying than it had any right to be.

Killian should put them both in the shower right now, if only to get his scent off the boy, but he couldn't bring himself to do it. Instead, he continued to stroke his hand up and down Chase's spine, letting the beta cuddle in close.

Any minute now, Killian would get up and fetch Chase some water and something to snack on, to make sure his physical state was as leveled out as his mental one. But that could wait.

For now, Killian's inner alpha needed to keep Chase close, tucked right into his chest. And Killian had learned long ago that after any scene, he needed to placate those deep instincts —that was *his* aftercare.

So Killian held the beta, and breathed in his own scent on the boy's skin, and tried not to worry that he'd just fucked over his whole life in one fell swoop.

6

___

Chase

Chase woke up at Burke's house. In Burke's bed.

It wasn't a slow realization, no confused blinking back to reality and wondering where he was. Chase knew *exactly* where he was. They'd fucked, cuddled, and he'd somehow fallen asleep afterward, still in Burke's arms.

Even if Chase hadn't remembered the whole incident with startling clarity, it was obvious, because these leather-and-cherry pheromones surrounding him didn't exist in Chase's bed. He wished they did. Wished he could smuggle a pillow out under his shirt and sneak it into his bedroom, fall asleep to that scent every single night.

So maybe it wasn't that surprising he'd fallen asleep, what with that thick cloud of comforting, contented pheromones surrounding him. What *was* surprising was that Burke had fallen asleep too. Chase was still cuddled into him, a hand resting on Burke's steadily rising and falling chest and a leg slung over his hip. Burke, for his part, had an arm around Chase's middle. He was still fully clothed.

Because he fucked you fully clothed, his pants only unbuckled and unbuttoned enough to release his thick alpha cock. Which shouldn't have been as hot as it was, Jesus effing Christ.

Anyway, Burke was still dressed. And Chase still didn't know what the alpha looked like naked, or even shirtless. And he wouldn't *get* to know, because Burke had been very clear that they wouldn't be doing this again.

And Chase had known that, so he didn't get to have his feelings hurt about it, even if the sex had rearranged something crucial inside him and he was still trying to figure out what exactly it was.

Slowly and carefully, Chase untangled himself, wincing at a telltale soreness between his legs—Burke's cock was *not* beginner-level; that was for sure. Neither was the way the alpha fucked, for that matter. Sex with Burke was some new realm of sensuality where brute force met careful consideration and a whiskey-soaked voice taunted and praised in equal measure.

Don't think about that right now, Chase told himself. *Just get out, quick and easy.*

Chase didn't have a lot of "slipping away in the middle of the night" on his sexual résumé, but he knew he couldn't face Burke right now, not while the alpha was conscious. If he did, Chase was going to do something stupid, like beg to do it all again.

For one brief moment, when Chase began to move away, Burke's arm tightened around him, as if he was reluctant to let him go. Chase stilled, not even daring to breathe, and after a moment, Burke's arm relaxed again. Chase was able to roll away and off the bed in one smooth motion, landing silently on his feet.

It seemed he'd finally found a non-sports-related benefit to his athlete's reflexes.

Chase grabbed his pile of clothes and his shoes and took them out into the front room, where he dressed quickly and silently. He felt mildly guilty about heading out and leaving Burke's front door unlocked for the night, but it was probably preferable to him staying and forcing the professor into an awkward morning-after conversation.

Once he was safely on the porch, Chase pulled up a rideshare app. It was approaching three in the morning, and the bars were already closed, but drivers were still out and working.

Chase chatted politely to the beta driver, Susan, who seemed pleasantly surprised and grateful to have a sober passenger at this time of night. She drove him to his car, still waiting at the bar, and then Chase took himself home.

He let himself into the house, trying to sort out what he was feeling. He was exhausted but also ... not exactly wired, but raw. On edge in a way that wasn't familiar to him.

Chase thought of Burke petting him, telling Chase it was necessary aftercare. How much worse would Chase be feeling if Burke hadn't taken the time to cuddle? With how soft and high and fuzzy he'd been feeling in his postcoital state, Chase could imagine the steepness of that drop.

He was grateful for what Burke had done to mitigate it.

And Chase was grateful now to see a light on in the living room, and to find Spencer sprawled out in a corner of the couch, watching something that involved a lot of alphas throwing fists at each other.

Spencer gave Chase a slack, drunken grin. "Chasey! You're back!"

Chase slipped off his shoes, heading toward the couch. "I am. I'm surprised you are."

With Noah working that night, Spencer had headed to an all-alpha frat for one of their legendary parties. Betas weren't exactly unwelcome, but it was usually more of an alpha-omega arrangement, so Chase had been given an easy excuse to bow out.

Spencer shrugged. "Had my fun and wanted to get home.

Unlike Noah." At Chase's confused look, Spencer's grin widened. "Didn't you see the text?"

Chase knew he'd received a text on the group chat, but he hadn't checked it yet. He looked now and saw a message from Noah letting them know he planned to be out all night and that he'd see them tomorrow. It was followed by ten or so messages from Spencer hounding Noah for more details.

"Wasn't he working tonight?" Chase asked, taking a seat next to Spencer on the couch.

Noah worked as a barback at the same place Spencer worked as a bartender. Spencer had gotten him the job.

"Must have met someone at the bar."

That didn't sound like Noah at all, but Chase let it lie. If Noah had gone home with who Chase thought he'd gone home with, he wasn't going to want them pressing him for details.

Spencer leaned in, maybe to scent mark Chase, and then froze in place. "Whoa." He sniffed the air. "*Whoa.* Did you change designations while you were out?"

Right. Because Chase absolutely reeked of Burke's alpha pheromones.

Chase tried for a casual shrug. "Just a hookup."

Spencer gave him a look. "Um, yeah. You've had hookups before. You've never come home smelling like an alpha in rut." He sniffed the air again, wrinkling his nose. "Intense. Who was he?"

"Just some guy."

Chase supposed he should be grateful Noah wasn't home right now. There was no way Noah wouldn't recognize Burke's distinct pheromones. But Spencer had never taken Burke's class, and he hadn't been there that day in the quad. Chase and Burke should be in the clear, even with Chase reeking of his former professor.

"You gonna see him again?"

This will be one time only.

"Nah."

"It's kind of a bummer sometimes, huh? The one-time things?" Spencer's bleary gaze had sharpened, and he was eyeing Chase with more scrutiny than usual.

"Yeah," Chase said with surprise. "Didn't think you felt that way though."

Maybe Spencer had smoked some weed with his booze. Sometimes that made him introspective.

Spencer leaned back into the couch again, throwing his head back with a sigh. "Sometimes after I nut, I get hit with this, like, gut punch of loneliness." He thumped a fist against his chest in demonstration. "Like, it hurts." He lowered his chin, meeting Chase's eyes with a loopy smile, like he hadn't just said something completely heartbreaking. "But then I have you guys to come home to, and it's fine."

This definitely wasn't the time to get through to Spencer about anything important, but Chase couldn't help saying something. "You know, there's this thing where some people hook up and then still hang out afterward, and it's not so lonely in the end."

Spencer rolled his eyes. "I know what dating is, Chase. Want me to help with that a bit?" He waved a hand at Chase, encompassing his whole being. Or, more likely, the pheromones drenching him. "You'll need to take a real shower to get it fully off though. I don't think my scent can really compete."

The thought of covering Burke's pheromones didn't sit right in Chase's gut. He cleared his throat. "No, I don't mind. I'll shower before I sleep."

Probably. Possibly. Maybe.

Spencer bolted upright out of nowhere. "Oh my god. Should we make grilled cheeses?"

Yeah, he'd definitely had some weed with his booze.

Chase shook his head. "I think I might go to bed, actually. I'm beat."

Spencer sank back with a disappointed sigh. "But I'm not tired yet." He gave Chase a hopeful look. "Wanna sleep out here on the couch while I watch my movie?"

Chase really, really did.

"Yeah, man, that sounds great."

Chase grabbed a spare pillow and shoved it against Spencer's side, laying down his head. He tucked his legs onto the couch, grinning when Spencer draped a blanket over him.

Long fingers petted through Chase's hair as the sound of alphas fighting on the TV screen filled the air again. "You're the best, dude," Spencer said with a happy sigh.

Chase wasn't anything special. But it was clear Spencer didn't want to be alone tonight, and for some reason, neither did Chase. He might not get the best sleep of his life on the living room couch, but at least he'd be with someone who cared, and that felt kind of important.

Even if Spencer's spiced pheromones weren't quite right, they were familiar. Comforting.

Chase closed his eyes and—for the second time that night—let himself fall asleep next to an alpha.

———

THE NEXT TWO WEEKS WERE ... fine. Totally and completely fine.

Chase went to class, studied less than he should have, and met some of his former teammates at the sandpits for a chaotic game of beach volleyball. He spent a ridiculous amount of time trying to convince Spencer that just because Noah was keeping his new relationship private didn't mean he suddenly hated them.

Chase even went to a terrible party and let himself be flirted with by a hopeful omega with pink hair and pretty freckles. That had also been ... fine.

So Chase had been busy. Time card full.

He hadn't seen Burke. Not once.

"Do you think this is real tuna? Or, like, the imitation stuff?"

Chase pulled himself out of his head to find Spencer peeling the top piece of bread off his sandwich, staring at the contents with suspicion.

They were at a coffee shop on campus they liked, one near the biosciences building that had terrible sandwiches but excellent outdoor seating. Noah was with them for a change, although he kept glancing at his phone with an enamored smile he should definitely be embarrassed about.

"I don't think imitation tuna is a thing," Chase told Spencer when Noah didn't offer up any words of wisdom. "You thinking of imitation crab?"

Spencer snapped his fingers. "Yeah, that's it." He narrowed his eyes at his sandwich. "Is that what this is?"

"You're asking if your tuna sandwich is made from imitation crab?"

"Yeah." Spencer held it out to Chase. "Try a bite."

It wasn't worth arguing. Chase grabbed the sandwich and took a bite, immediately letting it fall from his mouth into a napkin. "Jesus. Maybe it is, actually."

Spencer eyed Chase's turkey club hopefully. "Is yours good?"

"No, but it's not ... that." Chase pushed half of it toward him. "Have at it."

Spencer started eating happily, and they were silent for a bit. It was another beautiful day—sunny but not too hot—and Chase flipped his hat and tipped his head back, letting the sun hit his face.

He should be content. He was always content on days like this, when the weather was nice and his friends were at his side.

"Hey, Spence, are you on any apps lately?" he found himself asking.

"Like, dating apps?" Spencer answered, his mouth full of turkey. "Sometimes."

Chase tilted his head back down, raising a brow at his friend. "They any good?"

Spencer swallowed noisily and gave Chase a ridiculous grin. "Aw, Chasey, are you looking for love? A nice beta lady to have nice beta babies with?"

"Dick," Noah said immediately, finally looking up from his phone.

He and Chase had realized early on in the friendship that they'd need to come up with a code word for when Spencer was spouting dickish nonsense without realizing it. The one they'd come up with was ... not subtle.

Spencer managed to pull off an offended look. "I said *nice* beta babies."

"I think I'll wait until after college for the two point five kids, thanks. Just ... looking to hook up? I guess?"

"What about that alpha you banged. Was he any good?"

Of course Spencer remembered. He never forgot that sort of shit. Chase flipped his cap forward again, glancing to the side at Noah, but the other alpha didn't look suspicious.

Of course he doesn't. Why the fuck would he?

"He was—"

And like a fucking demon summoned from the depths, there was Burke. After two weeks of not a single sighting, he was there, across the grassy square, walking on the path that ran alongside the biosciences building. He was talking to another professor, an omega wearing a hopelessly dorky, floppy wide-brimmed hat.

As Chase watched, the two of them paused on the path, the omega gesticulating wildly.

Chase slumped lower in his seat.

"He was what?" Noah asked.

It took Chase a moment to realize both his friends were staring at him. "Who was what?"

"The alpha Spence says you banged," Noah said slowly, like maybe he'd been waiting for a response for a while.

"Oh." Chase cleared his throat. "He was ... good."

More than good.

Chase hadn't been able to stop thinking about *how* good. While in class. While not studying. While losing at beach volleyball.

He'd get these little flashes. *Perfect fucking hole. Touch yourself for me.* And he'd go all hot, and his skin would feel like it was too tight on his body.

Chase had never been sex-obsessed before, not like the majority of the alphas and omegas he knew. He'd even liked that about himself, how it made him chiller than most of the under-grads around him. Less volatile.

But now it was a problem. Because Chase didn't want dating apps. He didn't want a nice beta lady or their imaginary kids. He didn't want to go with the flow anymore, if the flow meant pretending that night had never happened.

What Chase wanted was to be held down and fucked within an inch of his life. He wanted crooning, growly words telling him he had a gorgeous body and a perfect fucking hole. He wanted to tear the dorky omega professor out of Burke's line of sight and—and *bite* him.

Burke, not the omega.

Why did it have to be one time anyway? They'd already done the bad, forbidden thing. So why not just ... keep doing it? Chase wouldn't spill to anyone. And Burke definitely seemed like the kind of man who knew how to keep a secret.

Salty ocean air. A firm hand on his shoulder.

"Hey man, are you okay?" Noah asked.

With immense effort, Chase tore his eyes away from Burke and the omega, giving Noah what he hoped was an easy grin. "Yeah, of course. Just have an essay I'm trying to figure out."

Noah didn't look convinced. He squeezed Chase's shoulder. "You can tell us if you're not, you know."

"Why?" Spencer suddenly looked devastated, his mouth full of turkey again. "What are you talking about? What's wrong with Chase? Was it the thing I said about beta babies?"

"No, dude. I'm fine. Promise."

Noah pulled Chase more firmly under his arm, scent marking him with more of his ocean-rich pheromones with the movement. "Of course you are. You're steady as they come. Tell us about the essay though. We can help you brainstorm."

Luckily, Chase really did have an essay in his American lit class he needed to figure out, so he relaxed into Noah's hold, spitballing ideas with his friends.

They'd sorted out a potential thesis when Chase felt something. A new weight on his skin.

He raised his eyes to find Burke, alone on the path now, staring at Chase from across the way. Before Chase could decide what to do—smile, wink, give him the finger?—the alpha professor whirled, striding off with a scowl on his stupidly handsome face.

What the fuck is his problem?

7

Killian

Chase Adler was waiting outside Killian's office door.

Killian had an entire hallway's worth of time to adjust himself to that fact. A blink and a step to assure himself it wasn't some manifested hallucination. Another step to categorize Chase's appearance: joggers, thin T-shirt, ever-present baseball cap hiding his green eyes in a way that was *not* filling Killian with any sort of rage, because he did. Not. Care.

"Mr. Adler," Killian greeted coolly when he arrived at his door one full eternity later. He dug out his keys to unlock it. The action put them close enough for Killian to note that Chase smelled of spiced tea and ocean air. Killian knew he would.

He shoved his irritation down deep.

It didn't matter that the beta smelled of other alphas. It didn't matter that the last time Killian had seen Chase, he'd smelled only of Killian. Thoroughly. Completely.

It did. Not. Matter.

Killian ushered Chase inside with a hand not quite touching the beta's lower back. "Take a seat."

After only a moment of deliberation, Killian locked the door.

Chase made a small noise, and Killian rounded his desk to his chair—a wall of wood between them seemed like a reasonable idea. "Nothing is happening here today," he said sternly. "I simply prefer my private conversations remain private."

"Of course, sir."

Killian huffed. That answered the question of whether one night of intimacy had done anything to lessen Chase's innate manners.

Killian wouldn't know, because Chase had been gone when Killian had woken.

The fact that Killian had fallen asleep in the midst of providing aftercare to a sub—had not gotten Chase water or made sure he'd eaten something before leaving—was unacceptable. What was even more unacceptable was Chase slipping out of Killian's bed in the dark, running off before Killian could feel ... settled about the whole affair.

That was why Killian had been on edge since, looking for Chase around every corner. Not the act itself, but the way it had ended.

Killian folded his hands on his lap and waited for Chase to tell him why he'd come here today.

But Chase didn't say anything. He sat in the chair across from Killian and stared back at him, completely silent. If Killian didn't know any better, he'd think Chase was employing negotiation tactics—staying quiet so his opponent would speak first.

Childish, really. Killian wouldn't fall prey to it. Chase had come to *him*. It was up to the beta to explain his presence here.

Except it was taking all Killian's concentration just to keep his pheromones in check, and the words slipped out without his permission. "I drove you to my home so that I would be the one driving you back. So that I could be sure you were all right before we parted ways."

Chase shifted slightly in his seat, wafting ocean air and spiced tea toward Killian. "Sir?"

"You left like a thief in the night before I could ascertain whether you were well enough to do so. Next time—"

Chase coughed, his expression hidden by his cap. "There's going to be a next time?"

"No."

Killian's swift denial left them in silence once again. Killian would maintain it this time. He'd said enough.

Except that damned hat covering Chase's eyes was driving him crazy.

"I don't like talking to people when I can't see their face."

Chase cocked his head, an unspoken question.

Killian gestured to Chase's head. "Hat. Off."

"Oh." As if it wasn't an unreasonable request in the slightest, Chase tugged off his cap and placed it on his lap.

There was no reason for his hair to still be silken and perfectly parted after being pressed down by a baseball cap all day. No reason at all.

For the first time since he'd arrived at Killian's office, Chase seemed slightly on edge. He'd started chewing nervously at his lower lip. He had beautiful lips, full and pink.

Killian had never gotten to see them wrapped around his cock.

Killian pressed two fingers to the space between his brows. Hard.

"Sir ... Are you all right?"

"What brings you here, Chase Adler?" Killian asked wearily, unconsciously repeating his question from the other night. The one that had started it all. "Are you looking for a repeat? After I explicitly told you once would have to be enough?"

Chase's brow furrowed, but he didn't respond. Somehow he didn't even seem stubborn about it, just ... calm.

Infuriatingly calm.

Spiced tea. Ocean air.

Unacceptable.

Killian grabbed a pen from his desk. Placed it back. Grabbed another.

"You will wait for my text tonight. You may drive yourself to my home, but you will *not* be leaving until the morning, when I can be assured that you're returning home in an appropriate state."

Chase's pretty green eyes widened, as if he was startled by Killian's words. What right did he have to be startled? *He'd* done this.

"You remember where I live?" Killian asked tersely.

"Yes, sir."

"Try. Again."

"Yes, Alpha." Chase had released his lower lip from the clutches of his teeth, and there was a small smile playing at his lips now. "I remember where you live."

"Good. Come here."

Chase rose, naturally graceful as ever. He came around Killian's desk, his hat held tightly in his hands. Killian gestured for him to place the damned thing back on his head, and then he took one of Chase's hands in his.

Killian wanted to stand, wanted to shove his face into Chase Adler's neck. But he took hold of the beta's wrist instead, rubbed his thumb there. Back and forth, back and forth.

"Your classes are going well?"

Chase nodded. "So far."

"Good. Other hand."

Chase gave him his other wrist, and Killian repeated the scent marking.

"Is this a good idea?" Chase asked, and Killian finally felt something settle in him at the slightly breathless way his question came out.

Still, Killian didn't release him. Not yet. "My pheromones are notoriously overpowering," he said quietly, moving up the inside of Chase's arm to the sensitive skin at the crook of his elbow. Chase's lips parted, his breath coming faster. "Sometimes they stick. No one will think anything of it." Killian narrowed his eyes. "You reek of baby alphas."

"My roommates," Chase told him, confirming Killian's earlier suspicions. "My friends."

His pupils were blown already, from something as simple as a casual scent marking. Poor thing. Killian tried not to let it get to him. He was halfway successful.

Killian made a noncommittal noise, then took stock. There was still a subtle hint of spice and salt, but Chase now smelled of leather and cherries more than not.

A tightness in Killian's chest eased.

"You may go." He released his hold on Chase's arm. "Keep your phone close."

"Yes, Alpha."

Without another word, Chase turned and left the room.

Killian could get angry right about now, convince himself he'd just been played. But he usually wasn't in the habit of lying to himself—at least not so egregiously—and the truth was, he'd played himself.

Chase had barely spoken a word, and Killian had folded. Again.

————

KILLIAN WAS A MORNING WORKOUT PERSON. Always had been, probably always would be.

He liked to sweat out the fog of sleep, work out any lingering tensions or aggressions before starting the day. Weights, treadmill, rowing machine. He kept it varied in an attempt to keep his own interest. He felt pretty strongly that this consistent yet flexible routine was part of what kept him calm, despite his designation.

Killian had already worked out that morning, of course. And yet here he was at the gym again, just before dinnertime, sprinting on the treadmill like the devil himself was at his heels.

Killian had been brought here by some sort of vague idea that he could sweat Chase Adler out of his system.

Sure, Killian had caved back there in his office, but if he could hold out—if he could choose not to send that text tonight—things would stop there. Chase wouldn't show up without Killian's express invitation; Killian knew that much. Not at this stage, not with Killian's "one time only" hanging in the air between them.

It was up to Killian to stay the course. Or to break.

And he'd just run three miles much more quickly than was wise, was now dripping with sweat, and was in no more control of his hormones than he had been a few hours before, with Chase Adler sitting pretty as he pleased in front of him, saying nothing and somehow asking everything.

Killian turned the treadmill off with a growl, easing himself off the damn thing and stalking to the gym's locker room. He took a freezing-cold shower that did nothing to dull his edge, then dressed back in his work clothes. He hated that—getting dressed in dirty clothes after a shower. But he hadn't been planning to go to the gym a second time that day, so he'd have to make do.

Killian would change at home. Something loose and comfortable. Soft clothes to soothe the savage beast, or something like that.

He was going to text Chase.

Fuck. No. No, I'm not.

He was.

Killian tore his belongings out of the locker and swiped through his phone, hitting the contact number of the one person who *might* talk him into reasonable action.

Prince picked up on the third ring.

"Killian," he drawled, and somehow Killian could tell Prince was horizontal on that massive monstrosity he called a sofa. "Joining us tonight after all?"

"I'm about to do something stupid," Killian announced, startling a beta woman leaving the women's locker room as he turned the corner to the gym's exit.

Silence on the other end.

"Hello?"

Prince cleared his throat. "Sorry, I was just making sure I hadn't misread my phone. Thought I was talking to Devon for a second." There was the sound of him setting something down, either a laptop or a beer bottle—both were equally likely. "How stupid are we talking here?"

"Potentially-blowing-up-my-life kind of stupid."

Chase may not have been *Killian's* student anymore, but he was still an undergraduate student at Killian's university. A situation that wasn't explicitly forbidden but not exactly approved of. It might have been a different matter if Chase were a grad student, but as it was, if he wanted to make trouble for Killian, he most definitely could.

Not that Chase seemed like the troublemaking type. More like the "sit pretty on his knees, suck cock like an angel, and thank his alpha for the opportunity" kind.

Fuck, Killian wanted to see that. He wanted to put Chase Adler on his knees and fuck his face. Wanted him to hold Killian's cum in his mouth and not swallow until told.

"*Well?*" Killian barked as he rounded to the corner of the

parking lot where his car waited. He needed some sense knocked into him, and he needed it now.

"Am I supposed to be the voice of reason here?"

"Yes. Obviously."

"Are you sure? Me?"

"It's you or Devon."

"Fair enough. I say ..." Prince stopped there, clearly pausing for suspense. Killian was surprised he didn't go for a drum roll while he was at it. "... Go for it."

Killian resisted the urge to kick at his car. "Son of a *bitch*."

Prince cackled brightly on the other end. "You had to have known."

"I despise you both."

"Poor Devon. Not even on the call and still catching heat. Should I get him on the line? I feel like this hissy fit of yours is a once-in-a-lifetime opportunity."

Killian whirled, pacing in the other direction. He wasn't ready to be seated. He needed ... movement. "This is hardly a hissy fit."

"For you, it might as well be." There was the sound of Prince pouring something. "So you met someone."

"In a sense."

"A fuck-up-your-life someone."

"Potentially."

Prince took a loud sip of his drink. "God, I'd kill to meet them."

"That isn't happening."

"A photo?"

"I need better friends."

"Glad to be of help." Prince took another loud sip. He was smacking his lips on purpose; Killian would bet his life on it. "Listen. You're loaded, you've got a good professional name for yourself, and you're not particularly attached to anything in your life. Go. Blow it up. I'm just happy to see you actually invested in something for once."

It was the exact opposite of the kind of pep talk Killian needed. He hung up the phone.

Killian made his way back to his car and got in, starting it and then sitting there with the engine running. It didn't seem wise to get moving just yet. Vehicular manslaughter wasn't a charge Killian was looking to add to his résumé.

It was time to look at the facts.

Killian had fucked Chase, and now the beta was under Killian's skin. Killian had attempted avoidance and then had caved at the first sight of him. Exercise as a substitute for sex was well and truly out. Killian had tried to speak to a voice of reason, but apparently he didn't know any of those.

He'd clearly taken a wrong turn somewhere when it came to the people he surrounded himself with.

That's because you're *the voice of reason, and you're losing it.*

So that was that. Killian was going to text Chase. Once was going to turn into twice.

But maybe they could leave it at that. Twice was still different from a full-blown affair.

How could they leave it at that?

Killian had to get those pretty lips around his cock, for one. That seemed ... incredibly important right now. It wouldn't do to be left with that missed opportunity hanging over his head again.

And Chase had to stay the night. That had been the other issue—unsettled alpha instincts from the beta slipping away too soon.

Killian needed to fuck him hard, then care for him properly, *then* send him on his way.

Feed him breakfast too. For good measure.

Killian could picture it perfectly, actually: Chase at his kitchen table, sleep-mussed and well-fucked, eating from a plate Killian had prepared.

Perhaps Killian would stop at the store on his way home.

Killian put the car in gear, suddenly feeling like he could be behind the wheel quite safely after all.

He let out a breath as he drove away.

Everything was under control.

8

Chase

A knock on Chase's open door had him looking up from his phone for the first time in an hour.

It was Spencer, dressed all in black, a jacket slung over one shoulder. "Last chance to tag along and claim me as your bartender wingman."

"I'm good," Chase told him. "Thought you weren't getting the good shifts anymore?"

"Deb changed her mind," Spencer said with a smirk. "Maybe she wants this again." He gestured down at his body, doing something annoying with his eyebrows.

"You gonna go for it?"

Chase personally thought it was a bad idea getting involved with coworkers Spencer had to see every day, but he'd already shared his thoughts on the matter. Spencer had let his dick lead the way, as per usual. And then paid the price when Deb had stuck him with the early weeknight shifts with all the shitty tippers.

But Spencer shook his head. "Nah. She got kind of mean when I didn't call. Even though I told her what it was." He frowned down at his feet. "It's always like that. Hella annoying."

"Hey." Chase straightened from his slouch. "You know you don't have to put up with that, right?"

"I kinda do. She's my manager."

"No, I mean ... People being dicks to you. If it's consensual and you made your boundaries clear, then don't let them guilt-trip you for what you don't want."

"Aw, you're such a sweetie pie, Chasey." Spencer grinned, immediately shaking off his funk. It was always that easy with him. Chase envied him the quick turnaround. "Hope whoever you're waiting on tonight treats you right." He pointed a finger at Chase. "They'll answer to me if they don't."

Spencer spun on his heel, his jacket whirling in the air as he walked away.

"Hey!" Chase called after him. "How do you know I'm waiting on someone?"

His only answer was the sound of maniacal cackling, then the front door closing.

Chase frowned down at his phone, then tossed it face down on his bed. Him staring at it like an idiot for hours was probably how Spencer had known Chase was hoping for a text from ... someone.

But Burke was either going to text or he wasn't, and Chase staying glued to his phone wasn't going to change the outcome. Chase needed a distraction.

He settled for organizing his closet.

Since Chase's parents were fronting the majority of their rent, Noah and Spencer had insisted on giving Chase the biggest room, which meant he had the biggest closet. Sometimes his roommates' stuff seemed to migrate into it. The thing was Chase had never seen either of them actually put anything in there. It was like the objects moved on their own in the middle of the night.

Like this Costco-sized box of condoms Chase had definitely *not* purchased himself.

He briefly considered pocketing some, but Burke had covered that side of things the night before. Tonight—if it happened at all —would probably be the same. And if it wasn't ...

What would it be like for him to fuck me bare?

All the blood in Chase's body rushed to his dick at the thought, and he swore, tossing the box of condoms to the side. *No thoughts of bareback alpha dick. You're supposed to be distracting yourself, not ramping yourself up even more.*

After he had categorized what was Spencer's and what was Noah's, there wasn't much to go through, but Chase had stuffed a bunch of textbooks and notebooks from the last semester in the back corner, too lazy to do anything with them. He took them out now, separating them into piles. He'd toss the notebooks and take the textbooks to the used bookstore tomorrow. He was always inexplicably tempted to keep it all, as if for some reason he'd need his illegible notes from Ancient Roman History five years down the line.

Chase sorted through what he could reach, then crawled further into his closet. There was a smallish cardboard box hiding in the back, and he couldn't remember what was in it.

It was his lacrosse uniform.

Chase rocked back on his heels, lid in hand, weirdly surprised to see it. He was pretty sure he'd been supposed to return it when he'd quit. Maybe he'd forgotten.

Chase lifted it out of the box, shaking out the thick fabric.

Lacrosse had been something he'd pretty much always played, thanks to a coach he'd had in elementary school, a man who'd been so warm and encouraging that Chase would have done anything to keep his attention. Including playing long after he was too old for the guy's team.

Chase had kept with it, maybe for the sake of those memories, or maybe just for something to do—a reason to be out of his cold, empty house in his high school years.

And when he'd caught the eye of some scouts and had been offered a scholarship to college, he'd thought that maybe it would feel good, to do something on his own like that. To pay for school with his own skills. He'd even thought that maybe his parents would be proud.

But in the end, it hadn't felt like anything at all. Chase had saved his parents money they didn't need or care about, and the sport he'd always enjoyed as an escape became some sort of transaction instead.

Chase had ended it as mindlessly as he'd started. He'd been at an oppressively quiet Christmas Eve dinner with his parents last year, and he'd wanted *something*. Without having planned it at all, he'd told them he was quitting. That they'd need to pay his tuition after all.

And his father had just said, "We'll let the accountant know," and taken another bite of prime rib.

And that had been that. No anger. No questions. No nothing.

Chase's coaches had been pissed, and his teammates had been disappointed, but it hadn't been any life-destroying thing. Chase was closer with Noah and Spencer than any of the guys he'd played with, anyway. So there'd been no consequences at all really, other than a vague sense of dissatisfaction with himself.

And now, staring at his uniform, Chase couldn't say how he felt. He missed his teammates every now and then. Missed the game some days more than others. But he wasn't sad, exactly. And he wasn't relieved either.

He should feel *something*, though, right? Something more than mild confusion.

Maybe in the end, he was just as empty as the people who raised him.

Chase shoved the box to the back of his closet just as his phone dinged.

It was a message from Burke.

> Professor Alpha: I'm waiting.

———

THERE WAS something intimidating about standing on Burke's doorstep.

The other night, Chase hadn't had to think about it at all. He'd gone to the bar on a whim, and then he'd just ... followed Burke's lead. Chase had followed him into the car, followed him *out* of the car, followed him into the house.

Even going to Burke's classroom today hadn't been a conscious decision. Chase had just ... ended up there, drawn to it like a magnet.

But now Chase had to knock. Deliberately. Or maybe press the doorbell.

Before Chase could decide on one or the other, the door opened to reveal Burke, a familiar glass of whiskey in hand. His brow furrowed as he took Chase in. "You've been standing on my doorstep for five minutes."

It had *not* been five whole minutes, but Chase couldn't find the words to argue because his brain had just short-circuited.

Burke was wearing casual clothes.

He had on a long-sleeved black shirt with the sleeves pushed up to the elbows and thin gray sweatpants that made it incredibly clear he wasn't wearing anything underneath.

Burke in casual clothes. Burke barefoot. Burke's big dick in sweatpants.

Burke stepped back from the door to make room for Chase. He

hadn't taken his eyes off Chase once, and the look in them was ... hungry.

It was that look on his face that did it.

Chase stepped inside.

Burke held out his hand as he led Chase into the living room. "Keys."

"I told you I'd stay," Chase told him, even as he dropped his car keys into the alpha's palm.

"And do you always do what you say you will, Chase Adler?"

"Yes."

"Mm." Without warning, Burke whirled and stepped close, shoving his nose into Chase's neck. Chase hadn't showered—hadn't washed Burke's scent off him—and Burke let out a satisfied grunt before stepping back. "Go to the bedroom. Clothes off, like before. I'd like you kneeling by the bed this time."

"Yes, Alpha."

There was no seduction. There wasn't even a kiss this time. But something hot swirled in Chase's belly regardless. They'd only done this once before, and already his body was associating Burke's orders with future pleasure.

Chase let himself into the bedroom and undressed, folding his clothes neatly and placing them again on Burke's bedside table. There was a different novel this time. Chase noted the title to look up later.

Naked, he knelt by the foot of the bed, his bare ass resting on his calves. After a moment of deliberation, he set his hands palm down on his thighs. The position would get uncomfortable fairly quickly, but that was fine. Chase didn't mind a bit of discomfort.

It didn't matter anyway—he wasn't left waiting long.

Burke appeared in the doorway after hardly a few minutes had passed, still fully dressed besides his bare feet, a mostly full glass in hand. He set it carefully on the bedside table next to Chase's clothes.

For the rest of his life, Chase was going to associate the smell of whiskey and leather with Burke, wasn't he?

Burke was hard now, his erection outlined obscenely in his thin sweats.

And that had Chase's own dick filling. Because they hadn't even really touched yet, so that meant Burke was hard and aching just from the *thought* of what he was going to do to Chase.

And what he was going to do became quickly apparent as Burke stepped up to Chase's kneeling form, the movement placing his erection directly in line with Chase's face.

Burke stroked Chase's hair back with gentle fingers, a sharp contrast to the ravenous look in his eyes. "Pretty as a picture, sweet boy."

Chase's belly swooped, his dick fully hard now from the combination of Burke's heavy scent and the promise of that clothed erection.

Burke gave a lock of Chase's hair a soft tug. "How are your dick-sucking skills, Chase Adler?"

"Average," Chase answered truthfully.

He was rewarded with a soft, husky laugh. "Mm, we'll fix that, won't we?" Burke murmured, his thumb tracing over Chase's lips. "You're such a good student. So attentive and eager to please. We'll get that score up in no time."

With his free hand, Burke lowered the waistband of his sweats, releasing his cock from its confines.

Chase's mouth watered instantly.

It was thick. So thick. Dark and ruddy in color, the dusky red head peeking out of its foreskin. It smelled like the most concentrated essence of Burke's pheromones combined with the musky scent of male arousal.

That was inside me, Chase thought dazedly. *Holy fucking shit.*

"Would you like a taste, sweet boy?"

Chase nodded without thought. He wanted it. Maybe needed

it. He'd never been particularly cock-hungry before, but now he was pretty sure he'd die if he didn't get Burke's cock in his mouth in the next thirty seconds.

Burke's thumb pressed down on Chase's lower lip. "Open."

Chase opened.

Burke eased his thick cockhead into Chase's mouth—just the tip resting on his tongue—and Chase lapped at it. Taking a taste, as he'd been promised.

Burke's flavor was salty and a little bitter. Like any other dick, probably, and yet Chase moaned, sucking on the head now, tonguing the foreskin back to get more of Burke's precum on his taste buds.

Burke's eyes were heavy on Chase's skin, his hand back in Chase's hair, toying with the strands. He wasn't pulling or tugging or telling Chase what to do—not yet, at least—so Chase let himself explore.

There was something vulnerable and incredibly hot about kneeling like this, his hands lax on his thighs, only his mouth in on the action. Like he was here to service the alpha in front of him. Here to be used.

He supposed he was.

Chase licked along the swollen veins of Burke's cock, sucked gently on the sides, spit and tongued at the loose skin where Burke's knot would eventually swell. Chase didn't try to swallow him down or suck his dick with any real sort of intent. He felt certain Burke would tell him when it was time.

By the time he got back to the fat, swollen head of Burke's cock—Chase's favorite part, he'd decided—Chase had relaxed into it, his whole body strangely comfortable as he lapped and sucked.

There was a sharp tug on Chase's hair. He leaned his head back, looking directly into Burke's molten eyes.

"*Fuck*," Burke swore, his chest rising and falling rapidly. He tugged Chase's hair again, gently shaking Chase's head with his hold. "I want to fuck your mouth."

Chase dropped his mouth open.

Burke groaned. "Have you ever had someone fuck this pretty mouth before?"

Chase had to close his mouth to answer. "No, Alpha."

He let it fall open again.

Burke swore again. Let out a hard breath. "Relax and let me lead. Pinch my thigh if you can't speak and want to stop."

Then he drove his cock deep into Chase's throat.

Chase gagged immediately, soaking Burke's cock with his spit. Burke pulled back with a mean smile. "Try again, sweet boy."

Chase opened his mouth and tried again.

He wasn't very good at it. He kept choking and gagging and coughing. But Burke didn't seem to mind. He kept swearing softly and shoving his cock back in anyway, and Chase sort of lost himself in it, a hazy mist filling his head.

And then Burke's hands were stroking his hair again, and Burke was sort of crooning at him. "Relax. There's no need to tense. No need to think at all. Just take what your alpha gives you, hm, baby boy?"

Chase opened watery eyes to find Burke staring down at him, the alpha's pupils so blown his eyes looked black in the dim light. Chase whimpered as something finally gave, his throat opening and letting Burke in all the way to the hilt.

"There it is," Burke murmured, cock pressing at the sensitive skin at the back of Chase's throat. "Look at you. Not a thought in that head."

Burke slowly picked up the pace, finally fucking Chase's throat with relative ease. Chase still gagged sometimes, but he didn't get caught up in it. He just readjusted and breathed through his nose and let Burke do what he wanted, his head fuzzy and his lips pleasantly sore.

At some point Chase had to put his hands on Burke's thighs to keep his balance, but he kept his fingers up, careful not to pinch.

"Fuck," Burke swore. "You're going to make me come, looking at me like that."

Chase hadn't even realized he was staring. He'd sort of lost any sense of space and time. There was only the weight of Burke's cock on his tongue, the smell of his pheromones invading Chase's senses. A leather-and-cherry-scented fog.

Chase realized he was hard as steel, his dick aching in the cool of the air-conditioned house. Could someone come just from sucking cock? Chase wasn't sure, but if this went on much longer, he'd probably find out.

And then Burke's cock seemed to get impossibly larger, and he tugged Chase's head back. Chase whined his distress—he wanted that *back*, damn it—and Burke clucked his tongue. "I'm going to come in your pretty mouth now, and you're not going to swallow. You're going to keep it all in your mouth for me. Understand?"

Chase nodded as best he could with Burke's hand holding him in place.

Burke slid his cock back into Chase's mouth, shallower this time. Chase immediately hollowed his cheeks and sucked, and he was rewarded with a deep groan and hot, thick cum filling his mouth.

Chase didn't swallow. He held the cum in his mouth even after Burke finally withdrew, panting, "Show me."

Chase opened his mouth. Some of the cum slipped out of the corners, despite his best efforts, but Burke didn't seem disappointed. He swept his thumb along Chase's chin, gathering what Chase had lost and slipping it back inside.

Chase sucked Burke's thumb, and Burke groaned again. "Good boy. Now you swallow."

Chase swallowed.

Burke withdrew his thumb. "Say, 'Thank you, Alpha.'"

"Thank you, Alpha."

Burke tucked his softened cock back into his sweats. The look in his eyes was no less hungry than before as he sat on the bed, patting his thick thighs. "Come here."

Chase scrambled up, hyperaware now of his painfully hard cock. He climbed onto Burke's lap, and Burke wrapped an arm around Chase's back and pressed Chase's head down until it was nestled into the crook of Burke's neck and all Chase could breathe were Burke's sex-rich pheromones.

A hand wrapped around Chase's cock. He whimpered.

"Sh," Burke soothed. "It's okay, sweet boy. I've got you."

He started jerking Chase off, and he must have put lotion or something in his hand, because it was an easy glide. He was still fully clothed, and Chase was naked on his lap. There was something vaguely humiliating about that, but of course that only made Chase's dick harder and his head foggier.

He wanted to come. He wanted Burke's cock in his mouth again. He wanted to tongue at Burke's balls because he'd forgotten to do that when he'd had the chance.

Chase settled for mouthing desperately at Burke's warm neck, huffing the alpha's pheromones like a drug as Burke jerked him off efficiently.

"You did so well, sweet boy. Your mouth was made for that, did you know? You earned every bit of that cum. You should be proud. So proud."

The words wrapped around Chase like a warm blanket, and he was lost.

He was barely aware of his own orgasm, his entire body already alight in strange, foggy pleasure. He bit down hard on Burke's neck as he trembled and spasmed, and Burke grunted.

"That's it. You deserve it."

And for a moment—spent and lust-drunk and in a strange headspace he'd never been in before—Chase believed him.

9

Killian

well-fucked, sleep-mussed Chase walking into Killian's kitchen was just as satisfying as Killian had imagined.

Well, almost.

Chase had already showered and dressed in fresh clothing he'd apparently had stashed in his car, and he walked in smelling like his enticing, minty self. Not a whiff of Killian's pheromones on him or his athletic shorts and T-shirt.

It was ... mildly infuriating.

Killian set down the coffee filter he'd started filling and strode over to rectify the situation, only to be halted by Chase's outstretched hand. "I've got a pick-up game with some of the guys from my old team in a few hours. I think one or two of them have taken your class."

As in, one or two of them would recognize Killian's scent if Chase showed up saturated in it.

Killian frowned. That was ... fine. Of course Chase wasn't going to walk out of his house reeking of his pheromones every single time the beta came over. That would be unmanageable.

Killian cleared his throat, stuffing down his ridiculous alpha instincts and returning to his task. "Coffee?"

"No, thank you. I don't drink it."

"Tea?"

"I should really—"

Killian whirled with a cut-off growl. "I'm making you breakfast. Only the choice of beverage is optional."

If Chase was surprised by Killian's insistence, he didn't show it. And really, Chase had every right to tell Killian off right now. To remind Killian that he was only entitled to boss Chase around in the bedroom, and even that much was conditional.

But the beta only nodded calmly. "Yes, Alpha." His gaze darted to the fridge. "Do you have orange juice?"

Some knot of tension in Killian's shoulders resolved itself. "Yes." He went to the fridge to fetch it. "Take a seat."

Chase sat at Killian's square kitchen table. Sat and stared, quite openly. For once, he wasn't wearing his ever-present cap.

"You're shirtless."

Killian glanced down at his chest. He'd only thrown on sweats before coming into the kitchen this morning. He'd expected Chase to sleep in a little longer, but it seemed the beta was an early riser. If he was a former athlete, it made sense. Most college teams had to keep to a rigorous training schedule, including early morning practices.

When Killian returned his gaze to the beta, Chase was still staring. Killian arched a brow. "Do you object?"

Chase's cheeks flushed pink as he shook his head. "You should teach classes like that, you know. You'd have perfect attendance."

Killian resisted a foreign urge to preen. "I'll stick to my usual methods of terrifying them into submission," he said, setting a glass of orange juice in front of his guest.

Chase grinned. "So you admit you're intimidating."

"Of course I do."

"Yeah." Chase let out a soft laugh. "Of course you do."

Killian set about making breakfast. He kept it simple: eggs and toast and some breakfast sausages he'd possibly bought expressly to feed his guest.

While he cooked, he let himself give in to his curiosity, just a little. "Old teammates, you said. You played a sport here?"

"Lacrosse," Chase told him, toying with the rim of his glass. "I ... had a scholarship."

"An injury took you out?" Killian guessed. Chase was still at the school, after all, and most athletic scholarships were protected against such things.

"No. I just—I just stopped." Something in the beta's voice had Killian turning, but Chase's expression was unreadable. "I wasn't all that passionate about it." He shrugged. "Maybe I'm just not passionate by nature." Killian gave him a look, and the blush returned to Chase's cheeks. "That's different."

"Is it?" Killian asked mildly as he set their plates in front of them, taking a seat across from the beta.

As expected, Chase ate with perfect manners, murmuring his appreciation in between delicate bites.

Killian had meant to put on a shirt before they ate, but he found himself too gratified by the way Chase's eyes kept darting to his bare chest to regret his lapse.

It was nice. Comfortable. Killian usually enjoyed his time alone in the mornings, but Chase's presence was by no means an intrusion. He lacked the chaotic energy of so many young men his age. He was calm and steady, and he seemed to fit perfectly at Killian's table.

When Chase made a move to stand and clear their dishes, Killian halted him with a hand on his wrist. Chase stopped what he was doing immediately, looking to Killian expectantly.

The instant obedience was ... heady.

Chase wasn't blushing now, or giving any sort of sly smile that could be taken as encouragement. He didn't seem to be angling for another invitation either. He seemed instead like he'd be perfectly content walking out of Killian's house with only a friendly goodbye between them. By all appearances, he could be nothing more than a polite and helpful houseguest, and not someone who'd slept wrapped in Killian's arms all night.

But he *had* done such a thing. Killian had stayed awake longer than he should have bearing witness to it.

Killian had thought it had been enough the night before, the way he'd fucked Chase's mouth like a madman and jerked him off just as ferociously. Killian had been sated and self-satisfied as he'd washed them both off in the shower, Chase pliant as stretched-out taffy under Killian's ministrations.

But then they'd returned to the bedroom, and Chase had smelled only of body wash and shampoo, and Killian had gotten ... irritated.

He'd plopped Chase on the bed, taken out a condom, and asked Chase his color in a gruff voice not at all his own. ("Green," Chase had answered immediately, dropping his legs wide open. "Green, Alpha.")

Then Killian had fucked the boy into a weeping mess.

Chase had been on his back this time. So Killian could see his face. So he could watch him go from calm but aroused to that same empty, glassy-eyed headspace as before.

And it had been just as addicting as it had been watching it happen with Killian's cock down Chase's throat.

Afterward, Killian had cleaned Chase up with only a washcloth, leaving the majority of his scent on the boy, allowing them both to drift off to sleep reeking of alpha pheromones and sex.

So that should have been it. Killian had gotten what he'd wanted: the sight of Chase Adler on his knees, pretty lips wrapped around Killian's cock. Killian had it burned into his brain for the rest of eternity. And he'd fucked him twice now, which was two times more than he ever should have.

That should definitely be it. He could put it all out of his mind now.

Except.

"I want to fuck you bare."

Once again, Killian didn't recognize his own voice. This gruff desperation wasn't at all him.

Chase's pretty green eyes widened only slightly in surprise. "Sir?"

Killian's mouth moved entirely without his permission. "I'm going to get tested, and you're going to get tested, and we're not going to fuck anyone else until this thing between us has run its course. Say yes if you agree."

"Yes," Chase said after a moment. He cocked his head. Killian still had hold of his wrist, but Chase didn't seem in any hurry to free his arm. "When will this thing have run its course, exactly?"

"Soon, I fucking hope."

Chase didn't so much as wince at the harsh words, and that made Killian feel ten times worse. He released his hold immediately. "I'm sorry. I'm an asshole before my second cup of coffee."

Chase shrugged. "I'm a student. You're a teacher. It's natural to be uncomfortable with it."

"That's no reason for me to be a dick. Come here."

Chase stood and rounded the table, and Killian pulled him onto his lap. He meant to say something comforting, but he somehow ended up kissing the beta, too hungry and demanding by half for eight in the fucking morning.

But Chase let him. He opened his mouth and sank into Killian's hold and let Killian fuck his mouth with his tongue as desperately as he wanted.

It was Killian who had to break the kiss, panting out the words.

"I'm not going to take that shit out on you. And if I try, you won't let me. Got it? Say, 'Yes, Alpha.'"

"Yes, Alpha."

"You can end it at any time."

Chase's eyes were unreadable as he answered, "I know."

Another knot loosened, this time somewhere in Killian's chest. The relief made him greedy. "I want to fuck you again before you drive home."

Chase nodded eagerly. "Okay."

Killian was already turning Chase to face the table on his lap, tugging down Chase's shorts and underwear and shoving his own sweats out of the way to free his cock, which was somehow an angry, leaking mess, like Killian was coming out of months of celibacy and not a night where he'd already blown his load twice.

He pressed a hand to Chase's back. "Lean forward."

He belatedly remembered to pull out the condom he'd for some reason stashed in his pocket, rolling it on frantically before he pressed a searching finger to Chase's hole. He was probably a little loose from the night before, but Killian would still need to—

Killian froze. "Chase?"

"Yes, Alpha?"

"Did you prep yourself in the shower?"

"A little." Chase cleared his throat. The tips of his ears were red. "I wasn't expecting— It was just in case."

"Fuck." Killian dropped his head to Chase's back. "You're dangerous."

"I'm really not."

Killian didn't argue the point. He wrapped an arm around Chase's middle and lined himself up, notching the broad head of his cock to Chase's prepped hole.

Chase groaned as Killian eased him down over his cock, his hand splayed across Chase's clenched abs. Someday very soon

Killian was going to be doing this without the condom. Bare skin to bare skin. Chase Adler, dripping with his cum.

And then perhaps ...

Visions assaulted Killian. Of this exact same position, only in his office this time. Chase in Killian's lap, his perfect ass clenching down on Killian's cock as Killian graded papers. Chase on his knees under Killian's desk, his eager mouth working desperately as Killian planned out his next lesson.

Killian grunted, tightening his arms around his beta. "You said a few hours?"

"Probably—" Chase stopped, letting out another desperate groan as Killian stood, kicking back his chair and bending Chase fully over the table. "Probably just an hour now."

"Don't worry, sweet boy," Killian soothed, driving his hips back and then sliding in, Chase's channel tight and hot and smooth as butter. "I'll wash my scent off afterward. You won't even be late."

Killian wouldn't have been able to make this last even if he wanted to. It was going to be quick and furious and beastly, because apparently that was what this unassuming beta had turned Killian into.

Fuck.

Killian was in so much fucking trouble.

10

Chase

Chase nursed his flat beer and tried not to stare at one of his roommates making out heavily with a beta girl who'd introduced herself approximately thirty seconds ago. Chase wasn't a natural voyeur, but also they were, like, right in front of his face.

"Do you think Spence has adapted to need less oxygen than the average human?" Noah asked next to him.

Chase shrugged. "That would be pretty quick work, evolution-arily speaking."

"True." Noah shook his empty bottle. "I'm going to get another drink. Want one?"

"I'm good."

Chase didn't even want the drink he had. He'd poured it over an hour ago—his first drink of the night—and he was barely halfway through it. As a beta, he wasn't particularly pheromone-sensitive, but for some reason all the mixed scents in the heavily populated house were making his stomach roil.

It was shitty of him to mope about it though. He was the one who'd dragged his friends out to this party.

Well, he'd dragged Noah. Spencer had been all for it, thrilled that the three of them were finally free on the same Friday night.

They were at a house party one of Chase's old teammates was throwing. Chase had always liked the guy's parties; they were a good time without going over the top. But it was also Friday night, and Chase had become accustomed to ... certain things on his Friday nights.

Basically, he and Burke had fallen into a routine the past month or so. Friday evenings, Burke would text him. Chase would show up. Burke would make him see God. Chase would stay the night. Burke would cook Chase breakfast. Chase would leave, stomach full and body well used.

They kept it to one night a week, and for some reason it was always Friday night, and that had been working fine. Chase only thought about the alpha professor 90 percent of the time otherwise, but he'd been making do with fantasies and anticipation.

Until today, when Burke had texted Chase, not *I'm waiting*, but *I'm unavailable this evening. You owe me double orgasms, sweet boy. I'll wring them out of you one way or another.*

And yeah, the last part of the text had made Chase's belly swoop and his dick fill, but still, what the fuck?

It was Burke's damn fault Chase had developed a Pavlovian response to Fridays, anyway.

As soon as Chase woke up Friday mornings, his skin was hot and sensitive, and he only ever barely made it through classes without drifting off into horrifically explicit daydreams that had him fighting erections in public.

And now tonight he was all worked up with nowhere to put it. And Spence was being Spence, and Noah was clearly missing his own omega professor, and everything was just ... not ideal.

"What did Mr. Whiskers ever do to you?"

Chase pulled himself out of his sulky thoughts to find the host of the party—Carter Bishop—standing beside him, red plastic cup in hand.

"What?" Chase asked.

Carter gestured to a small white porcelain cat on a floating shelf that Chase had apparently been directing his gaze toward. "Mr. Whiskers. You're glaring at him pretty intently." He sipped his drink thoughtfully. "I don't think I've ever even seen you look angry before, so he must have done something bad."

Chase cocked his head, studying the little feline. It was beyond out of place in what was essentially a frat house. "Maybe I was just shocked by the big, bad lacrosse captain having a secret porcelain kitty-cat fetish."

"Former captain," Carter corrected mildly. "And I have layers."

Chase huffed a laugh. He liked Carter. He always had. The alpha had been a good captain until he'd been taken out by an ACL tear shortly before Chase had quit the team. Carter hadn't seemed as angry about his fate as he could have been, but maybe that was because his athletic scholarship had been protected against injuries.

"I was never going to play professionally," he'd told Chase once with a shrug, his postsurgery knee thick with bandages. "And classes will be easier now that my schedule's open."

So yeah, Chase liked him. Everyone liked him though. Carter was a classic all-American alpha catch, with thick brown hair and sharp blue eyes and an honest-to-God dimple on his chin. He was friendly to everyone without being a pushover, and he was generous with his time and money. He didn't have to be captain of the team to have social clout.

Which meant any moment ...

And sure enough, a gaggle of omega sorority sisters suddenly materialized in front of them, giggling to each other as one of them asked Carter if he'd mix them up some drinks.

Chase flipped his cap back to the front and gave Carter a nudge. "Good party, man. Catch you later."

He sidestepped Spencer sucking face and slipped out the front door. The night was comfortably cool, and Chase let out a relieved breath, making his way to the side of the house and taking a seat on the dry grass. He set his half-full beer on the ground.

Why had he come here, anyway? He should have asked the guys to stay in tonight, maybe have a movie night and order pizza. That probably would have been more his speed with the mood he was in.

Except it would have been just the same, wouldn't it? Because that still wouldn't have been *right*. It wouldn't have been the Friday night Chase had become accustomed to. He wouldn't have been fucked or held or told he was good and perfect and beautiful.

Jesus.

Chase pulled out his phone, but there was nothing. Of course there wasn't. Burke had already backed out—he had no other reason to text. Chase frowned down at the blank screen.

But what gave Burke the right, anyway? Shouldn't he have given Chase a little more notice? More explanation? Chase had—he had *needs*. And if Burke was going to bail on him, who was to say Chase wasn't going to try to get those needs met elsewhere? This whole situation was a ... mutual compulsive attraction thing, not a dating thing. Chase didn't owe Burke anything. He could go back to the party now and try to find someone else to scratch this incessant itch.

Except it wouldn't be what he'd come to expect, if Chase found it elsewhere. Not the sex and not the moments after. It wouldn't be the same with anyone but Burke.

Unless it was *Burke* who was getting his needs met elsewhere.

A wave of nausea hit Chase out of nowhere. Burke wouldn't do that to him, though ... right? He'd said they'd be exclusive until this thing ran its course.

Was tonight Burke's way of saying this thing *had* run its course? Maybe he'd gone to the club he used to go to, no longer satisfied with Chase's performance or something.

Maybe he was fucking some obedient omega right now, as Chase wallowed by himself in the grass, none the wiser.

Chase jumped up, only half aware of kicking his beer onto the grass. Before he knew it, he'd dug his car keys out of his pocket and was heading down the street to where he'd parked.

There was one sure way to find out if Burke was home or not.

———

BURKE TOOK LONGER to answer the door than Chase was used to. Which made sense, since Chase had been explicitly told that Burke was unavailable tonight, and thus was not expected to be here.

Chase frowned at the thick wooden door in front of him.

Oh fuck. What was he even doing here? Why had he come? What the fuck was he hoping to accomplish?

He turned to leave just as the door opened. And there was Burke, his dark brow creased in concern. "Chase? Is everything all right?"

Chase froze in place for a moment, then pivoted back to face the door fully. Burke looked good. Really good. He was dressed casually but still nicely, somewhere between his teaching clothes and those sweats that made Chase go a little feral. His dark hair was falling in front of his face, and his pheromones were mellow in a way they rarely were when Chase first arrived at the door.

When Chase said nothing, Burke's frown deepened, although he seemed more confused than angry. "I told you I was busy tonight, didn't I?"

"You did."

Classical music drifted out of the open door, as did the distinct smells of a home-cooked meal. Chase glared over Burke's shoulder into the house. What exactly was going on in there?

Burke sighed and looked out past Chase to the street, then gestured inside. "Come in, then."

Chase stepped inside the house and then immediately wished he hadn't. There were two wine glasses on the living room coffee table, both of them half full. And with the music and the food—

Chase whirled on Burke. "Is this a date?"

Just then a man somewhere around Burke's age walked in from the direction of the dining room. He was handsome and blond and dressed in a suit, and he was followed by an equally attractive bearded guy holding a beer. Chase was pretty sure they were both alphas, but it was hard to tell with Burke's heavy pheromones already saturating the house.

"*Is* this a date, Killian?" the blond guy asked, pressing a hand to his chest in faux shock. "You rascal, you should have told us! I would have worn a sluttier shirt."

Burke pinched the bridge of his nose. "As I said, I'm occupied tonight. Chase, this is Devon and Prince." He pointed to the blond and the bearded guy respectively. "Please ignore anything and everything they might say."

The bearded guy—Prince—now had a massive grin on his face. "Holy shit, it's the fuck-up-your life someone, isn't it?"

Burke cleared his throat, sliding an unreadable look Chase's way. "As I said, ignore everything."

Oh fuck. Chase had definitely fucked up, hadn't he? He'd just barged in on some sort of middle-aged boys' night. "Burke, I—"

"You call him *Burke*?" Devon asked with clear delight, a Cheshire grin on his face.

"You call me Burke?" Burke echoed.

Chase supposed he'd never said it out loud in Burke's presence. It was always "Alpha" or "sir" when they were together. He shrugged. "I guess I do, in my head." He was beyond flustered now, and it made his voice uncharacteristically sharp as he added, "It's your name, isn't it?"

Burke gave Chase another look, this one very, very clear.

"Sir," Chase added immediately.

"Oh my god," Devon groaned, snatching up one of the half-empty wineglasses. "I wish I had a camera."

"You have your phone," Prince suggested.

"But what if Killian decides to break it over my head? I can see the smoke pouring out of his ears as we speak." Devon wagged a finger at Burke. "So this is why you wanted to move dinner to Saturday." He stepped to Chase, his hand held out. "Devon Carmichael, longtime friend of your *Burke* here. Absolutely delighted to make your acquaintance."

Chase shook the man's hand. "Chase Adler. Pleasure to meet you, sir."

"Oh." Devon glanced to Burke with a sly smile. "I get it now."

"You didn't get it from the face alone?" Prince asked, giving Chase a not-very-subtle wink when Chase looked his way.

Burke treated his friends to a truly terrifying glower and then pulled Chase to the side. He placed his hands on Chase's shoulders, rubbing them up and down his upper arms briskly as he looked him over. "You're really all right?"

"Yes, sir. Sorry. I'm—I should get going, huh?"

There was a long silence as Burke studied him. "No," Burke eventually said, shaking his head slowly. "You'll stay. But you'll need to be punished, sweet boy. I set a boundary, and you ignored it."

Chase hadn't expected Burke to call him that—sweet boy—in front of other people. But Burke had, and very clearly. He hadn't even lowered his voice when he did it. Chase shifted in place, not sure if he was pleased or embarrassed.

"Color?" Burke asked, his thumbs sweeping over Chase's biceps.

"Green," Chase answered instantly.

Burke's pheromones sharpened, the leather growing richer, and a smile graced his lips, there and gone again. "Would you like to join us, or wait for your punishment in the bedroom?"

So matter of fact, even with his friends blatantly listening in. It made Chase hot and squirmy. He cleared his throat before speaking. "I'll wait in the bedroom."

"Do you need a book?"

Chase gave him a look. "I have a phone."

Burke arched a dark brow. "Try it again without the sass. I'm not in the mood for brat taming."

"I have my phone to keep me entertained, Alpha."

"There's my sweet boy. Go."

Chase turned toward Burke's bedroom, ducking his head to avoid the amused stares of Devon and Prince.

"Chase," Burke called after him.

Chase turned. Burke's gaze was hot enough to burn. "You can call me Killian, if you like. In your head, that is."

Chase hurried down the hall. Once he was safely enclosed in Burke's bedroom, he climbed onto the bed, fully clothed for now. He didn't know how long Burke would be, and Chase didn't fancy having either of Burke's friends wander in and find him naked.

Chase took his phone out but didn't unlock it just yet. He could hear the murmur of voices through the wall, as well as some light laughter. None of it sounded angry or mean-spirited.

Chase inhaled deeply. Leather and cherry. He was warm all over, and only part of it was embarrassment. Or arousal.

He'd fucked up tonight. He'd been unforgivably rude, barging in when Burke had told him he was busy. And Burke—*Killian*, Chase corrected, trying to get used to the change—hadn't sent him away. He hadn't threatened to deprive Chase of his company until he got his act together. He wasn't going to end things because

Chase had gotten difficult. He'd even offered to let Chase join him and his friends, for fuck's sake.

Chase didn't know what to do with that.

Growing up, the few—very few—times Chase had acted out, he'd only ever been ignored all the more, brushed off to be sequestered with the nanny for days on end. He'd learned quickly that rebellion didn't lead to anything good. At least if he'd behaved, his parents had sometimes remembered to shoot him some sort of acknowledgment.

Chase had been taught that it was easier to go along with things, no matter how bad they felt, and live with the crumbs of affection that got him.

But Killian hadn't ignored Chase tonight. Kind of the opposite, actually.

Because when the alpha came back to this bedroom, he was going to mete out the punishment he deemed necessary, and then he was going to probably—judging by the heat in his eyes just now—fuck Chase like there was no tomorrow. And then he was going to hold him and sleep beside him and make him breakfast in the morning. All because …

Because why?

Because maybe Killian cared.

And maybe Chase cared too.

11

Killian

Killian had never so badly wanted to shove his friends out a window. Preferably one that overlooked two or more stories.

Devon was smirking over his wineglass, and Prince was looking incredibly self-satisfied, sprawled in his chair like a graceless oaf. The two of them weren't saying a word, which was somehow so much worse.

Killian let out a deep, weary sigh. "All right. Have at it."

"Why, Burke darling, whatever do you mean?" Devon cocked his head, the picture of innocence.

Prince let out a guffaw, then covered it by tearing into a bite of his dinner. "Steak's great, Kill," he said with his mouth full. "Perfectly cooked."

The two of them were here for the group's monthly dinner. Killian had tried to push it to Saturday. (Because he'd gotten used to a certain routine, was all, not because of any other reason.) But Devon had insisted he was unavailable any other night this week.

"Yes, perfectly cooked," Devon purred, although he hadn't touched his steak since the interruption. "Are you going to bring sweet Chase any?"

Killian had to force himself to unclench his jaw. "I'm sure he's already eaten."

"Oh, you know the youths. Always missing their dinners." Devon took a sip of his wine. "How old is he, anyway?"

"Old enough."

"Aha!" Devon leaned over the table, pointing his finger like he'd caught Killian out at something. "Old enough for *what*, exactly?"

"Ignore Devon," Prince said, his mouth full of yet another bite of steak. "He's just happy to see you so smitten."

Killian gave him an incredulous look. "I am not smitten."

"Yes, you are."

"Says who?"

Prince waved a hand. "Your face. Your pheromones. The way that boy looks at you. You've got to be treating him awfully nice to have him looking at you that way."

Killian decided to focus on his wine. It was bright and peppery, a surprisingly good balance to the steak. It was a meal he might have prepared for himself on a particularly decadent night.

Yes, that was it. He could pretend he was alone. That he had no friends to speak of.

"It's fine if you're *not* smitten," Devon said easily, running a hand through his blond hair. "Bring him to the club some night, then. I wouldn't mind a little taste. Neither would Prince, if the drool is any indication."

An alpha growl rang out, followed by the sound of glass breaking. Wine sloshed over the tablecloth in front of Killian's plate.

Killian stared down at the table in front of him. Apparently he'd set his wineglass down too hard, and the stem had snapped.

That wasn't—Killian didn't *break* things. He didn't get *angry*.

Neither of his friends looked at all surprised. Prince threw his napkin over the spill and then got back to his steak.

"What's the problem?" Devon asked, all teasing gone. "He's lovely, and he clearly adores you."

Killian wasn't sure where they were seeing *that*. Outside the bedroom, Chase was frustratingly difficult to read.

Although, he had come here tonight.

Why had Chase come here tonight?

Sex? Comfort? Routine? A simple check-in to make sure Killian was adhering to the terms of their arrangement?

Killian cleared his throat and set the broken cup of his glass carefully on his plate. "Like you said, he's young. And a student."

"*Your* student?"

"He was."

"Psh." Devon shrugged. "Past tense. Who the fuck cares?"

Killian didn't, not really. He wasn't sure why he'd even brought it up. The age gap, maybe. The fear that, with the years between them, their compatibility in the bedroom wouldn't extend elsewhere.

The problem was, Killian already had a sneaking suspicion it did.

Killian didn't usually like having anyone in his space for a prolonged time. He wasn't used to it, and any disruption to his accustomed way of doing things tended to put him in a foul mood. But it was disconcertingly easy to have Chase at Killian's side on Saturday mornings. The beta just ... fit. The same way he had at that bar. Chase was comfortable in himself in a way that was absurdly sexy in someone so young, especially someone who fell apart so easily under Killian's hands.

What would it be like to have Chase at his side at a dinner like this? He'd do well, Killian knew. He'd be polite and interested in the company, and Killian could easily picture how sweetly embarrassed he'd be at Devon's teasing. And he'd have Prince eating out of the palm of his hand by the end.

Killian wanted that. It was frustrating how much he wanted that.

And the compatibility in the bedroom couldn't be dismissed so easily anyway, could it? The first time Killian had taken Chase bare, he thought he'd been transported directly into heaven. He'd spent what felt like hours afterward fingering the boy, pushing his cum back inside and watching it trickle out, coaxing another and then another orgasm from the weeping beta. It had soothed some feral alpha piece of Killian, breeding him like that.

Killian startled when he realized Prince was at his side, taking the sopping napkin and plate with the shattered glass away from him. "We've broken him," Prince said, presumably to Devon, before heading off to the kitchen.

"You haven't. I'm just ... adjusting."

Devon set his wine down with a sigh. "We should be off anyway. You have a sweet boy awaiting punishment. It would be bad form to stick around."

Killian ran a hand over his face. "Stay a little longer," he said. "He likes the anticipation, and I need to be a little ... steadier before I go in there."

Devon gave him a shrewd glance. "You're always steady."

"That's what I thought too."

Killian was pretty sure he had been too. Until Chase Adler had appeared in his life.

————

A HALF HOUR LATER, Killian had sent Devon and Prince off, neither of them having been ejected from any windows in the process.

Killian stood in front of his bedroom door and pushed up the sleeves of his thin black sweater. He hadn't missed the way Chase always looked at his forearms, and Killian considered it a good weapon to have in his arsenal.

Perhaps Killian didn't know why Chase had come here without an invitation, but he certainly knew what he wanted to do with the beta now that he had.

Namely, take Chase apart piece by piece until he was a whimpering mess, then cover him with Killian's scent and stuff him full of Killian's cum until there was no part of him—inside or out—that wasn't claimed.

Killian let out a breath and opened the door.

Chase was standing next to the bed, in the process of folding his recently removed shirt. He lifted his head at Killian's arrival, and his flushed cheeks were evidence enough that he was aware of his misstep.

Killian crossed his arms, tutting loudly. "Still dressed, sweet boy?"

"I thought— Your friends ..." Chase trailed off, then cleared his throat. "I'm sorry, Alpha. It won't happen again."

"It won't, will it?" Killian asked, soft and dangerous.

Chase let out a stuttered breath, then quickly removed his pants and underwear, folding them carefully even in his hurry.

The air was thick with anticipation, and Killian drank it in. They hadn't done anything like this before, any sort of punishment. Chase was so sweetly obedient it hadn't been necessary.

When Chase's clothes were neatly piled, he clasped his hands behind his back. "Should I kneel, Alpha?"

Killian shook his head. "Come here."

Chase took careful steps to stand in front of Killian, his poor cock already rising from the attention, though Killian hadn't so much as laid a finger on him.

Killian cupped Chase's throat, stroking his thumb along his jawline. "You were very naughty tonight, weren't you?"

He could feel Chase's swallow. "Yes, Alpha."

"But you're still a good boy underneath, aren't you?"

Chase's green eyes were fierce as he answered, "*Yes*, Alpha."

"So you're going to take your punishment, and that will be that. All forgiven."

"Just like that?" Chase asked, a strange note of hopefulness in his tone.

"Just like that."

"Can I ask …?"

"Spanking," Killian answered. "Ten strokes."

Chase's brow furrowed. "And that's enough?"

Killian's grin was all teeth. "That's enough. I'm not any sort of devotee of impact play, but you have a gorgeous ass, and I can admit I won't mind seeing it flushed red with my handprints."

"Oh." Chase swallowed again, and his gaze took on a glassy sheen.

"Color?"

"Green."

After a gentle squeeze, Killian removed his hold on Chase's throat. "I'm going to sit at the head of the bed, and you're going to lie in my lap."

The pink flush had traveled down to Chase's chest now. "Yes, Alpha."

Killian got into position, his back against the headboard, his cock now straining painfully against his zipper. It couldn't be helped. A nude Chase, flushed and embarrassed after hardly a word, was enough to drive anyone a little mad.

Chase didn't hesitate or delay. As soon as Killian was seated, he climbed onto the bed and laid himself face down over Killian's lap with his usual grace. After a moment, he folded his arms and rested his chin on them.

Killian slipped a hand under Chase's hips, adjusting Chase's erection to lay flat against his lap. He gave it a rough stroke while he was at it.

"A-Alpha?"

Killian released Chase's cock, turning his attention to those firm, muscular cheeks. "Yes, sweet boy?"

"What if I come?"

"Then you come." Killian grinned, squeezing at the round flesh. "I look forward to it."

He continued to squeeze and stroke and caress, warming up the skin. Chase sighed and relaxed into the touch, his body losing any remaining tension and melting over Killian's lap.

Killian would have to remember that. He should massage the boy more often.

But that would come later.

Killian gave Chase's ass a single, firm swat. Chase's body immediately tensed up, and he let out a choked gasp.

Definitely his first spanking.

"That was one," Killian told him. "Count for me."

It took Chase a moment to speak. "One, Alpha."

Killian immediately swatted him again.

"*Ungh.*"

"I'm waiting."

"Two, Alpha."

"Good boy," Killian praised, and he was rewarded with the sight of a full-body shiver taking over all those muscles.

Killian spread them out after that, keeping his strokes unpredictable. It was partly by intention—a way to increase the anticipation for his sweet boy—and partly because he quickly became obsessed with patting and squeezing at the reddened flesh in between each hit. Obsessed with the way Chase whimpered and wiggled to avoid his touch, only to grind his erection against Killian's lap in his efforts to get away.

Between a rock and a hard place, the poor thing.

After the fifth, Killian began to dip his hands between Chase's legs, stroking at his taint, caressing whatever tender skin he could reach. Chase's squirming quickly became a determined rocking against him.

By the eighth swat, Chase's skin was bright pink. Killian gave him the last two spanks in quick succession, putting more strength in them than the others. Chase's back arched as he cried out, "Nine! Ten! Oh god!"

His voice was thick, and he'd started sniffling some time ago, tearful even as he desperately tried to get friction against his hard cock.

"All done, sweet boy," Killian praised. "And you took it so well. Now what do you say?"

"G-Green."

Killian grinned. It was possible he hadn't stopped grinning since Chase had climbed onto the bed and presented his ass for punishment. "Not that, sweet boy."

It had become a kind of addiction, these moments in time where Chase tried to figure out what was expected of him. He almost always got it right. His intuition was remarkable.

"Th-Thank you, Alpha," Chase said after another moment, and his voice was thick and more than a little dazed. "Thank you for—for my punishment."

"Mm, there it is." Killian was lightly petting at Chase's reddened skin now, resisting the mildly disturbing urge to lean down and bite Chase's ass. Hard. "You may come now, if you can manage it like this."

Despite the continued sniffing, Chase immediately began to hump against Killian with new desperation. It was a kind of torture for Killian, hard and aching as he was, but he'd be fucking Chase full of his cum soon enough. It wouldn't kill him to practice a little self-restraint.

Probably.

Killian slipped his fingers into the shadowed furrow of Chase's ass, petting at his hole, and Chase came with a shudder and a drawn-out moan, his cum spurting half on Killian's thigh and half on his bedspread.

And then Chase was scrambling up to straddle Killian's lap, his arms tight around Killian's neck, his body racked with forceful sobs.

Killian wrapped his arms around Chase's back, holding him just as tightly in return.

He'd already known there was pain in Chase Adler, something deep and raw and possibly unexamined. The few comments Chase had made over their time together pointed in the direction of his family. And weren't familial wounds almost always the case?

Maybe it was a good thing Chase had acted out tonight. A bit of catharsis never hurt. Chase didn't seem the type to engage in it often enough.

And here he had Killian to tend his wounds afterward.

"There we go," Killian soothed, rubbing his palms up and down Chase's trembling muscles. "Let it out, baby boy. Let it all out."

12

Chase

Chase couldn't remember the last time he'd cried.

Well, he could. It was sometime around the last time Killian had fucked his face. But he couldn't remember the last time he'd really let go and sobbed it out. Crying wasn't exactly something the Adler household approved of, and Chase had gotten used to the lack.

But it was easy right now, with Killian holding him so tightly. Like a dam had broken somewhere inside Chase, broken apart bit by bit with each slap of Killian's palm against Chase's ass.

Was that a thing? It must have been, because Killian didn't exactly seem surprised by this turn of events.

Chase hadn't realized how good it would feel to cry. How freeing, how emptying.

But eventually his sobs subsided and he was only being held, his face tucked into Killian's neck.

"Did it hurt that badly?" Killian asked softly, rubbing at Chase's back.

"No," Chase told him. His voice was thick from all the water-works. "It felt good. Really, really good."

It had. Chase hadn't been expecting it, the way the sharp stinging slaps on his bare ass had made his cock fill. Hadn't expected the hungry way Killian had groped him, like he was getting just as much pleasure out of Chase's punishment as he did out of fucking him. Hadn't expected the intense, almost painful sense of release as the punishment had ended. Hadn't expected how his mind had gone hazy and his body had gone hot and the tears had escaped as easy as breathing.

"You have a lot of pain hiding in there, don't you, sweet boy?"

Chase let out a stuttered breath. He didn't talk about that. Not ever. He knew how privileged he was. How lucky. No one needed his whining.

But just for this moment, Chase was spent and empty in a way that made it easy to admit, "Yeah. Maybe more than I thought."

Killian stroked a firm hand down Chase's spine. "Thank you for giving it to me. Your pain."

It was such a nice fucking thing to say that Chase couldn't come up with a response. He could feel Killian's hard length underneath his ass, and even though Chase was tear-streaked and snotty, he couldn't help shifting against it.

"Did the crying ruin the mood?" he asked, and he was too worn out to be embarrassed by how desperate the question came out.

Killian barked a sharp laugh. "If you think a few tears are going to stop me from stuffing you full of my cum, then you're not the bright student I thought you were."

Well.

That answered that.

It was a good thing too. Maybe it was weird to want sex after the kind of catharsis Chase had just experienced, but he did. Chase craved the comfort of it, the familiar ecstasy of Killian manipulating his body and dictating his actions. Craved that empty-headed space where there was no thought, only easy obedience and the pleasure that came with it.

There was a tug on Chase's hair, and he lifted his head to meet Killian's blue eyes, dark with arousal. "You're going to come again with my cock in you, baby boy," Killian warned, rough and low.

"You think?" Chase asked dumbly.

"I do." Killian pushed him gently off his lap. "I want you kneeling with your hands on the headboard. I want to see my handiwork while I fuck you."

Chase stayed where he was for a second, craning his neck as he looked backward and tried to get a peek at his own ass. "Can I ...?"

Killian understood the unspoken question. He always seemed to. "Mirror or photo?"

Chase didn't let himself think too hard about his answer. "Photo."

Killian nodded his head at the headboard. "Into position."

Chase scrambled to the head of the bed, kneeling there while he gripped the top of the headboard. He heard the telltale sound of someone taking a picture with their phone. His belly swooped. He was going to have evidence now. Evidence of what Killian had done to him. Something to look at when they were apart and Chase got antsy for his alpha's touch.

The bed dipped as Killian climbed back on. And then strong hands were on Chase's ass, groping without a bit of delicacy. Chase gasped.

"Sore?" Killian asked gruffly from behind him.

"Yes, Alpha."

"Mm."

Killian kept right on groping, the pleasure-pain of it sending hot licks of fire from Chase's tender skin straight to his dick. Killian started kissing at Chase's shoulders, his mouth as hot as his touch. And then a lubed finger was pressing at Chase's hole, and Chase leaned into the headboard, pushing his ass out in a way that was probably much too eager.

Damn it. Chase was impatient for it—that hot press of Killian's dick inside him. He should have prepped while he'd waited. He hadn't thought of it, too turned around and in his own head from the twists and turns of the night.

"This would be easier if I was an omega, wouldn't it?"

Chase had no idea why he said it. Maybe because he was still raw and vulnerable, split open in a way that had some strange, nagging insecurity coming out. The rumors had always said Killian fucked omegas. He was an alpha, after all. Most alphas preferred them when it came down to it.

Killian paused for only a moment before he went back to opening Chase up. "Do you know why I usually fucked omegas at the club?" he asked, his tone conversational.

"Because you had a t-type?" Chase guessed, trying to hold on to the thread of conversation as Killian mercilessly worked a second finger into him.

"Because their pheromones make them easy to read. It's like a cheat code for a scene. Less risky with a new partner, having another way to sense limits. And do you know why that doesn't matter with you?" Killian's hard cock brushed against Chase's hip as he added a third finger. He must have been planning to take Chase hard—he was rarely ever patient enough to get beyond two.

He'd asked Chase a question, hadn't he?

Chase made some sort of vague, garbled negative sound in his throat, still pushing his ass out like a desperate slut.

Killian let out a low chuckle, running his nose along the back of Chase's neck, sending a shiver down Chase's spine. "Because as inscrutable as you are out in the world, in here, with my hands on you, you're an open fucking book. I don't need your pheromones,

Chase Adler. This pretty face and this responsive fucking body of yours tell me everything I need to know."

Killian withdrew his fingers, pressing his broad, muscled body against Chase's back, rocking him into the headboard. His hard cock slid against Chase's crease, a tease and a promise. "And you're such a good, good boy that I know you'll tell me 'red' if you need to. Isn't that right?"

Chase was hot all over, probably flushed from his toes to the tips of his ears. Whatever Killian was talking about, it was only with him that Chase was like this. Only with Killian that he became this open, desperate thing. But it was too mortifying for Chase to say out loud, even now.

"And who the fuck needs slick?" Killian asked, tugging Chase's hips out again and giving one a firm slap. "That's what lube's for. Keep your hands where they are."

And then the blunt head of his cock was pressing in, and he was filling Chase with the whole thick length of it.

God, it felt good, the way Chase's body stretched around that girth. The way Killian's potent pheromones wrapped around him as his insides were rearranged.

Killian didn't wait for him to adjust, didn't pause for Chase to take a breath. He started slamming his hips like he was as desperate for this as Chase was, like he'd used up all his patient goodwill and now it was his time to rut and fuck and claim.

And Chase fucking melted, like he always did.

There was a stinging burn where the wiry hair on Killian's groin and thighs was brushing against the sore skin of Chase's ass, and the edge of pain was doing something weird to Chase. It was like he couldn't get a handle on his own arousal, couldn't make it fit into any manageable space.

And Killian's hands were roaming everywhere, tugging at Chase's hardening cock only sporadically, never lingering anywhere for too long.

And he smelled good. He always smelled so fucking good.

Maybe that was part of the problem. Part of what had Chase wondering about omegas. Because Chase *liked* the fact that Killian was an alpha. He liked Killian's big frame and his thick cock and his overwhelming scent. He liked the animalistic growls Killian let out when Chase's body was satisfying him in just the right way. Liked the press of blunt teeth at the nape of his neck.

Wait. No. Actually, that part was new.

Chase froze, his cock so hard it ached now. Killian's teeth were teasing at the spot where a mate bite might lie. Even betas could be mated, though the bite had to be refreshed every few years.

The pressure increased, just a touch, and then the teeth left Chase's nape, and Killian was nibbling at Chase's ear, laughing lowly at Chase's desperate moan. "I'm going to knot you one day, Chase Adler," he breathed, sounding hungry and frantic and maybe a little mean.

Chase's orgasm came out of nowhere.

Killian's hand wasn't even on Chase's cock, and Chase was still gripping the headboard like he'd been told. But his balls drew up, and his whole body started shaking, and his cock spurted completely untouched all over Killian's fancy pillows.

"Oh fuck," Killian swore, broad hands gripping hard at Chase's hips, slamming Chase back into each thrust. "What a good fucking boy you are. I knew you could do it, baby. Your body knows what's best for it, doesn't it? Knows it needs to come with this big alpha cock inside it."

He slid a hand around and cupped Chase's dick as it softened, hips still pumping away until suddenly he slammed in deep and let out a harsh growl.

He came a lot, as an alpha. And he seemed to like that part especially—how much he came inside Chase. So Chase wasn't surprised when moments later he was drawn away from the headboard and rearranged on his side with Killian behind him, the weight of his gaze on Chase's ass a tangible thing.

"Is it an alpha thing?" Chase asked idly, feeling loose and spent and empty in the best way. "Like breeding your omega?"

"There's an idea for role-play," Killian murmured, parting Chase's cheeks, presumably so he had a better view. "But I don't think I need to be an alpha to find my cum trickling out of you immensely satisfying."

He watched for a little while longer before shuffling closer and spooning Chase, not seeming to mind the mess. "How are you feeling, sweet boy?"

"Good." Chase let out a long, satisfied breath. His ass burned, he was lying in a wet spot, and he had sweat cooling and sticking all over his body. "Really good."

"I'm glad." Killian wrapped a firm arm around Chase's waist. "I'm going to ask you some questions now."

"A pop quiz?"

Killian bit Chase's shoulder none so gently. "Very funny. Tell me why you came tonight."

And Chase was warm and safe and relaxed enough to tell the truth. "Fridays. I'm used to Fridays."

"Fridays will be our day, then," Killian said easily. "No exceptions. What else?"

Was he talking about demands? That wasn't exactly Chase's forte—asking for things. Except ...

"When it's done, you have to tell me," Chase requested quietly. "Explicitly. Don't leave me guessing."

"Good," Killian said, like maybe he meant it. Like maybe Chase asking him for things was a privilege and not a burden. "I won't leave you guessing. What else?"

Chase shifted on the bed, but he was locked in place by Killian's hold. "I don't know. That's it, I think."

"I have a few for you."

Chase tilted his head back in surprise. "You do?"

Killian's gaze was steady, even as his lips curled into a half smile. "I'd like to see you more often. Fridays will be ours, like we said. But would you be opposed to other nights? Or staying longer some Saturdays? Perhaps Sunday afternoons?"

Chase was so taken aback he couldn't overthink it. It didn't help that Killian looked unbelievably good, all flushed and sweaty with his dark hair hanging over his brow.

"Um, no. I'm not opposed."

Killian cupped Chase's face, pulling him in for a filthy kiss. "It's settled, then," he said afterward, and there was no mistaking the satisfaction in his voice. "Let's draw a bath, shall we? And then you're eating some steak. I've been told I cooked it to perfection, and I won't sleep until you have a taste."

Chase let himself be drawn up from the bed and led to the bathroom, following Killian's lead in some sort of daze.

So that was it. They were ... dating? Fucking? Seeing each other in secret, only more so? But not exactly secret, because Killian's friends knew now.

They were *something*; that was for sure. Something Chase should maybe push to define, but he shied away at the thought of it, like a sore spot he couldn't bear touching. To define it would be too ...

Chase didn't know, actually. It didn't matter anyway. He'd be getting to see more of Killian; that much was clear. Getting more of this thing between them. And that, for Chase, was enough.

That was more than enough.

13

Chase

"You have any idea why Noah called this meeting?" Chase asked Spencer, shoving the alpha's sock-clad feet off his lap for the tenth time in a minute.

"No idea." Spencer popped his feet right back in Chase's lap, wiggling his toes. "But you can give these bad boys a rub if you like, maybe help pass the time."

"Oh, can I? Can I really?"

But Chase found himself digging his thumbs into Spencer's arches anyway while they waited for Noah to arrive. Persistence like that should really be rewarded.

It was Friday morning of their spring break. All three of them had stayed in town: Spencer to work, Noah to make up his missed midterms, and Chase because he had nothing better to do. Well, he'd *planned* to have better things to do, but he hadn't seen as much of Killian as he'd hoped. It turned out professors had a lot of grading to do during the break. Plus, Spencer had wanted to hang out with Chase as much as possible when he wasn't working, since Noah had been so caught up in schoolwork.

But the distance was surprisingly difficult.

Things had changed between them since the night Chase had shown up unannounced. They'd ... deepened, maybe. Chase knew stuff about Killian now, both big and little. The novels on his bedside table were spy thrillers, for one, most of them set in World War I or II. Killian made his way through them voraciously, despite his impressive workload at the university. He was an early riser but often taciturn and grumpy before he'd had at least two cups of coffee. He took speaking engagements in the summer as a way out of the Phoenix heat, and he often consulted with other professors who needed help with any tricky statistics in their research. He liked feeding Chase, and he liked reading with Chase under his arm. He preferred when Chase reeked of him and nothing else.

What Chase *didn't* know was whether Killian was as unsettled by this time apart as he was.

But of course he wasn't. It had barely been a week.

Spencer groaned in approval as Chase worked his feet over, bringing Chase's attention back to the present. "Probably has something to do with why Noah ran off and disappeared for a week, though, right?" Spencer guessed. "Like, why he missed all his midterms? You think his omega went into heat?"

"I think he'll tell us that if he wants to."

Spencer patted Chase's baseball hat. "Sweet, considerate Chasey."

Just for that, Chase stopped his massage.

Spencer's whine of complaint was interrupted by Noah rushing into the apartment. His pheromones were off the charts, bright and bursting with happiness, and he smelled kind of like a margarita, his salty ocean scent now saturated with lime.

He looked happy, too, that wide grin of his stretching from ear to ear.

He stopped in front of the couch, not bothering to greet them. "I have an announcement!"

"You're pregnant!" Spencer yelled, lifting his feet from Chase's lap and setting them on the floor. "And it's twins!"

Noah's smile didn't even falter. "So the omega I've been seeing ..."

"You're letting us meet him?" Spencer asked, his excitement genuine this time.

Noah rubbed a hand on the back of his neck, his grin taking on a sheepish edge. "Actually, yeah. And, um, his name is Eli Miller. He's a professor. My professor."

"Holy shit!" Spencer's mouth dropped open. "Holy— You sneaky— Holy shit!"

He jumped up, slapping his hands on Noah's shoulders and shaking him like Noah really had just announced he was pregnant with twins. Then he was demanding Noah's whole story, and Noah spilled it all, by all accounts relieved and grateful to finally share everything about the man he was so smitten with.

"It still has to be on the down-low," he ended with. "Until next year at the earliest, but we're letting in our closest people."

"That's us!" Spencer crowed, kicking at Chase's leg in his excitement.

Chase grinned back at him absently. Or he thought he did. He was pretty sure his face was doing the things it was supposed to do. It was just ... everything felt strangely far away, like he was watching through a window.

Noah and his omega were going public? Or semipublic, at least. Chase hadn't expected it for some reason. Or maybe just not so soon. And he and Spencer were going to meet him, apparently. Because Noah and Eli were in it for the long haul. Together. Really together.

Why did Chase feel so strange?

"Next up is Chase revealing his secret hookup," Chase heard Spencer say, and he looked up from his feet to see both his roommates were watching him.

"Oh. Yeah." Chase cleared his throat, which was suddenly way too dry. "That's a different thing though. We're not, like, in love. It's just sex."

Spencer's brow furrowed. "Yeah, but—"

"Hey," Noah broke in, wrapping an arm around Spencer's shoulder. "Go easy on him. He's got dinner with his folks tonight."

"Oh. Right." Spencer winced apologetically at Chase. "You sure you don't want us to go with you?"

Chase's parents had called the day before to let him know they were flying into Phoenix for a business meeting and expected to see him for dinner tonight. And while it was sweet of Spencer to offer, Chase already knew his roommates weren't included in the invitation. His parents had made it clear they didn't find it necessary to know his friends.

"Yeah, I'm good. They're easy."

Spencer and Noah exchanged looks but didn't press.

Until suddenly Spencer whirled to face Chase, pointing an accusing finger. "Wait! Why aren't you more surprised by this?"

"Oh." Chase exchanged a look with a wide-eyed, panicky Noah. "I didn't know for sure, but I sort of guessed. I'm in the same class, and Noah is ... not subtle around Miller."

"Betrayal!" Spencer shouted, lobbing throw pillows at both of them. "Betrayal on all sides!"

"Fuck, Chase," Noah groaned, dodging a large, tasseled pillow. "Couldn't you have just pretended?"

Chase was too busy climbing over the arm of the couch to crouch underneath it, allowing Spencer's pillow missiles to fly overhead. Why did they have so many throw pillows anyway? They must have come with the couch his parents had bought.

Chase's phone buzzed, and he pulled it out of his pocket to find a text from Killian.

> Killian: Grading's finally done. I'm scheduled for a massage this afternoon. It's a standing monthly appointment. Apparently I carry quite a lot of tension in my shoulders.

> Chase: I bet you do.

> Killian: Come over afterward.

> Chase: I have a dinner thing. It could take a while.

It took Killian longer to reply this time, and Chase bit at his lip. Fridays were supposed to be their night, but this dinner hadn't exactly been a request he could refuse.

> Killian: Sleep over, then.

> Chase: Can I let you know after dinner?

> Killian: Promptly.

> Chase: Yes, Alpha.

Chase sighed, tucking this phone back in his pocket. He peeked around the front of the sofa to find Noah had Spencer in a headlock.

Chase grinned at the sight. It was almost enough to soothe the weird unease he couldn't seem to shake. He should have just said yes to Killian and let the alpha fuck it out of his system, but he wasn't sure what state he was going to be in by the time dinner was over.

Or why he felt so weird about Noah and Eli going public.

Maybe Chase had just spent too many days holed up in the house, eating leftover pizza and playing video games with Spencer.

Yeah, that was probably it. He'd get out of the house, get some fresh air, and he'd feel better. Because Chase was fine. And Noah and Eli going public was fine. And dinner with Chase's parents was going to be ... just fine.

———

CHASE'S MOTHER greeted him outside the restaurant with a kiss to his cheek that was miles away from actually touching his skin. His father made do with a distracted nod in Chase's general direction, more focused on the valet and his potential to scratch their car.

The two of them looked good. They always did. Money had a way of softening any harsh edges of aging, and Chase's parents weren't afraid to use that to their advantage. His mother's hair was immaculately dyed and coiffed. His father was tanned and healthy-looking, trim as ever due to his regular appointments with a personal trainer.

"How are you, darling?" his mother asked Chase absently.

Before Chase could answer, she was already turning to his father. "Robert, forget the car. It's a rental—who cares what happens to it? I'm famished."

His father let out a grunt and wrapped an arm around his wife, ushering her inside. Chase followed behind them, wondering if they'd notice if he just ducked away and skipped the whole thing.

The restaurant was familiar, a place his parents had taken him to before. It was just their type—expensive but not too opulent, with well-cooked food that never bordered on too adventurous. So dinner was predictably delicious.

And predictably quiet.

After a few perfunctory questions—"Your grades are acceptable? No trouble with the house?"—his parents mostly talked between themselves, rehashing the business dinner from the night before. Chase's father was apparently looking to expand into more Phoenix real estate, possibly something commercial.

There were no more questions directed to Chase. No queries about his roommates, his close friends of three years now. No follow-up about his life without lacrosse, a sport he'd played since he was a child. And not a single inquiry into his dating life, although Chase wouldn't have been truthful if asked.

Chase had never figured out exactly what was wrong with him.

It had been this way since he was so young—it couldn't possibly have been anything he'd *done*, right? Sometimes he theorized that it was his beta designation that was the problem. His parents were a classic alpha-omega pair. Maybe they'd wanted a sweet omega to coddle, or a burly alpha to take over the family business. Maybe a beta was too much of a blank slate, and they didn't have enough in themselves to fill him up with normal familial affection.

It didn't much matter either way—it wasn't like there was anything Chase could do about it—but it was a theory, anyway.

Chase ate his pasta politely and made interested noises when his parents remembered to direct a comment in his direction. Maybe he *was* the problem, with the way he just accepted the status quo. If he were Spencer, he'd be acting loud and obnoxious, just for the attention. If he were Noah, he'd probably be calling them out firmly for acting ice-cold with a son who'd never done anything to deserve it. Either way, he wouldn't be sitting here, acting out the same old dynamics in the way they always did, again and again and again.

But Chase wasn't Noah or Spencer. He was just himself, and he smiled and nodded and wondered why it never changed, and why he was stupid enough to hold out hope that it would.

Dinner lasted forever. The meal itself was four courses, and then there was dessert, and after-dinner coffee. Chase wasn't sure why they were lingering—maybe some deeply buried guilt over them not caring that he was there at all?

Or maybe his father just really wanted a coffee.

"You can get your own car back, can't you, son?" his father asked when they'd finally made their way outside again. "Your mother's worn out. We need to get back to our hotel."

Chase hadn't driven himself. He'd been dropped off by Spencer at his parents' request. They'd claimed they wanted to drive him back themselves and see the state of the house, check in on their investment. He hadn't questioned why they couldn't have picked him up too.

Chase just nodded. "Yeah, I can find my way."

His mother blew a kiss that was maybe supposed to be aimed his way, but she was already turning to the valet approaching with the car. "I told you about summer, right, darling?"

"Yes. I'll stay here."

His father clapped him on the back. "We'll see you for Christmas, son."

Apparently Thanksgiving was out, then. Chase idly wondered where they'd be for it as he stood there, watching them drive off.

His eyes were dry but weirdly hot as he pulled up the rideshare app on his phone. He wished he had his cap to tug down, but baseball hats weren't polite for dinner, as he'd been told many times in the past.

Before he could think too hard about it, he swiped out of the app and hit Killian's name instead.

Killian picked up immediately. "When are you coming over?" he asked before Chase could even greet him, his voice gruff with impatience. "I've been waiting too long, sweet boy."

It was oddly painful, to have his presence craved so badly after barely feeling like a person for the last three hours. Like Chase's whole body was pins and needles after being numb for too long. He had the strange desire to hang up.

But he didn't. He couldn't.

"Actually—" Chase paused, clearing his throat. The words kept getting stuck somewhere on the way out. "Can you come get me?"

Killian didn't hesitate, and Chase could hear the jingle of him grabbing his keys. "Send me the location. I'm leaving now."

14

Killian

K illian had maintained the same monthly massage with the same masseuse for coming on two years now.

Tonight, instead of getting scolded for working too many hours hunched over a computer, he'd been told for the very first time that he had fewer knots than usual.

"Whatever relaxation techniques you've learned," his masseuse had said with surprise, "keep them up."

Killian intended to.

But he also had a feeling—as he broke half a dozen traffic laws speeding to the restaurant where Chase was waiting—that every single knot he'd gotten worked out was now bunched up tightly again.

Chase had sounded ... wrong over the phone. Detached in a way that was somehow distressingly different from the beta's usual cool reserve. It was sending Killian's instincts spiraling, the need to protect and fix whatever had gone awry.

Killian parked at the curb in front of the restaurant, waving the valet off. Before he could unbuckle and leap out of the car dramatically, Chase was already climbing into the passenger seat.

"Thanks for picking me up."

Killian turned in his seat and took stock as Chase buckled himself in.

His beta still sounded off. Chase's eyes were dry but glassy, and his expression was oddly blank. He might even have looked serene if Killian hadn't known him better than that.

For once, Killian wished Chase had pheromones for him to read.

"What happened?" he asked, making no move to set the car in gear.

"I just needed a ride," Chase told him, his gaze fixed on the windshield in front of him.

Killian turned off the car.

Chase frowned at the keys in the ignition, although his reaction was delayed by a notable second. "What are you doing?"

"What. Happened?"

Chase blinked at Killian. "It was nothing. Just ... dinner with my parents."

Ah. The family. Killian was glad he'd turned off the engine. Something was going on there, and he was no longer satisfied with staying in the dark. Not if the parents were now making visits and leaving Chase like this, whatever *this* was.

"What did they do?"

"Nothing," Chase repeated, managing to sound genuinely surprised by the question. When Killian only arched a brow, he frowned. "I mean it. Nothing."

"Why didn't they drive you home?"

Chase shrugged. "They were tired."

That was bullshit. The house Chase shared with the baby alphas was only ten minutes from here. Killian had looked it up once, after coaxing the address from his beta one lazy Sunday morning.

Killian's answering silence seemed to throw Chase off. He shrugged again, the movement jerky, with none of his usual natural grace. "They're not— When it comes to—" He broke off. Let out a breath. Tried again. "They just don't like me very much. They never have."

It was strange, the anger that ran through Killian. Hotter than anything he'd ever felt, and yet it left him ice-cold. "Explain."

Chase trapped his lower lip between his teeth. Let it out again. "They're not terrible or anything," he eventually said. "They just ... aren't that interested in me."

"And they never have been," Killian repeated.

"No."

Killian had to unclench his teeth with determined effort to ask, "And when you were a *child*?"

"I mean, I had a nanny. I wasn't neglected." Chase drew back, startled by whatever he saw in Killian's face. "Why are you looking at me like that?"

"You just told me you were a child completely devoid of parental affection. How should I be looking?"

"No, no." Chase shook his head. "You've got the wrong idea. It's not that bad. Like, he doesn't talk about it, but Spencer grew up really struggling with money, and his mother is, like, mean." Chase's leg was bouncing now. Killian had never seen him so jittery. "That's hard, you know? That's real."

Meaning his own struggles weren't.

Killian wasn't equipped for this. He was used to comforting with actions, not words. But words were necessary here, and he needed to step the fuck up. "Suffering is relative, Chase," he said, trying to keep his tone as neutral as possible. "There's always going to be someone who has it worse. That doesn't mean you can't hurt."

Chase's leg stopped its bouncing, and he seemed to sit with Killian's words for a long time.

Jesus fuck. Had no one ever told him that before? Not a single person? But of course not, if he'd never shared. If he'd kept that pain tucked close to his chest, secret and contained.

Killian thought of Chase's sobbing breakdown the night of his punishment, the release and the relief there. It was no wonder. And it made it that much more disturbing now, Chase's dry eyes and lack of reaction.

Who had trained him to be so stoic? Or was that just the natural result of a lifetime of neglect?

Finally, Chase spoke. "I thought pulling out of my scholarship would be big enough to merit a conversation," he said, almost absently. "I don't even know why I wanted that. Why do I still care? It's pathetic."

"It's not," Killian said firmly. "It's normal to crave a parent's love and affection."

Chase met his gaze. "You seem fine."

It was true that Killian wasn't close with his parents. They were very different people, and their relationship reflected that. But he'd never doubted he was loved.

"I'm older than you," he explained. "As we age, those relationships ... shift. People start gravitating toward the affection of partners. Friends."

"Is that what you do?" Chase asked, cocking his head.

Killian scrubbed a hand down his face. "I don't think I'm the paragon of mental health that you think I am."

"You seem to be doing all right to me."

"I get by." They were too far away from each other for this conversation. It was no longer remotely tenable. Killian moved his seat back as far as it would go. He gave his thigh a pat. "Come sit on my lap."

"In the car?"

"Yes, in the fucking car."

Moving far too slowly for Killian's liking, Chase unbuckled his seat belt and climbed over the center console, arranging himself until his thighs were straddling Killian's, his head hunched down to avoid the car's ceiling.

"This is ridiculous," Chase complained, although he made no move to go back to his seat.

"It isn't." Killian clamped his hands around the backs of Chase's thighs, keeping him exactly where he was.

Chase glanced out the window. "The valet can see us. His name's Jason."

"I'm aware."

Of the former, obviously. Killian had had no idea about the latter.

Chase let out a noise that was somewhere between a laugh and a sigh, and then he was pressing his face into the crook of Killian's neck as hard as he could. "They barely noticed I was there," he said, the words muffled. "And I didn't do anything about it. Didn't stand up for myself. Didn't make a scene. I just sat there."

Killian swept a hand through Chase's silken hair, then grasped the back of his neck firmly. "Because you, Chase Adler, are a good boy, aren't you? You aim to please. And it's their own fucking fault they can't appreciate it."

Chase's answering sigh was hot against Killian's skin. "Why are you so nice to me?"

"It's the easiest thing in the world, being nice to you."

Chase turned his head, just enough to make his next words clear. "They never scent marked me growing up. I had a nanny when I was really young, but she was another beta. We're learning in Omega Studies ... betas crave scent marking too. From our old pack days. They've done brain scans. There are—there are real benefits."

It was growing damp against Killian's neck, although there

were no other signs of Chase's tears. No sobs this time. No shaking shoulders.

"That's why I'm on you like a dog in heat all the time," Killian told him. "The brain benefits."

There was a moment of silence, and then Chase leaned back with a watery laugh. "You just made a joke," he told Killian, some of that horrible blankness finally gone from his wet eyes.

"I did." And while Killian could have stayed here forever, with Chase taking comfort on his lap, remaining parked at the curb of a random restaurant was probably not ideal. "Come, let's get you home." At Chase's look, Killian clarified. "My home."

"Yours. Okay." Chase glanced out the window again, then smirked at Killian. "You sure you don't want to give Jason more of a show? Seems like your type of thing."

Killian gave his hip a firm swat. "Don't be a brat. Back in your seat."

———

KILLIAN HAD OWNED the lounge chairs in his backyard for ages. They'd come with the patio furniture set he'd purchased with very little thought. He only occasionally remembered to use them.

But now, lying in the early morning sun with a book in hand, his coffee within reach, and Chase Adler lying boneless between his legs, curled up against Killian's chest, Killian was gaining a newfound appreciation.

"I'm surprised you don't have a pool," Chase mused sleepily, his breath warm against Killian's shirtless skin.

"Mm. I've thought about it. But I already use the pool at my gym."

"And you leave for some of the summer. For your speaking engagements."

Killian smiled into his book. Chase had remembered. "Often, yes."

Of course, Killian had quite a few universities still waiting for his answer this year. He'd been holding off finalizing his summer schedule, and he wasn't skilled enough at lying to himself to even pretend to wonder why.

Chase was staying in town for the summer, he'd told Killian. And that thought had already been tempting enough before, but now that Killian had learned about what a bullshit, indifferent home life Chase had endured, a new protectiveness was surging through him.

Even without what Chase had shared with Killian the night before, it all still probably would have been inevitable. They'd been spending more time together, and whether they wanted to keep it casual or not, a certain amount of intimacy had taken place.

And Killian had been taking an inordinate amount of pleasure in learning more about his young paramour in small, stolen bits.

Chase was studious but didn't stress overly about academics. He had an incredibly tight bond with the baby alphas Killian always saw hanging off him. (Which might have filled Killian with a certain amount of jealousy before, but for which he was now grateful, since it meant Chase wasn't wholly alone in life.) In almost every scenario, Chase maintained a quiet confidence that could be mistaken for aloofness. Except he learned the names of everyone he met, always had a moment for a friend in need, and had a knack for sussing out small tasks that needed to be done and doing them without a word.

And he was horrendously easy to spend time with, but Killian had already known that.

Chase set his phone down on the lounger, peering up at Killian with green eyes narrowed against the sun. He'd left his hat inside, and Killian would either need to fetch it or make sure he put on sunscreen soon. Chase was fairer than Killian, and Killian didn't want him burning.

"Can you keep a secret?" Chase asked.

Killian set down his book, arching a brow. "You have to ask?"

Chase didn't crack a smile, just bit at his lower lip before saying, "My roommate, Noah. He's been dating a professor. Professor Miller."

"*Eli* Miller?" Killian asked with surprise. He'd met the man a few times at various university functions. The omega had used to cart around an older husband—a smarmy, annoying bastard, that one—but that must have been a thing of the past.

Killian had an email from Miller in his inbox, actually, asking to pick Killian's brain about publishing academic books for the masses. Killian had put out a moderately successful guide to popular statistics a few years ago.

"Yeah. They're not *public* public, but they just came out to their friends. To us."

A surge of ... something ran through Killian at the news. Before he could process it, Chase let out a sigh. "I'm bored."

Killian was too affronted to question the change of subject. "Excuse me?"

Chase gave him a cheeky smile. "I just mean, I didn't bring my school stuff. I'm just doomscrolling on my phone here."

Killian tilted his head toward the house. "Go get one of my books to read. And your hat while you're at it."

"One of your precious spy novels?" Chase asked, his grin widening as he sat up.

"Mm. Try *Eye of the Needle*. World War II. There's a good film version. We can watch it when you're done."

"All right." Chase hopped off the lounger with disturbing agility and went into the house. Killian craned his neck to watch him go. The beta was wearing nothing but his boxer briefs, and a lazy sort of lust swam through Killian's belly at the sight.

There wasn't any urgency to it. Not yet, at least. Chase wouldn't be leaving before the evening—Killian had already exacted his promise to stay. There would be time to fuck him into a weeping mess *after* they'd had their relaxing morning.

Killian hadn't done it the night before. He'd decided a rejuvenating bath was in order—warm water to soothe the soul, or something like that—and by the time they'd figured out how to fit two grown men into his tub, lazy kisses had turned to determined frotting, and then Killian had jerked them both off to completion. They'd rinsed off in the shower, and Chase had been demonstrably exhausted, his eyes barely staying open by the time Killian had turned the water off. He'd fallen asleep curled into Killian's chest as Killian had read his book, the same spy novel he was reading now.

It had all been ... quite domestic.

A teacher and a student going public.

It was a thought. Definitely a thought.

Killian could have his scent on Chase whenever he wanted. Chase could leave the house absolutely dripping in his pheromones, and there would be nothing anyone could say about it.

Killian cleared his throat, adjusting his cock.

Chase returned, his baseball cap in place and a book in his hand. He climbed back onto the lounger, fitting perfectly into his earlier position. He rubbed experimentally against Killian's erection. "This wasn't there when I left."

Killian gave him a swat. "Hush. Read your book."

"But—"

"If you get through three chapters, I'll let you ride me on this lounger." Killian smirked down at him. "At least until you beg me to flip you over and fuck you like the eager little beta you are."

"Really?" Chase arched a brow, maybe trying for coy, but his squirming gave him away. "Outside? Where your neighbors can hear?"

"Oh, sweet boy," Killian crooned with mock sympathy. "Did no one ever tell you how loud you are when you're getting fucked properly? The neighbors can *always* hear you."

Chase ducked his head into his book, but Killian didn't miss the delicious pink flush that traveled all the way to the tips of his ears.

There was no sign of the empty despair from the night before. No trace of the pain Chase's parents had unearthed within him. But Killian remembered.

He wouldn't be forgetting it anytime soon.

15

Chase

After that one morning when Killian had attacked Chase after his shower and fucked him back into smelling like a leather-and-cherry explosion, the alpha had generally been more chill about Chase leaving his house scentless.

And Chase particularly hadn't been expecting a problem *this* morning because he'd already stayed one night longer than he was supposed to, letting Killian pamper and fuck him intermittently until he'd basically forgotten his own name, let alone what day it was.

He was kind of surprised his roommates hadn't called the cops after him—it was already Sunday, and he hadn't seen them since after their classes Friday afternoon.

Although, Spencer and Noah were blowing up his phone now, so maybe they were starting to consider drastic measures.

Chase had planned to text them his reassurances over breakfast, but as soon as he walked into Killian's kitchen—freshly showered and ready to be fed a ridiculously wholesome morning meal before heading home—Killian sniffed the air and *growled*.

Chase froze mid-step, his body reacting to the alpha threat before his brain could. "Um. Everything okay?"

Without a word, Killian took the pan of eggs he'd been scrambling from the stove and turned off the burner. He stalked over to Chase, blue eyes blazing.

And then Chase found himself turned around and bent over the kitchen table, his hat tugged off and thrown onto the floor, his sweats and underwear unceremoniously shoved down. Killian kicked Chase's legs apart roughly with a frustrated grunt.

"Um ..."

"Color?" Killian's voice was gruff, practically unrecognizable.

But Chase's answer always seemed to be the same. "Green."

And then Killian spit on him.

He spit on Chase's hole, to be exact. He spread Chase's cheeks wide, and he spit right in the center, rubbing it in with his thumb with another wordless grunt. And then he did it again. And again.

He'd already fucked Chase that morning, a slow, sleepy grind when they'd both been barely half awake. So Chase was relatively loose and open already, his tender skin hypersensitive to Killian's rough, commanding touch.

"Need my cum back in there," Killian mumbled, and Chase honestly couldn't tell if the alpha was talking to Chase or to himself.

Chase was prepared for the next thing at his entrance to be a hard, alpha cock—nothing about Killian's current vibes were shouting "slow seduction"—but instead, Killian dropped to his knees behind him and shoved his face right into Chase's crease, tonguing him furiously.

Chase groaned at the hot, wet touch. His dick was being crushed against the kitchen table painfully, but he could still feel himself hardening despite the discomfort. Killian's mouth was just so ... hungry. Greedy. Messy.

The alpha kept pausing to rub his face over Chase's cheeks and upper thighs, scent marking his lower half like it was an urgent need. Killian hadn't shaved yet that morning, and his stubble prickled at Chase's skin.

When Chase was soaked with spit, inside and out, Killian rose back up, notching the fat head of his cock at Chase's entrance. He paused there, like he was waiting for permission. Like for once, Chase's color hadn't been enough. "Need my cum in you," he growled again.

"Okay," Chase soothed, or maybe whined, who the fuck could say. "You can fuck me, Alpha."

Killian let out a rumbling purr of satisfaction, and then he pressed in.

It was a slower drag than usual without any extra lube to ease the way, but it wasn't painful. Chase was open enough from earlier, and he'd been half-assed about cleaning himself out in the shower. And Killian had worked enough spit into him to fill a fucking swimming pool, so ...

Chase choked on air as Killian started driving into him roughly, pulling back and slamming in again over and over. There were none of his usual whispered words, no seduction. It was a mindless, determined rutting. Like he was completing a task, not fucking Chase so much as doing what he'd said he needed to do: get his cum back inside.

And for some reason, it was driving Chase just as wild as the low, crooning praise he usually received. His hard cock ached where it was pressed against the table, and the low, punched-out moans he was letting out with each thrust of Killian's hips were loud enough to echo in the large kitchen.

It didn't take long; Killian was too worked up. After a few more frantic pumps, he drove in hard, his hips shuddering against Chase's ass.

Filling him up, just like he'd promised.

And then Killian jerked Chase upright, his back against Killian's chest, and stroked Chase's cock like a man on a mission. It was rough and kind of painful, and Chase came almost immediately, spurting all over Killian's fist, barely able to breathe as he let out a strangled, gasping cry.

Fuck. His knees were weak with it.

Killian grunted his approval, then pulled up Chase's sweats and underwear, wiping the cum coating his hand onto a spare paper towel.

Killian's own cum was still seeping out of Chase's ass. Chase's underwear was going to be wet and sticky until he could get home and change.

Killian turned Chase around by the shoulders. His eyes were still hot, and his dark hair was in disarray, with color high on his cheeks. He looked kind of wild. Feral.

"You can't shower here," he told Chase, his chest rising and falling rapidly.

Chase blinked at him. "Okay."

"You can shower when you get home. When I'm not there." After a beat, Killian added, "Sorry."

"It's no problem."

Killian let out a harsh breath. "It's possible I'm close to my rut."

Chase raised a brow. "You think?"

Killian laughed ruefully, rubbing a hand over his face. "I thought I'd be good until summer break, but it seems to be arriving early. I'm guessing in a few days at best." He lowered his hand, meeting Chase's gaze squarely. "I'd like you to be here. To spend it with me."

For just a moment, something indescribable twisted in Chase's chest. It was a big deal, to be invited for an alpha's rut. Chase knew more than a few couples who'd spent them apart in the early days, worried the intensity would be too much for a fledgling relationship.

Chase squashed the weird feeling down. Hard.

He and Killian were no strangers to intense sex; that was all. It wouldn't be as big of a deal for them as for some people.

Killian misread Chase's hesitation. "I won't let you get hurt, Chase."

Because Chase was a beta. Because Killian would need to knot him.

Killian's going to knot me.

All Chase's blood rushed south, and his spent dick twitched.

Chase swallowed. Cleared his throat. "I'm not worried about that. But, um, isn't it *you* that could get hurt? If I can't ... satisfy?"

From what Chase knew, it was painful for an alpha to go through an unresolved rut. There were some who wouldn't even try with a beta or another alpha. They considered it better to go it alone—with medication and the proper toys—than be left unsatisfied.

Killian's eyes blazed with something unreadable. "You'll satisfy," he said, low and rough as a whispered promise.

"Okay. Yeah." Chase found himself nodding. "I'll spend your rut with you."

Killian's whole body sagged with relief. He really must not have liked spending ruts alone. "Good," he said gruffly. He set Chase's cap back on his head, brushing a hand over Chase's neck in a much more casual scent marking than his earlier efforts. "That's good, then." He turned back to the stove. "Sit down. I'll start a new pan of eggs."

And when Chase left that morning, he left with Killian's cum trailing down his thighs and a key to Killian's house burning a hole in his pocket.

———

CHASE HAD ALREADY KNOWN he wasn't going to get away with it. It was almost noon, and both his roommates were definitely home; they'd been texting him nonstop about joining their *Mario Kart* marathon while he'd been finishing breakfast with Killian.

So Chase wasn't surprised to find them both out in the common area when he arrived. And obviously Chase smelled like an alpha's cum dumpster so ...

"Someone's been getting laaaaid," Spencer sang out the moment Chase stepped into the living room.

Noah laughed, all beaming smiles as he had been ever since he'd told them about Miller. Then he stopped, wrinkling his nose. He sat up from his slouch and set his controller down. "Wait. Is that—?"

Chase cleared his throat. Now or never, he supposed. "I'm fucking Professor Burke."

He was 90 percent sure at this point that he was allowed to admit that to his roommates. Killian had told his friends almost months ago, and he no longer seemed all that concerned with secrecy in general.

Chase had already thought about telling them before, that weekend after the disastrous dinner with his parents, but something had stopped him. It had all felt too ... sensitive, then.

"What?" Spencer asked, dropping his controller on the floor. "Wait, what?" He looked around the room for some reason, as if Killian might be there, hiding behind the couch. "What?"

So Spencer was broken. That was Chase's bad—maybe he should have eased them into it.

"The stats professor?" Noah asked slowly, sniffing at the air again for confirmation.

"Yeah." Chase tugged his cap down a little, then flipped it backward. "For a while now."

"So you're *both* dating professors?" Spencer asked.

"Fucking," Chase corrected. "It's not— We're not like Noah and Eli."

Eli, who'd hosted a pool party at his house last weekend because he was so eager to be on good terms with Noah's people now that they were out in the open. Eli, who looked at Noah like he was all the good in the world distilled into one person.

"Okaaay ...," Noah said, drawing the word out, like he was trying to process too much information at once.

Which was silly. It wasn't even that much information to process. Chase was fucking Killian. He was tired of hiding the pheromones. So what?

Chase slumped down in the armchair across from the couch. He really should shower, but first ...

He leaned forward, resting his forearms on his thighs as he looked between his two besties. "Tell me about your ruts."

Spencer choked on air. "What?" he asked when he'd recovered.

Chase had spoken pretty clearly, so he didn't repeat himself. "You're not, like, completely gone, right? You still have some of your senses?"

Noah held up a hand. "Wait, you're spending Professor Burke's rut with him?" he asked.

"Yeah."

"But you're not ... dating."

"No." But then for some reason, that felt like a lie, so Chase shrugged. "I don't know. Maybe a little."

His roommates exchanged a glance, and then they were silent for a while, staring at him. Chase waited them out. It wasn't hard; he had more patience in his pinky finger than the two of them had in their whole bodies combined.

"I mean, I've only ever spent them alone," Noah eventually told him, after one last glance in Spencer's direction. "Eli and I haven't ... not yet." And then he blushed all adorably, like he was still a total virgin talking about his upcoming wedding night or something.

Spencer sighed and scratched at his neck. "I mean, I paired with an omega through heat services once, but it was kind of embarrassing."

"Why?" Chase asked. It must have happened over a summer or something, for him and Noah not to already know about it. The campus heat services ran year-round for students who stayed in the area, pairing trained alphas and omegas with those who either couldn't or didn't want to use medication during heats or ruts. "You were too aggressive?"

"Nah. I got really needy. Whiny. I think maybe I cried?" Spencer shrugged, clearly unashamed of recounting it to his friends, at least. "I spend them alone now. Heat services gives me meds to get through them. Sometimes I use toys for funsies."

Chase leaned back in his chair and tugged his cap back down to the front again, considering. None of what they'd told him was really all that helpful, was it?

"Um, I've been reading up on it to prepare for my next one with Eli," Noah said. "There'll be a lot of scent marking." He gave a pointed cough, waving a hand in the air, though he did it with a smile. "Seems like you'll be used to that."

Chase flipped him off.

"Some alphas are big on submission," Noah continued, ignoring the gesture. "Get real riled up if their partner isn't, like, pliant enough to their whims or whatever."

Chase hummed noncommittally. That wouldn't exactly be a problem for him, would it? Killian only had to crook his finger and he'd have Chase dropping to his knees without a word.

"And if there's a ... connection," Noah added, giving Chase an unreadable look. "There will be some mating ritual elements. Like hand-feeding and über-protectiveness and stuff. Alphas in rut like making sure their ... partner is taken care of."

Chase tugged at his lower lip, thinking all that over. So basically it would be like how Killian acted already, only with the intensity ramped up a bit.

And the knotting. He couldn't forget the knotting.

Chase shifted in his seat, wincing at the immediate reminder of the mess in his underwear. Jesus, he couldn't believe he'd sat down to chat like this. He needed a shower, like, yesterday.

He stood. "Okay. Thanks, guys. Lemme clean up and I'll join the game."

"Um, Chase?" Noah stopped him with a gentle hand on his wrist, although he didn't try for a scent mark. "You good?"

"Yeah." Chase gave him a vague smile, already turning toward his room. "I'm always good."

16

Killian

"I really appreciate you meeting with me."

Killian grunted out something that might have sounded like "no problem" if his jaw had been a little less tense.

He was getting too close to his rut, and he really should have been spending as much time home as possible, not out in public. But he'd needed to take care of something first. Or he'd thought he'd needed to. It was possible he hadn't been thinking quite clearly when he'd arranged this meeting.

Eli Miller looked the same as ever. Short and slender and fine-featured—an ideal omega in the old-fashioned sense of it, if one ignored that he was whip-smart and clearly professionally ambitious, seeing as how he had locked down tenure by the age of thirty-four.

He was sipping the coffee Killian had given him and pretending not to be confused as to why Killian had summoned him to meet in person.

Killian was possibly wondering the same thing. It had been a last-minute decision he was now regretting. He'd just ... wanted to see. Wanted to *know*.

Although, *what* he'd wanted to know wasn't coming to mind at the moment.

Eli sniffed the air, blanched noticeably, and set down his cup. He cleared his throat, leaning forward in a way that seemed to imply he was getting down to business. "You know, I was wondering why you didn't just make this an email, but then my boyfriend told me this morning that we actually have a mutual acquaintance."

It took a moment for that to register. Killian sat back in his chair. "Chase told Noah about us?"

Eli cocked his head. "You seem surprised."

"I am."

"But not upset."

"No."

Killian was anything but upset, even though he hadn't known that Chase had spoken to his roommates. Killian was fighting not to immediately read too much into it, actually.

Something had shifted for him when it came to their relationship, that night he'd picked up Chase from the restaurant, when Chase had finally shared some of that pain inside him and where it came from. And Killian's impending rut was only stirring it all up that much more.

Killian was done with restraint, with secrecy, with playing it safe. He wanted to claim his beta. Officially. Publicly. He was fairly certain with the slightest bit of encouragement he'd be ready to move Chase into his home this very day.

But even with his hormones raging and impatience running through his veins, Killian knew Chase wasn't ready.

He wasn't ready, and it was driving Killian crazy.

Chase was just too ... far away. Not physically—although, with his rut so close, Killian did very much want Chase right here, right now, at all times—but emotionally.

For all that Chase melted like putty in Killian's hands during sex, and for all that he put up with all Killian's demanding, bossy care afterward, there was still a wall there. Something practically solid and opaque standing between them and a future together. The most clear sign of it was how quickly Chase changed the goddamn subject anytime Killian tried to talk to him about anything surrounding their relationship. It was a new habit of his, as if he sensed how desperate Killian was getting and was managing to sidestep the issue entirely.

And Killian didn't know how to break through that wall without scaring Chase away.

Chase was too self-possessed and too self-contained, and Killian could too easily picture him walking away, keeping everything they'd shared together tucked deep inside and never letting it out again.

But why Killian had thought meeting with Professor Miller was the key to his problem, Killian didn't quite know. Except that Eli had done it—he'd had a relationship with a student, kept it secret and safe, and now was integrating their lives like any other couple, if the things Chase had told Killian were true.

Surely the omega had some sort of insight?

The look Eli was giving Killian bordered on pitying. He'd obviously realized Killian had no interest in discussing work today. He gave him a small smile. "You know, I really don't know him that well yet. We've only spent a few evenings together. Although, he did come over for a little pool party a bit ago."

Oh, Killian knew all about the goddamn pool party. He'd been seething with something remarkably close to jealousy at the thought of a sun-soaked, water-slicked Chase lounging about completely out of Killian's reach, and he'd left a massive, indiscreet hickey on Chase's neck. Killian hadn't even had an impending rut to blame then.

It hadn't been his finest hour.

He could make up for it now. He could say something reasonable and polite to Eli and get back to the business at hand—helping Eli navigate the publishing industry.

Instead, Killian found himself asking, "How did it fall apart with you and your ex?"

"Richard?" Eli's eyes widened with shock, then narrowed in indignation. "Is that really any of your business?"

"No." Killian sighed. "It isn't."

Eli stared at him for a moment. Then he sat back in his chair, mirroring Killian's posture. "He was selfish, and he tried to make me something I wasn't," he eventually said, and Killian must have been looking truly pathetic for the favor Eli was doing him in his honesty. "That and the rampant cheating."

Well, that wasn't helpful. Killian was selfish with everyone *but* Chase; he liked Chase exactly as he was, and he had absolutely no desire to fuck another non-Chase person for as long as he lived.

Eli propped his chin on his hand. He had warm eyes. Kind eyes. A direct contrast to Killian's gaze, which he'd been told more than once was steely. "You know, if he wants you to go slow, just go slow. Although, I know that's ... challenging for alphas."

Killian cursed quietly, swiping a hand over his face. In terms of advice, it was the opposite of what he'd been looking for. "I apologize for ... today. This. I'll email you all the details of how I got my book out there. I can even get you in touch with my agent. She'd be thrilled. Your reputation precedes you."

"Thank you." Eli was still studying him. "Can I say something indelicate?"

Killian waved a hand. "Go right ahead. Decorum hasn't exactly been the theme of this meeting."

Eli nodded, then folded his hands in his lap. "Maybe wait until your rut has passed to make any big relationship moves."

Wise. Fucking. Words.

Killian leaned down to fish a small bottle out of his desk drawer. He shoved it in Eli's direction. "Scent-neutralizing spray. It's not a perfect fix, but—"

"I appreciate that." Eli took the bottle and rose from his chair, and Killian idly wondered how long this slipup of his would take to get back to Noah, and if Noah would share it with his beta best friend.

Eli paused at the door. "I don't know enough to know if I'm rooting for you or not, but either way, good luck."

"Thanks." Killian resisted the urge to slam his forehead down on his desk repeatedly. "I think I might need it."

———

THE DRIVE HOME WAS A BLUR, Killian too frustrated with himself to pay proper attention to the road.

What had he been expecting Eli to give him, *The How to Go from Fucking Your Student to Forming a Life Partnership Handbook*?

Killian had made a fool of himself for no reason, and the only thing he'd gained was the reminder that he wasn't in the right headspace for any big decisions.

Which was also bullshit, because Killian *knew* what he wanted. It was convincing Chase of the same thing that was the issue.

Killian stormed into his house, beelining to the coffeepot, since it was too early for whiskey. He needed to send some emails. He was too close to his rut and clearly in no state to teach his classes for the rest of the week. He had some prerecorded lectures to fall back on, and a TA would have to do the rest.

Killian could feel things building, could feel himself getting more aggressive, more protective over what was his.

And horny. He was getting fucking horny.

He didn't need to be off hounding random omegas about how to woo Chase. He needed Chase *here*.

The thing was, Killian had a feeling that if he simply told Chase, in no uncertain terms, "We're dating now. It's official. You're mine," Chase would allow it. He'd go along with Killian as he always did, pliant and eager and a good fucking boy until the end.

But Killian couldn't do that with everything that came their way; it couldn't always be his decision. If they were going to build something real, Chase had to be an equal partner. He had to want it just as much as Killian.

Even half as much would be acceptable at this point.

Killian couldn't go around ordering, "You're moving in."

"We're getting married."

"I'm claiming you."

A claiming bite. A perfect, bite-shaped scar on the back of Chase's perfect, unmarred neck.

Fuck. Killian's dick was hard. Rock fucking hard.

He abandoned his coffee and went straight to the couch, undoing his buckle hurriedly. He shoved his hand into his pants and grasped his cock. Tugged it. Growled in frustration.

This wasn't right. It wasn't right at all. Killian needed something hot and wet and tight around him. Chase's pretty pink mouth. Or Chase's hole, spit-soaked and lubed to all hell. Or fuck, he'd even take Chase's thighs, muscular and firm and squeezed tight around his cock. They hadn't done that yet, but Killian was already planning to during his rut, when Chase needed a break from his knot. Killian was going to lube those thighs and squeeze them together and fuck into them like a madman.

Fuck. Killian was hot. Too hot. His clothes were terrible too. He'd thought they were good quality—fucking expensive as hell— but they itched at his skin.

He took them all off.

The smell of the coffee was aggravating now too. Killian rose from the couch and strode naked into his kitchen. He turned the coffee pot off and dumped it all out in the sink.

No foreign scents, even coffee scents. Only Killian's pheromones. And his beta, wrapped up in them so tightly everyone knew he was Killian's.

Where *was* his beta?

Chase was supposed to be here. Naked. Safe. Only Killian would get to see him wet and flushed and desperate. Killian would make sure all the windows and doors were locked so they wouldn't be interrupted. Because he was going to knot his beta, and that would take time. Killian was going to be careful. Gentle. No hurting him. Because Chase was strong, but he was also fragile. And he was ... not here?

His phone. Killian needed his phone. And lube. There needed to be lube everywhere. His bedroom. The living room. The kitchen. Because he was going to knot Chase, and he wasn't going to hurt him. Not once.

Killian went back to the couch and gathered his clothes. He took them to his bedroom and set them on his bed. Chase might want them. He might want to be surrounded by soft things that smelled like Killian.

They needed more blankets.

Killian went to his closet and started gathering the extras he kept there, setting them with his clothes. He added his robe to the pile, the one he wore on cooler winter mornings.

There. That was good. Chase could arrange them however he wanted. He would like that, wouldn't he? A soft pile of nice things that smelled like Killian?

Where *was* Chase?

Right. Killian needed his phone.

He went back to the bed and took his phone out of his pants pocket.

> Killian: Come here.

> Killian: Come now.

There. His beta would come.

Killian went to the kitchen. He needed to make sure he had enough food on hand for his beta. Good things. Sweet things. Easy things. Fruit and nuts and those energy bars they made to fuel omegas during their heats. He'd stuff his beta with his knot, and he'd feed him delicious morsels, and he'd take such good care of him that Chase would never want to come off.

After a minute Killian went back to his bedroom. He grabbed his phone again.

> Killian: Rut.

17

Chase

Letting himself into Killian's house was the first time Chase had used his key, and the act felt ... significant. But that was probably just Chase's nerves talking.

He hadn't been sure, with Killian's first two messages, if it had only been Killian acting especially bossy and demanding.

Come here.

Come now.

But then the third message had made it perfectly clear.

Rut.

Chase had showered quicker than he ever had in his life—he'd been at school all day, and he had a feeling the scents of the other students would bother Killian in his current state—and then he'd rushed over.

Killian's house was quiet as Chase stepped inside. Unnervingly so, despite relative silence being the norm in Killian's neatly ordered world. But there was pressure in the air now, something taut and heavy.

"Hello?" Chase called, closing the door carefully behind him. "Killian?"

He'd known Killian could be silent on his feet when he wasn't wearing his fancy dress shoes, but Chase hadn't realized *how* silent until Killian was just ... there. In the hallway, facing Chase.

Completely naked.

And ... *damn*. Chase had thought in the past months that he'd adjusted to the animal magnetism of this alpha. They'd fucked hundreds of times at this point, after all. Chase had seen Killian in every stage of undress and vice versa.

But yeah ... none of that compared to a naked, horny Killian in all his rut-induced glory.

His pheromones were like a dark fog rolling in, potent enough that, even as a beta, they made Chase's head spin. Killian was standing ramrod straight, his massive, hard cock bobbing in the air in a way that maybe should have been ridiculous, except for the look in his eyes ...

No one had ever looked at Chase like that. Like he was sex incarnate. Like he was prey. Like he was everything.

Chase set his bag on the floor, some subconscious warning reminding him to make his movements slow and easy.

"Hello, Alpha," he said, calm and even as he could. "How are you feeling?"

Killian cocked his head. His hands clenched into fists and then unclenched again. "Beta," he eventually ground out, his voice so deep and rough that Chase had trouble distinguishing the word.

Chase stayed where he was, locked in a moment of uncertainty. Was that supposed to mean something in particular? Was Killian ... disappointed? Had he forgotten that the person he'd asked for wasn't an omega?

"That's right," Chase said after a moment. He swallowed hard and forced himself to ask. "I'm a beta. Do you still want me to stay? Or I could—"

There was a blur of movement, and then somewhere around two hundred pounds of alpha muscle was hurtling straight toward him.

Holy shit. Maybe Killian *was* pissed. Maybe Chase was about to be knocked on his ass for the presumption of his arrival.

Before Chase could even brace himself properly, he found himself upside down and staring at an impressive pair of bare, muscled butt cheeks flexing as they moved.

For a professor, Killian really did have an insanely nice ass.

And Chase was getting up close and personal with it because Killian had apparently thrown Chase over his shoulder, and he was taking him in the direction of the bedroom with long, decisive strides.

So Chase was staying. Good to know.

It wasn't long before Chase was dropped to his feet near the foot of the bed. And then Killian was stripping off Chase's clothes, muttering something under his breath. It almost sounded like he was saying the word *gentle* over and over.

If so, he was maybe missing the mark a little—Chase's shirt definitely ripped in like three different places as Killian tore it off him—but Killian *did* seem to be trying to keep himself contained, his movements jerky with the effort.

He was also emitting an insane amount of heat, pressed against Chase's back as he tugged Chase's jeans down, and Chase was glad to be rid of his clothes. He was going to be a sweaty mess in no time with a living furnace like this rubbing against him.

Chase's underwear was the last to go, and Killian held them up, *sniffed* them, and tossed them on the bed, where Chase now realized there was a pile of blankets and clothes spread over the covers.

Chase stood there for a second, staring at that pile as Killian huffed and grunted behind him. It was kind of odd to see such a mess in Killian's space, which was usually so neat and clean. Chase's underwear didn't seem to be the only preworn piece of clothing in the bunch either.

Killian stayed where he was as well—pressed close to Chase's back—but he was anything but still. His hands kept stroking and touching bits of Chase's skin, and he kept nuzzling his head into the back of Chase's neck and shoulders. Scent marking him with impatient grunts as he slid his hard cock up and down between Chase's cheeks, like he couldn't help himself from rutting a little.

But he didn't try to shove that big dick inside him, and he wasn't tugging Chase onto the bed and mounting him, so Killian had to be at least a little bit self-aware.

Chase turned his head to check in with him, and there was Killian's handsome face *right there*, his pupils blown so wide his blue eyes looked completely black.

"Is that—"

Chase wasn't able to finish his question because Killian promptly shoved his tongue in Chase's mouth, kissing him furiously with no preamble, apparently fucking *starving* for it. His arms wrapped around Chase's middle, and he lifted Chase onto his tiptoes, like he needed Chase's mouth as close to his as physically possible. Like even the few inches of difference in height between them wasn't allowed.

Chase was panting by the time Killian backed off to nuzzle at his shoulder again. Panting and hard. So fucking hard. It didn't seem to matter that the kiss had been sloppy and desperate and nowhere near as artful as what Killian usually had to offer. Chase had been hard since the moment Killian had appeared in the hallway, his pheromones so dark and rich they were like molasses moving through Chase's lungs. And if Chase were an omega, he had no doubt he'd be gushing slick every-fucking-where right about now.

It took Chase a minute to remember what he'd been trying to ask, what with Killian's hands roaming all over his body again, leaving a trail of fire in their wake.

"Is that for my nest?" Chase managed to get out this time.

Killian made a vague, grunting sound of affirmation, nudging his nose against Chase's jaw.

"Killian, I don't—I'm a beta," Chase reminded him.

Killian made a wounded noise, and Chase tried to figure out how to navigate this.

Apparently it was important to Killian that Chase make a nest, but Chase was a beta, and betas didn't nest. They didn't have the nose for it, and given that Killian *did*, Chase had a feeling that some half-assed pretending wasn't going to work. Not with Killian already this worked up.

Chase set his hand over Killian's, where it was currently tracing patterns on Chase's lower belly, stilling it for the moment. "Alpha, will you do it for me?" he asked. "Will you build me a nest?"

Chase held his breath as Killian growled, pressing his cock harder against Chase's crease, the slippery head catching at Chase's rim as Killian ground against him.

And then Killian was moving away to the bed, where he immediately began to rearrange the messy pile.

Chase let out a sigh of relief. That seemed to be a compromise rut-Killian was amenable to.

It was also a tempting bit of eye candy, actually, watching a naked Killian bend and growl and sniff as he worked. But Chase only made the mistake of touching his own cock once, and Killian turned around immediately—like he had some sort of sixth sense surrounding Chase's arousal—and growled at him so fiercely that Chase didn't try again.

No touching. Got it.

Eventually Killian let out a satisfied grunt and stood at the side of the bed, presenting the nest to Chase. It was mostly flat, with the blankets forming the lower layers and what looked to be Killian's worn clothes forming the top. Which Chase supposed made sense, because Chase would basically be rolling in Killian's scent, those dirty clothes covering whatever bits Killian's hands missed when it came to scent marking him.

Chase didn't know what to do or say, so he nodded. "Very nice."

Killian puffed up with pride—and fuck, why was that the most adorable thing Chase had ever seen?—and then he grabbed Chase and plopped him on top of the nest, pressing down on Chase's chest until he was flat on his back.

And then Killian scent marked the ever-living shit out of him.

Killian had always been especially hot on the idea of Chase smelling like him, and Chase had thought he'd already gotten the Extreme Scenting Treatment from him, but this was another level. Not a millimeter of Chase's skin was spared. Killian paid special attention to his neck and groin, of course, but he also covered Chase's armpits, and the insides of his elbows, and the dip of his belly button.

And it turned out it was a special kind of torture to have Killian rubbing his cheeks and hands all over Chase's dick without actually putting any pressure or friction on it.

Does my cock really have to be scent marked? Chase wanted to ask. *When we already know you're going to have your hands and mouth all over it?*

He held his tongue. He wasn't going to provoke an alpha in rut over unimportant shit, like the fact that Chase might cry if he didn't come soon.

And then Killian flipped Chase over and did it all again on the other side.

By the time lubed fingers pressed to Chase's crease, Chase was a strange mix of pliant and overstimulated. His cock was dribbling precum all over the nest, and all he could think about was getting fucked. Fucked hard and fucked fast.

And he really thought he would be too. Really thought the prep would be rushed and insufficient and possibly a little painful, given Killian's state of mind.

But Killian started chanting to himself again, those soft, rumbling "gentles," and then he took. His. Fucking. Time.

One finger. Two fingers. Three. And then his mouth was on Chase's ass, Killian seemingly not caring about the lube he'd just worked into him. And then back to three fingers. Then his mouth again.

By the time Killian got to four fingers, Chase was whimpering into his folded arms, trying not to buck and writhe against the teasing, because it only got Killian more agitated, and then he would start the process all over again.

Chase knew because Killian had already done it. Twice.

But *fuck*, Chase wanted to come. He wanted to come so fucking badly. And he knew if he touched his cock, Killian was going to lose it, or even worse, make that sad, wounded noise again. But four fingers was a fucking lot—Killian's hands weren't exactly dainty—and Killian wasn't making any attempt to stroke Chase's prostate or force him to come a million times like he usually did. He was just ... stretching him.

It didn't hurt—not with the lengthy amount of time Killian was taking with it—and there was something intoxicating about being stretched so full with Killian bent over him, nuzzling at Chase's skin and biting into Chase's ass with blunt teeth in warning any time he dared move too much.

But it was intense, and when Killian wiggled and scissored his four fingers, Chase had one brief, terrifying moment where he thought, *Holy shit, is Killian going to* fist *me?*

And before he had time to process how he felt about that possibility, Killian suddenly pulled Chase's hips up and back, pressing Chase's weight down on his forearms. It was the same position an omega would take when presenting to their alpha, and Killian seemed to like that, growling low in satisfaction when he had Chase contorted the way he wanted.

And then those fingers were finally leaving Chase's ass, and a familiar fat cockhead was pushing at Chase's entrance, sliding in easy as butter.

Chase moaned, louder than he ever had in his life. He didn't care that he sounded like a desperate slut—it felt so good after so much teasing. So much goddamn ass play without any relief.

He felt absurdly shameless as he let his voice tip into a whine, "Want you to touch my cock, Alpha."

Killian usually liked when Chase asked for what he wanted— rare as the occasion was—and even now, Killian's broad hand gripped Chase's cock immediately, stroking once before he let go with a frustrated grunt.

Well, it had been worth a shot.

And then the rough, brutal fucking Chase had been expecting finally began.

Chase lost his mind immediately. His load followed right after.

It turned out Chase didn't need Killian touching his cock. It barely took two pumps of Killian's hips, and all that tension and building heat finally broke over Chase like a storm, his cock spurting all over the nest as he screamed into his folded arms.

Killian seemed to like that fine, if the way he put his weight into fucking Chase into the mattress right after was any indication.

And maybe betas really did respond to rut pheromones in their own way because Chase's cock began to fill again almost immediately after his surprise orgasm, even as his toes were still curled into the mattress, shaking with the force of it.

What followed was animalistic and primal and almost frightening—the bed pounding against the wall so hard it sounded like the wood might crack—but maybe Killian was just as worked up by fingering Chase as Chase had been, because it was quicker than usual when he slammed his hips into Chase with a stuttered growl and bit hard into the crook of Chase's neck, just to the left of where a mating bite might lie.

Chase could feel the hot spurt of Killian's cum—more than Chase was used to—and then ... pressure.

For once, there was no cautious half withdrawal after orgasm, no effort to keep that swelling knot outside Chase's tender rim. This time, Killian's knot was growing inside him, locking Killian's cum in place as it pressed harder and harder against Chase's inner walls. It was painful but not at the same time. Intense in a way Chase had maybe expected but had no way to prepare for.

Chase made a noise he'd never made before, something shaking loose deep within him.

He was full. So full. As full as he could get without breaking into a million pieces.

But Chase didn't break. He took it all, his cock spurting weakly again as his prostate was mercilessly pressed by that unforgiving bulk.

Killian was letting out a constant, low growl from above him—almost like a purr—as he stroked his hands up and down Chase's sides, nuzzling at the bite mark he'd left in Chase's skin.

"Good beta," he rumbled, the words clearer than anything he'd said so far that day.

And Chase whined, low in his throat. He sounded exactly like an omega in heat, and he was too overcome by the pressure to be embarrassed by it.

Killian let the bite mark be and nuzzled Chase's cheek. His ear. His hairline.

"Good beta," he said again. As if it was confirmation Chase had needed to hear.

And maybe it was, because Chase finally found it in himself to relax around the immense pressure holding him in place. He let his body go limp in the nest Killian had made for him, Killian's impressive weight on top of him.

Killian's rumbled approval grew louder, and Chase let his eyes fall closed, secure in the knowledge he'd pleased his alpha.

———

AFTER THE SECOND or third time, Chase's mind went somewhere else. Some place floating and far off and perfect.

Everything was sensation. Everything was fucking.

Killian knotted him twice more before falling asleep for a brief rest, and when he woke up, he lubed Chase's inner thighs, folded Chase in half, and rutted between them, pressing them together to squeeze his knot as he came, rumbling and growling as he used Chase's muscles to massage himself.

Next he carried Chase to the kitchen and fed him fruit by hand, and then he pushed Chase to kneeling and fucked Chase's face, bringing Chase's hands up to squeeze his knot as hard as he could manage.

It became clear over the next few days that Killian was giving Chase as many breaks as he could bear to give him. But then Killian would get twitchy and growly and hungry for it, and he'd inevitably fuck Chase again, knotting him with a groan so deeply satisfied it sent shivers down Chase's spine every single time.

And Chase fucking ate it up, soreness be damned, because when they were knotted together it was like heaven, that crazy pressure and Killian's stroking, roving hands, his mumbled words that were only clear half the time. Words like "my beta" and "sweet mate" and "gentle, gentle" over and over.

Occasionally Killian seemed hungry for something else, and then he sucked Chase's cock with feral intensity, and once he spit

Chase's cum back into Chase's mouth, watching carefully until Chase swallowed it all. And then he smiled, both tender and wolfish, and stroked Chase's cheek. "Pretty," he crooned, and Chase blushed like a brand-new fucking virgin.

Sometimes Chase would cry when he was knotted, and he didn't even know why. But Killian seemed to sense it was something cathartic and not pained, because he never got distressed. He would only make that weird, rumbling alpha purr and lick the tears off Chase's face if he could reach them. Which was sweet and sort of hot in a way that only made Chase cry harder half the time. It was a whole cycle, really.

And Chase would have to remember to do more research later because he *did* seem to be responding to the rut pheromones, at least as much as his body was able. Chase might not have had slick, but he'd never tolerated this much sex in his life before, and yet he kept coming and coming, his body responding to each of Killian's many demands.

Although, Chase *was* growing a little weaker, maybe. And a little more sore. And tired. So fucking tired, the catnaps they'd been taking in between bouts nowhere near enough sleep to keep him actually rested.

Maybe *this* was what all those years of athletic training had been for. Not to be some sort of lacrosse champion, but just to survive this rut without breaking into pieces.

Things began to slow down on the third night. It was hard to tell at first, but then after the last knot, Killian finally fell asleep and *stayed* asleep for three hours without stirring. Chase let out a sigh of relief even as he held his alpha close, stroking Killian's sweaty hair back from his face. (Chase had learned quickly that just because Killian was sleeping didn't mean he didn't want Chase *right there*, within arm's reach.)

Chase was apparently going to make it out of this after all.

Who would've thought.

And yet he couldn't help feeling that something important had shifted. Something deep and unnameable that Chase couldn't look at too closely in his raw, overstimulated state. He wondered if he'd be able to find his feet when they both got their senses back, and what would happen if he never did.

For now, Chase slept.

18

Killian

Killian came back to his senses wrapped around Chase so tightly it was a surprise the beta was able to breathe comfortably in his arms.

Chase was sleeping on his stomach in the nest with his head turned to the side. Killian was on top of him, his half-hard cock nestled in the cleft of Chase's ass.

Killian shifted up onto one arm and took stock.

There were dark circles under Chase's eyes, and bite marks littered his neck and shoulders, though Killian had managed to avoid any placement that would have made things more ... permanent. Chase smelled so strongly of Killian's pheromones that they were no doubt embedded under his skin.

Killian tried not to take too much pleasure in that—he'd been a brute, hadn't he?—but it was hard to keep his inner alpha from gloating. It was incredibly satisfying having Chase looking and smelling like *his* in the nest Killian had built for him. He looked like a proper alpha's mate, and it was doing something to Killian.

Killian reluctantly withdrew his cock from its warm den and parted Chase's cheeks with a gentle touch. Chase's hole was reddened and puffy—definitely well used—but with no obvious signs of tearing. His inner thighs were also pink and chafed, and there was dried cum streaking them. Killian supposed that part wasn't surprising. They hadn't bathed at all during his rut—Killian's instincts hadn't liked it, the few times Chase had suggested it. Although, Killian did remember Chase wiping them down in between bouts as best he could.

Chase shifted and half turned, blinking bleary eyes up at Killian. "What— Is it—" He blinked some more, his shoulders sagging with relief. "I can see the blue in your eyes again."

"Rut's over," Killian told him. He cleared his throat. His voice was hoarse, no doubt from all the incessant growling he'd been doing. "Are you— You're all right?" he asked.

Killian remembered it all, though some parts were a little foggier than others. (The feel of Chase's channel squeezing his knot definitely wasn't something Killian was going to forget anytime soon.) Killian knew he hadn't taken it easy on him, that even his attempts to give Chase a break from his knot—fucking his face, fucking his thighs, sucking his cock like a devil—had been rough and possessive, despite Killian's constant inner mantra to be gentle with his beta.

Chase rolled over onto his back, still halfway beneath Killian. "I'm fine," he said softly. Whatever he saw in Killian's face had him cupping Killian's cheeks. "I'm *fine*, I swear. Really. I came so hard and so often I think there's nothing but dust left in there."

But he was trembling as he dropped his hands, and his eyes had gone glassy. Killian had seen him like this before. Many times before.

It was a drop from whatever headspace Chase had gone into during Killian's rut. He was crashing now that it was done.

Lucky for them both, Killian knew about aftercare, especially when it came to his sweet, self-possessed beta.

Killian stroked Chase's dark-blond strands back from his face. For once they weren't baby-soft, too coated in dried sweat and who knew what else. "You did so well for me, Chase Adler," Killian murmured, and he knew he'd hit the mark when Chase took a deep breath, almost a gasp, his pretty green eyes softening. "You were a perfect fucking beta for me, weren't you? You took my knot over and over. I've never been so satisfied during a rut. Not once in my life."

Chase caught his bottom lip between his teeth, gazing up at Killian through his lashes in a way that might have been coy if he hadn't looked so exhausted and raw. "Really?"

"Mm." Killian lowered until he was lying between Chase's parted thighs. He scratched lightly at the beta's scalp, pleased when it made Chase's lids lower in pleasure. "I remember it all. The way you squeezed around me. The way you opened your legs and your mouth to me whenever I wanted. The whimpers and whines you made while I fucked you."

Fuck. Killian was making himself hard, his cock filling more and more with every deliciously filthy memory that came up. He'd really used this boy, every bit of his beautiful body.

And he wanted to do it again.

Chase felt it too. He tucked his chin down and eyed the space between their bodies warily. "Fuck no. I can't."

Succinct. To the point.

Killian sighed, rising onto one arm again as he grasped his hard cock with his free hand. "I don't need you to," he assured, stroking himself with a fast, rough touch. "You've already been such a good boy, taking me as often as you did. I'm going to coat you in my cum one last time, and then we're going to shower and nap and eat everything in this house."

Killian should let Chase shower already, but he needed to finish this first. His rut hormones were still settling, and while

Killian wasn't going to fuck Chase—they'd need to take a break from penetration for a while as Chase's body recovered—he liked the idea of marking him one last time, saturating him before Killian was forced to wash those rut pheromones off his skin.

Chase went lax underneath him. "Oh. Okay."

He watched Killian touch himself with a keen interest that bordered on hunger. As if maybe he wasn't sick of Killian's cock or his touch, despite having had both of them on him constantly for the last three days.

It was a quick, efficient jerk-off session before Killian was spurting all over Chase's belly, rubbing the cum into his skin before he could stop himself. God, the beta really did look wrecked. Taken apart by alpha cock and somehow still smiling at Killian so sweetly as Killian led him to the shower.

Killian took great pleasure in not allowing Chase to lift a finger, washing Chase's hair and body for him, keeping his touch as gentle as he could. He took even greater pleasure in finally articulating all his many thoughts about how good Chase was, how perfectly responsive his body had been, how he took a knot like he'd been born for it.

Chase squirmed under the attention and praise at first, but he relaxed into it quickly enough, like he always did, letting the water and words wash over him like the good boy he was.

By the time they sat down in Killian's kitchen to eat something more substantial than hand-fed fruit, Chase was looking flushed and happy, no longer trembling, his eyes bright if a bit tired. They'd need to nap after eating. Chase hadn't had nearly enough rest in the last few days; Killian knew that much.

Maybe Killian could talk him into staying a few more days for sleep and care.

Or just never let him leave.

Fuck.

Killian had really thought that maybe after his rut, some of the possessiveness that had been building inside him would wane, but if anything, it was the opposite. Killian couldn't crush this feeling that they'd crossed some line that made Chase *his*. Permanently. Irrevocably.

Killian wanted to keep this man. *Needed* to keep him.

"If he needs you to go slow, go slow."

Killian sighed, shifting Chase on his lap and giving him another bite of omelet, one Killian had packed with veggies and cheese and smothered with avocado, hoping to get as many calories and nutrients into his beta as he could.

It was going to be a battle, wasn't it? Keeping his cool and not fucking everything up by railroading Chase. But Killian could do it. Small steps forward, no steps back—that would be his new mantra when it came to his beta.

And Killian had already decided the first step would be convincing Chase to let Killian take him out to dinner. In public.

That was what people did when they were dating, right? What Killian had done once upon a time. They went on dates. And so far Killian and Chase had been confined to Killian's house for the duration of their relationship. And while Killian liked having Chase in his house very much—on his couch, at his table, in his bed—he needed things to shift. He didn't want Chase convincing himself this was only a matter of sex.

Maybe it had started that way, but it sure as fuck wasn't ending that way.

It was ending with a ring on Chase's finger, if Killian had anything to say about it.

But that was getting ahead of himself. For now, the important thing was that they were fucking boyfriends, goddamn it, and Killian had to make sure Chase was on board with that or he was going to lose his goddamn mind.

Killian's gaze caught on the bite marks and hickeys that were scattered over Chase's skin.

Well. Lose his mind more than he already had.

———

IT TURNED out it wasn't difficult at all to convince Chase to go out to dinner.

That was possibly because Killian had suggested a restaurant far from campus—and far from the one he'd picked Chase up at the night he'd had been so upset—or it was possibly because Chase had seemed to be in a bit of a daze all day long.

The rut had clearly taken it out of him, and Killian had been doing his best to mitigate the effects. There had been quite a lot of scent marking and petting and foisting as much hydration on Chase as he would allow (he'd accused Killian at one point of trying to drown him from the inside out, and Killian had eased up a tad).

But maybe getting out of the house would be the answer. They'd been cooped up for days, and as much as Killian had been doing his best to air out his home, the rut pheromones were still thick as hell in certain areas.

They parked in the restaurant's tiny parking lot, and Killian led Chase inside. He'd been deliberate in his choice: a casual spot with the best pho Killian had found so far in Phoenix. He thought something hot and filling and not too heavy would be good for someone still feeling a bit ... fragile.

The hostess seated them at a booth, and Killian slid in after Chase, choosing to sit next to him rather than across. It was their first time out of the house since the rut, and Killian needed to be close to his beta with those possessive urges still so close to the surface.

Although, it did help that Chase still smelled of Killian. Not the rich sex pheromones of a rut—they'd showered thoroughly, using scent-neutralizing soap to aid the process—but the usual leather-and-cherry scent that always coated Chase after effusive nuzzling and petting.

Killian ordered beers for them both—he'd drink Chase's if the beta wasn't up for it—and slung an arm around Chase's shoulders.

Chase startled, then relaxed into the touch. He tilted his head to peer up at Killian. "You know, this is a really elaborate way to trick me into eating chicken soup."

Killian grinned. "Nonsense. I was going to suggest the rare steak pho. It's the better option here."

Chase shook his head, seemingly unconvinced. "I'm really fine, I promise." He took a swig of his beer, letting out a small, contented sigh, his weight resting against Killian. "But this is nice. Thank you."

Killian grabbed his own beer. "Were you getting a bit stir-crazy, sweet boy?"

"Maybe it's just nice to breathe in some fresh air."

Killian huffed out a laugh. "I'm going to choose not to be offended."

"Please. You know I like your scent." Chase toyed with the corner of his menu. The tips of his ears had gone pink. "I'm covered in it often enough."

"Are you?" Killian asked mildly.

"I don't even have to look at you to know you're looking very smug right now."

It was true—Killian was looking quite smug. He couldn't have helped it even if he'd wanted to, which he didn't. He had his beta out on a date, in public, and they were flirting. And practically cuddling, since Chase hadn't made any move to wiggle out from under Killian's arm.

This was progress. Killian was sure of it.

They ordered their food—Chase blushing becomingly when he ordered the chicken pho after all—and then they settled in to wait.

"Did you always know you wanted to go into academia?"

"Mm." Killian considered. "From fairly early on. I enjoyed college in a way I hadn't been expecting. I wanted to continue learning. And once you go for a doctorate, teaching is the obvious path."

"And you're good at it," Chase added.

"Some would disagree."

Chase rested his head against Killian's shoulder. "I don't know what I'm good at."

"I recall you being a very good student," Killian told him, trying not to sound like a complete pervert and failing miserably.

"Yeah, maybe, but I'm the same in all my classes. I'm a decent student, but I don't excel at anything in particular."

"And you're not going into the family business? I'm not dining with a future real estate mogul?" Killian teased.

Chase shook his head without so much as a smile. "He's never mentioned. And—" Chase lifted his head, tensing under Killian's arm. "Um. Well. Speak of the devil."

Killian followed Chase's alarmed gaze to find a middle-aged man approaching their table. "Is that your father?"

Killian didn't know what he'd do if it was. From the little he'd learned, he'd come to loathe Chase's parents. Killian didn't think he could be the slightest bit civil, even for Chase's sake.

"No." Chase sat up straighter, but Killian kept his arm around him because fuck if he was going to let some stranger scare him into doing otherwise, and he knew Chase was too polite to blatantly shrug him off. "It's one of his business acquaintances. I've had to sit through so many dinners with him."

The man arrived. He was one of those aggressively fit men in their late fifties that Phoenix overflowed with in the winter, overly tanned in a way that suggested many hours spent on one golf course or another. "Chase, my boy," he boomed, louder than Killian deemed necessary. "I thought that was you."

Chase smiled at him politely. His voice, when he spoke, was firm and easy. "Mr. Hansen. It's good to see you."

Mr. Hansen's gaze kept darting between the two of them, and while he was too mannered to blatantly sniff the air, Killian saw his nostrils flare. "I hope I'm not interrupting?"

Chase cleared his throat. Perhaps he was realizing that he reeked of Killian's pheromones. "Oh, no. Mr. Hansen, this is—"

"Professor Killian Burke, pleasure to meet you," Killian broke in, holding out the hand not currently wrapped around Chase's shoulder.

Mr. Hansen didn't attempt to hide his surprise as he shook Killian's hand. "Professor, you say? Pleasure, I'm sure. Well, I'll let you two get on with it. Until next time, Chase." He made as if to leave, then turned back, a slight edge to his voice. "I can't wait to tell your father I ran into you. He'll be so ... delighted."

Chase made some vague sound of assent, and Mr. Hansen walked off with a beaming smile, joining a small group leaving the restaurant.

Chase watched him until he was out the door. "I guess he's going into Phoenix real estate too," he said dully.

Their food arrived shortly after, but the easy flow to their evening had been altered. Chase was clearly distracted. He seemed to be waiting for the other shoe to drop, as if Mr. Hansen was going to return at any moment and interrogate him further.

Killian wasn't sure what the issue was, exactly. It could be weeks before the smarmy asshole spoke to Chase's father, and Chase's father didn't seem that interested in his son's life in the first place.

But Killian didn't press. If the publicity was what Chase was worried about, it was possible going slow was no longer an option.

For now, Killian put it out of his mind and focused on helping his beta relax again.

19

Chase

Chase was feeling almost normal by the time they got back to Killian's house for dinner.

Seeing Mr. Hansen had been ... odd, and not just because it had been so unexpected. The guy wasn't exactly Chase's favorite business associate of his father's by any means. He was one of those alphas who seemed to think the world was their oyster based solely on the natural advantage of their designation.

And he'd looked at Chase in a way Chase hadn't liked, back at the restaurant. It had been subtle, but there'd been a kind of calculating, judgmental tinge to it. It had set Chase on edge, when he'd been so happy and relaxed just moments before.

But that might have been Chase's raw nerves making themselves known. Killian's rut had been intense, to say the fucking least. And while part of that had been the way Chase had been pushed to his physical limit, part of it had just been ... Killian. The way he'd cuddled and hand-fed Chase whenever his knot went down. The way he'd checked in with bleary eyes and slurred words during his few moments of lucidity. The way he'd triple-checked the locks every time he'd been alert enough to make the rounds, growling at every vague sound from the street.

It had been a concentrated dose of everything that already made Chase weak for him: the intensity of his focus, the strength of his desire, the softness he exuded after he exercised the aggressive lust for Chase that was always simmering just underneath the surface.

So ... yeah. Chase had been a little raw. But the chicken pho and getting a breather from the rut pheromones had helped all that a bit.

And Killian was now in an alarmingly good mood, like Chase agreeing to have dinner with him had been some sort of boon he'd been dying for. Which was ridiculous, since he'd never even asked before.

When Chase's phone buzzed shortly after they'd gotten situated in the living room—Killian flipping through his book while Chase chose something for them to watch—Chase thought it might be one of his roommates. He'd let them know he'd gotten out of the rut safely, but he wouldn't have been surprised if they were impatient for more details. Spencer had already been dropping not-so-subtle hints in that direction. (*Yo, Chasey,* one of his texts had read. *How was that alpha rut D?!?!*)

But it wasn't one of Chase's roommates at all.

It was his father calling.

Chase blinked down at his phone in surprise, and Killian—still a little hypersensitive in the vestiges of his rut—tensed beside him on the couch. "What is it?"

"My dad."

It was strange for his dad to be calling though. Not just because Chase rarely heard from his parents and hadn't been expecting a call, but because it was usually his mother who handled the family communication.

Maybe they were coming for another visit?

Chase took a breath and accepted the call. "Hey, Dad."

"Chase," his father said. He sounded ... curt. Pissed, maybe. "I've heard a disturbing rumor."

Chase straightened, making some space between him and Killian on the couch. "Um. Okay."

"Chet Hansen says he saw you tonight." Each word leaving his father's mouth was clipped and decisive, like an evening news report. "Says you were canoodling with a much older man. He did his research, and he says this man teaches at your university."

"Oh." Chase's mind went blank in a very strange way. Of all the ways for him and Killian to get caught, he'd never imagined his parents being a factor.

"Well?"

Chase shook his head, trying to follow. "Was there a question in there?"

"Don't act smart," his father chastised, even though Chase hadn't been acting smart at all. "Are you carrying about with some pervert alpha professor like a two-bit rent boy, is the question. Did your mother and I not tell you I was pursuing business in Phoenix? Did you not consider what this might do to my reputation?"

Chase was at a loss. He'd never been in trouble with his parents before, even the few times when he'd wanted to be. They'd never noticed enough for him to manage it. So of course he hadn't considered their reaction. Why the fuck would he?

He tried to think back to what had been so horrendous about him and Killian at dinner. Chase had smelled like Killian's pheromones, sure. And Killian's arm had been around him, hadn't it? And the age difference had probably been obvious enough. But still, they'd only been eating dinner together. It wasn't like Chase had been blowing him under the table.

When Chase took too long to answer, his father sighed heavily.

"Are you screwing one of your teachers, Chase?" he asked, each word said so slowly, like Chase was too stupid to understand otherwise. "Publicly?"

"It's not—"

"Your mother and I have given you a remarkable amount of free rein, young man."

Chase frowned down at his lap. "I never asked for that."

"Excuse me?"

"The free rein. I never asked you to—"

"The amount of *money* we have—"

And then the phone was being plucked out of Chase's hands, too quick for him to protest. He wasn't sure if he would have, anyway. He wasn't sure he could take any more of whatever this was that was happening.

Had he wanted them to be mad at him before? Had Chase really thought negative attention was better than none at all? Because actually, it sucked. He hated it.

Killian held the phone to his ear, and Chase had never seen him look so angry before. "Mr. Adler?"

Chase startled. It was weird to hear Killian calling his father that.

"This is the pervert alpha professor. I'm afraid you've interrupted our evening together. You'll have to call back another time. Preferably when you've cooled down and gotten your head out of your ass." His gaze darted toward Chase, his steely blue eyes softening the slightest bit. "You have a wonderful son. I wish you deserved him."

He hung up, then pressed a few more buttons on Chase's phone, clearing his throat. "I've blocked his number until you're ready to speak with him."

"Oh. Okay." Chase blinked at him. "That was strange."

Killian's expression was unreadable now that the anger had

leached out. "You're trembling," he said, his tone nothing like the gruff, pissed-off voice he'd used with Chase's father.

"Am I?" Chase held up his hand, and yeah, it was visibly shaking. He tucked it under his leg. "I'm okay. I thought I wanted him to pay attention, but that was—" He tried to shrug and didn't quite manage it. "I didn't like that, I guess."

"Of course you didn't." Killian reached out as if to touch him, then redirected and swept a hand through his hair. "Christ, Chase. You shouldn't have had to listen to any of that."

"Can I maybe— Do you have—?"

Killian nodded, as if Chase had actually managed to formulate a question. "I'll make you some tea."

Chase had been about to ask for a beer, actually, but he supposed tea would be fine.

He'd be fine. He just ... needed a minute.

———

A HOT DRINK and half a movie later and Chase was fine. Really. He'd even told Killian that five or six times, although the alpha didn't seem inclined to believe him.

But he was.

Sure, the few times Chase had imagined him and Killian going public, he hadn't exactly pictured his father yelling at him over the phone and calling him a collegiate prostitute or whatever, but maybe he'd just been lacking in imagination.

They'd paused the movie so Chase could use the bathroom, and he took the opportunity to stretch and set his cup in the kitchen sink. Killian followed him in—he seemed reluctant to let Chase out of his sight, and Chase supposed he should count himself lucky Killian hadn't tried to follow him into the bathroom too.

Chase turned to lean his back against the sink. He needed to say something, if only to get that concerned look off Killian's face. "I'll just tell him it's over."

Killian blanched. "Excuse me?"

"My dad. I mean, they're never around, and it's not like we're out in public very often." Chase shrugged. "Seeing Mr. Hansen was a fluke. If it really pisses him off that much, I'll tell him I ended it and that will be that. They'll forget."

"No."

Killian's refusal sounded calm enough, but there was a finality to it that even Chase, in his slightly numb state, could hear.

Chase ... hadn't been expecting that. "What?"

Killian folded his arms. "That doesn't work for me."

"Why not?"

Killian stared him down for a minute, then cocked his head. "What exactly do you think we are, Chase?"

For some reason, the question had Chase flushing. He suddenly felt hot. Too hot. Why was Killian putting him on the spot like this? "Um. Lovers?"

He immediately wanted to die. For fuck's sake, he wasn't the heroine in some tragic romance. Couldn't he have chosen a better word for it?

But Killian didn't laugh. He only nodded. "Yes and no. I don't think it's any secret, after the rut we just shared together, that I have some very intense feelings for you, Chase Adler."

That hot feeling intensified, centering in his throat now. Chase wanted to loosen his collar, but he wasn't wearing a collar. He never wore a collar. He was a T-shirt guy. "W-What?"

Because what the fuck did Killian mean, it wasn't a secret? It sure as shit felt like one to Chase. No one had told him that. *Killian* had certainly never told him that.

But he's telling you now.

Killian kept staring at him, his arms crossed and his stance wide, the very picture of a stubborn, commanding alpha. "Chase."

And it was horrible the way he said it. Softly. Kindly.

Whatever Killian was looking for, he didn't seem to find it on Chase's face. He uncrossed his arms, running a frustrated hand through his hair. "Let's try this: What do you *want* us to be?"

Now it was Chase's turn to blanch. That hot feeling was replaced with a sudden wave of chill, like a bucket of ice-cold water had been poured over his head. "I don't know." He tried for a laugh, and it sounded all wrong. "Aren't *you* in charge? You tell me what to do and I follow? Isn't that how this works?"

Killian shook his head. "No, sweet boy. Not for things like this."

Chase couldn't look him in the eye anymore. His gaze dropped to his feet, and Killian seemed to take pity on him.

"*I* can tell you that I want us to be partners or boyfriends or whichever you prefer to call it," Killian said. "I can tell you I want to be even more than that someday. But is that what *you* want?"

This was somehow worse than the angry phone call. Worse than that soul-killing dinner with his parents. Worse than anything. Because there were things Chase thought he wanted to say—things that maybe he wanted to ask for—but it was like he physically couldn't. It all got stuck in his throat, no room for it with all that hot panic, and he didn't see any of it making its way out anytime soon.

What was *wrong* with him?

"Chase," Killian said again, in that soft, kind way.

And it was too much. His attention, his kindness, the things he wanted Chase to know and talk about and ask for.

"I should probably go," Chase said, wiping at his eyes. They were dry, though, so he didn't know why he bothered.

Killian didn't look angry. He looked kind of sad, which was somehow worse.

"I can— Let me think," Chase told him, turning back to face the sink. He should rinse out his mug, shouldn't he? It was rude to just leave it there. "For a while. And then I can ..." He trailed off. He didn't know what the end of that sentence was.

Killian's silence lasted an unbearably long time before he asked, "Are your roommates home?"

There. That was a question Chase could find an answer to, wasn't it? He dug his phone out of his pocket and checked his texts. "Yeah. They're home."

"Then go straight there," Killian commanded, his voice thick. "Let the baby alphas comfort you."

Something loosened in Chase's chest. Yeah. He could do that. That was straightforward. Easy.

He turned back around, and there was Killian, looking kind of devastated, and suddenly it wasn't easy anymore.

When Chase froze, Killian stepped forward, cupping Chase's face in his broad hands. He spoke clearly. Firmly. "I'm going to give you space because you asked for it, and I want to give you all the things you ask for. But I'll be waiting. Do you understand?"

Chase nodded, although he wasn't sure he did. He didn't think he understood anything right now. He wasn't sure what had just happened. He wanted to turn back time, and go back to when they were just waking up from Killian's rut. He wanted to say no to dinner and order takeout instead. He wanted to be on the couch right now, curled up in Killian's arms, watching something neither of them cared about.

He didn't know how to say any of that.

Killian gave him a hard look. "Text me when you're home safe. Immediately, or I'll be coming to check on you. The space starts after."

And somehow that was that.

Chase left.

20

Killian

Killian was well on his way to being very, very drunk.

Past that, probably, if he was being honest. Prince and Devon had already confiscated his phone and keys some time ago, declaring him a flight risk, but they had yet to confiscate the whiskey. Perhaps they'd realized he needed some ... mellowing.

Killian had called them shortly after Chase had left. He'd known he couldn't be alone. Had known that, left to his own devices, he would have done something ill-advised. Smashed something irreplaceable. Followed Chase home. Flown to whatever Midwestern town his beta's parents were hiding in and set their expensive house on fire.

Just as an example.

But instead Killian was drunk and chaperoned and full of frustration and regret.

It hadn't been the right time to push Chase. Killian had known that, even as he'd done it. But he hadn't been able to bear it—that calm, stone-faced decision to deny their relationship to Chase's parents. It had been too many steps back after not enough steps forward. The straw that had broken Killian's lovesick back.

"You're too quiet over there," Devon complained from his spot in Killian's best armchair. "What tragic things are you thinking about?"

Killian rubbed a hand over his face with a sigh. He was sprawled on his back on his living room floor, and if Chase could see him—under different circumstances, of course—Killian knew the exact shade of quiet amusement that would paint his beta's face at the sight.

"I still can't believe he hesitated, with how gone he seemed over you," Prince mused unhelpfully from his own horizontal position on Killian's couch.

"He has these walls," Killian told him, setting his glass on his chest, more than ready to expound on the subject.

"Oh my god," Devon groaned. "Enough about the goddamn *walls*. We heard you the first hundred times."

Killian frowned at the ceiling. The walls were important, so he didn't know why Devon was being an asshole about them. "He doesn't know how to be loved, I don't think. Doesn't know how to ask for it," he finally said, and he must not have repeated that one quite as often, because his words were met with a respectful silence.

It wasn't exactly right, but it was close. Chase allowed certain gestures of affection, some of them more easily than others. The physical sort was of course always allowed, as well as Killian's favorite, commanding sort of care—shared baths and hearty meals and quality time that he kept sneakily expanding. But not ... declarations, aside from specific praise that was very of the moment.

Killian could tell Chase he was a good boy, that he was a perfect fuckhole, but not that he wanted to cherish him for the rest of his life. Apparently.

What Killian should have done was tire him out first. He should have gotten Chase spent and comfortable and content, faced away from Killian in his arms—eye contact could be hard for Chase during these types of conversation—and *then* approached the subject.

But he hadn't. And Chase was gone. Back to his other alphas.

"Except those friends of his," Killian amended, aware that he sounded unbearably morose. "He lets *them* love him."

"Well, it's different with friends," Prince said, waving a hand to encompass the room. "Fewer expectations, you know. Easier."

Killian supposed Prince knew something about that; he hadn't had a particularly happy childhood himself.

Devon groaned again. "It's becoming contagious, I can hear it in Prince's voice—you're both getting maudlin now. It's time for us to go."

And maybe to someone else, that announcement would have seemed unkind. But Killian's friends had let him ramble and mope for hours, and forcing him to get some rest might have been the kindest thing they could do now.

And maybe Devon was also right about the timing, because Killian's eyes had shut at some point, and it was surprisingly difficult to get them back open.

He couldn't sleep though. Chase was gone. He had to stay awake to remember that.

Killian kept blinking up at the ceiling as he felt someone pry the whiskey bottle out of his hand. And then there was a determined sort of rummaging sound from somewhere, but Killian didn't bother to look.

He'd scared his beta away. What if he never got him back?

An eternity later, Killian heard the telltale sounds of Devon tugging Prince off the couch. Prince wasn't drunk—not like Killian —but he *was* quite lazy when he got comfortable somewhere.

"I've hidden your liquor," Devon told Killian. Or at least, Killian presumed Devon was talking to him, since it was Killian's house they were in. "Don't want you drinking yourself into a coma. We're off to the club to rid ourselves of the scent of your despair. Prince is going to lure some unsuspecting soul into his sadistic clutches with his kind eyes and easy smile, and I'm going to—well, you know."

"Make a pretty omega cry?" Killian answered for him.

"Precisely."

And then it was Killian who was getting tugged off the floor. Firm hands led him to his bedroom, then pushed him gently into bed. Warm lips pressed to Killian's forehead—a kiss, how nice— and then Devon told him, "Don't go doing anything stupid. We'll check on you in the morning."

Killian was asleep before he heard the front door close.

———

KILLIAN WOKE up with a pounding behind his temples and a mouth drier than the desert he lived in.

That was what he got for turning to whiskey when he was this close to forty—his body was rebelling in the aftermath, as it fucking should.

Killian let himself wallow in the physical torment for a few minutes—a decent distraction from any other kind of torment that might be lying in wait under this heaviness in his chest—before gingerly turning his head and searching for his phone on his nightstand.

There was a glass of water there. Devon's doing, no doubt. Killian made himself chug it down before checking his texts.

There was already a new one on the group message with Devon and Prince.

> Devon: We're giving you until noon to suffer. If we don't hear from you by then, we're coming over with something greasy to revive you.

Killian sent a quick text back.

> Killian: Alive. But you should've hidden the whiskey earlier.

He couldn't help but check his messages with Chase. As if somehow he might have missed one.

But there was only the one from the night before. The last one.

> Chase: Home safe.

Killian hadn't responded. Because he'd said he wouldn't, and even drunk and rambling to his friends, he'd known better than to go back on his word so quickly. Because he'd said he'd wait, and that meant not making the first move.

And yet there was some inner, instinctual part of him that was already rebelling.

Fuck that, it whispered. *Get him. Bite him. Claim him.*

That part of Killian insisted Chase was *his*. He'd shared a rut with the boy. He'd knotted him again and again. They were mates, bite mark or no.

Killian understood suddenly why Eli had counseled him to go slow, despite having no evidence of Killian doing otherwise. *This* was why so many people were still wary of alphas. Because they could be demanding, possessive assholes. Some might even argue it was in their very natures.

But that wasn't what Chase needed from Killian right now. It wasn't what he deserved. He deserved to be given space to think about what he wanted. He deserved to be given what he'd asked for—namely, time.

The key was for Killian to keep his cool and not fuck it up by getting all aggravated. Nothing had ended. It was only a pause.

So Killian didn't text Chase demanding an update. Didn't ask, *How did you sleep?* Or, *Are you in love with me yet?*

Instead, he hauled his tired, sad body out of bed and shuffled to the bathroom, where he brushed the awful taste out of his mouth and got the shower started, turning the taps to blistering hot and stepping under the spray.

Killian used his own shampoo because Chase had never left anything else for him to use instead. Because Killian had always liked Chase smelling like him and only him. But now that meant there was no scent of Chase in his house. No lingering pheromones. No special soap.

Only Killian's leather and cherry, bitter and heavy.

When had the situation transformed from sex with someone Killian couldn't resist to this all-consuming thing?

It had been a steady, unassuming encroachment, he was pretty sure. Much like Chase himself. The way he just ... fit. In Killian's house. In Killian's life.

The way he made Killian laugh without trying. The way he made him softer and sweeter than Killian was used to being. The way he made him want to be a real partner in a way Killian hadn't wanted to be in a really long time. Possibly ever, given his history.

Killian should have said those things. He should have said more than the incredibly insufficient phrase, "I have very intense feelings for you."

Very intense feelings? What did that even *mean*?

Ah, fuck, Killian was going to mope all day, wasn't he?

He shut the shower off, rubbing himself dry with a towel before returning to his bedroom.

He had a text waiting on his phone. Not from Chase, but from Devon again.

Devon: Remember. Nothing stupid.

Killian wished he felt like he didn't need the reminder.

21

Killian

Killian was fairly certain what he was doing counted as something stupid, despite Devon's daily reminders not to act out. But it was a new day, and Killian was still painfully sober, as he'd been since that first unfortunate night. And he'd been showing a remarkable amount of restraint, so perhaps his lapse could be forgiven.

It had been a week.

A week since Killian had gotten drunk off his ass and fallen asleep with a mountain of regrets crushing his chest. A week of giving Chase space and time, which Chase seemed to be taking ample advantage of, without sending so much as a single text after that last, *Home safe*.

And it was Friday, and Friday was *their* day. And Killian couldn't be at home, waiting for a message he was fairly certain he wasn't going to receive.

There was a knock on Killian's car window. He jumped in his

seat with a curse, turning to find a familiar face on his driver's side, although it was one he'd only seen from a distance so far.

Spencer, last name unknown. Undergraduate alpha. Room-mate to one Chase Adler.

Killian rolled down his window, and Spencer grinned at him as the heat of the day rolled into Killian's car, combating the air-conditioning he had running.

Spencer was obnoxiously handsome, tan and lean and muscled in his loose tank top, with his dark hair in disarray and a tongue piercing peeking out between his bared teeth. He had the sort of obvious, cocky swagger that should have been a front but that he seemed to back up with his good looks and—from what Chase had told Killian—innumerable notches on his bedpost.

Killian could name half a dozen doms who would probably trade a fucking kidney to bring this kid to his knees.

"Professor," Spencer greeted, somehow making the word sound like a taunt, although his smile was friendly enough.

Killian sighed, fighting the urge to roll his window right back up. "You know who I am."

That was unfortunate, as Killian was currently parked outside the home Spencer shared with Chase and Noah. Killian hadn't even parked around the block in some attempt to be stealth. His car was idling barely thirty feet from their front door.

As he'd said: something stupid.

Spencer set his folded arms on Killian's lowered window, leaning in. The gesture wafted his spiced-tea pheromones into Killian's space in a way Killian didn't much enjoy, but he felt like this might be a test of some sort, so he kept his growl in check.

"Hell, yeah, I do. I looked you up like ten seconds after Chasey told us about you." Spencer gave Killian a thorough once-over. "Not bad."

Killian had nothing to say to that, and Spencer's grin widened. "He's not here, you know."

"I'm aware." Chase's car wasn't in the driveway, and if Killian had been thinking straight in the first place, he would have realized Chase still had hours of classes left. But he hadn't been thinking straight for a week, so ...

Killian should leave. Nothing good could come of this conversation.

Instead, he cleared his throat. "I came at him too hard. Too fast."

Spencer laughed brightly. "Oh, you gotta do that with Chasey. It's a funny balance, pushy but patient. I was shit at it at first, but Noah helped balance things out." He cocked his head, glancing toward the empty house and then back to Killian. He lowered his voice to a whisper, despite there not being anyone else on the street. "His parents are dicks, did you know that? Like, serious dicks."

"I know."

Spencer scratched his neck. "Like, my mom's mean as hell, but at least she acknowledges I exist." He blew out a breath. "And he never talks about it. Not ever."

"I gathered."

Spencer cocked a brow. "So you might have to be patient for a little while longer, is what I'm saying. Keeps those emotions locked down tight, our Chasey."

Was Killian really going to take advice from this cocky kid? But he found himself nodding. "I will be. Patient."

Despite his current lapse in judgment, Killian would wait months if he had to. If that was how long it took for Chase to gather what he wanted to say.

Fuck, he hoped he didn't have to wait months.

"Mm-hmm." Spencer grinned at him amiably. "No offense, but you're parked in front of our house like a stalker right now."

Killian's hands tightened on the steering wheel. "Fair point."

He was trying to be agreeable, but a familiar, territorial aggression was building inside him. Some primal response to another alpha telling him what to do with his beta. Never mind that the alpha was young—somehow Spencer seemed so much younger than Chase, without any of Chase's air of self-possession—and a long-standing friend of Chase's. Killian's reaction was unreasonable, and yet he couldn't shake it.

The scent of rich leather filled the car, free of any cherry sweetness.

Spencer sniffed the air, then laughed again, obnoxiously loud. "Aw, don't worry, Professor. Chasey is like a brother to me." He poked his tongue piercing out between his teeth, wiggling his brows. "I mean, don't get me wrong, he's a handsome dude ..."

This time Killian's growl couldn't be contained.

Spencer's taunting smile took on an approving cast. "You're possessive of him. That's good. He deserves that."

His smile immediately dissolved into a thoughtful frown.

Mercurial little fuck, wasn't he? Killian could barely keep up.

"You know, Noah and I thought at first that you'd ended things." Spencer's spiced pheromones took on a sharp edge as his frown deepened. "I was all ready to kick your ass and get expelled for the trouble. But then we realized, if that had been the case, Chase would have just shut it all down and packed it in some secret feelings box and not even shown us he was hurting. So we figured out pretty quick that something else was up."

He suddenly straightened, slapping the car door in a definitive way. "So, you know. Keep up the good work and get the fuck out of here."

Killian was left reeling. Like he'd been given too much information and not enough at the same time.

He leaned out the window as Spencer started walking away, his backpack slung over one shoulder. "Wait!"

Spencer turned, brow raised expectantly.

"How is he?"

"Oh, he's miserable. Really, super-duper sad." Spencer held up two thumbs in the air. "So there's hope."

And weirdly, for the first time that week, Killian felt like there might be.

He sat there for a few long moments, watching Spencer head toward the house. He watched as he was intercepted by another alpha at the driveway, one with a broad build and loose blond curls. He watched as the newcomer turned toward Killian's car and locked eyes with him, grinning wide. His smile was less mocking and more welcoming, but it still had Killian cursing under his breath.

That was both Chase's roommates who now knew Killian was a fool.

Killian rolled up his window, letting the air-conditioning blast in his face before setting the car in gear. It was time to head home and find a few more scraps of patience within himself.

22

Chase

Chase hurried into the house, desperate to escape the late afternoon heat. He didn't bother to see if anyone else was home, just rushed into his bathroom—his was the only room with an en suite—and got cold water running in the sink.

Chase was too worn out to shower fully, but he wanted to wipe off some of the day. He'd been getting irritated lately with the scents of all the students smothering him on campus. Which didn't make any fucking sense, because he was a fucking beta and it shouldn't be affecting him at all, but it still helped to wash it off, even if it was all in Chase's head.

He splashed water on his face first, rubbing it down to his neck, then grabbed blindly for a hand towel. He ran it under the water and lifted his head, breaking out into a curse as he jumped, "Jesus fuck!"

Spencer grinned at him in the mirror's reflection. "Afternoon, Chasey."

He was leaning against the doorjamb, holding a bag of his favorite protein chips, and he popped one in his mouth, managing to keep his grin as he chewed. He looked smug as all hell, which was a change from the abnormally subdued concern he'd been failing to hide the rest of the week.

Chase gave him a look as he held a hand to his heart, willing it to slow down. "I'm not going out tonight. You and Noah can stop asking."

His roommates seemed to think that—after a week of moping —going to a party or five was going to pull Chase out of his funk, but Chase had no interest. It was Friday, and there was only one place he wanted to be. One person he wanted to see.

One person he was *afraid* to see.

"Your professor was just here, you know. Stalking you like a creep."

It took longer than it should have for Spencer's words to register. What he'd said was so unexpected that for a second, Chase had convinced himself his friend was speaking another language.

His professor.

The ache in Chase's chest made it hard to breathe, but he managed. Barely. He shut off the water, turning to face Spencer. "He was?"

Spencer popped another chip into his mouth. "I told him what's what."

"Oh, Jesus." That could mean so many things in Spencer's world, and Chase was now worried about all of them.

"He's really got it bad for you, huh?"

"It's ... good sex." The words felt wrong coming out of Chase's mouth, but he'd been repeating the mantra for so long that he didn't know how to stop. *It's just good sex. Intense sex. Sex, sex, sex.*

But it seemed like, for once, Spencer wasn't letting him off the hook with that. He cocked his head. "Is that it? Just good sex?"

"No." Chase ran a hand over his face, shaking the water drops off afterward. "I don't know." The silence was deafening, and his mouth moved without permission. "He wants to date me."

"Isn't that what you were already doing? Even with the secrecy, it was kind of obvious." Spencer laughed, not unkindly. "You spent his rut with him, Chasey."

Obvious. Of course. Chase's relationship with Killian seemed to be an obvious thing to everyone but him. Like how Killian had thought Chase should just know that Killian had been growing feelings for him. And apparently Spencer and probably Noah thought the same thing.

But Chase *didn't* know. How did anyone know?

When Chase had been too little to have better sense, he'd asked his nanny why his parents didn't love him like his friends' parents seemed to love them. His nanny had told him that *of course* his parents loved him. All parents loved their children.

But that had been a lie, one it had taken Chase almost his whole life to figure out. Trying to parse through why the love his parents felt for him didn't feel like love at all.

And why did everything have to come back to them? *Fuck* them. Fuck his dad's narcissistic self-interest. Fuck his mom's enabling and her cheek kisses that never touched skin. This was about Killian. Chase and Killian.

Standing seemed suddenly a little too difficult to manage, and Chase slid down until he hit the floor. Spencer, being Spencer, sat down across from him in the doorway. Chase rested his head against the wall. "How do you do it, Spence? Put your feelings out there over and over?"

It wasn't like Spencer was proclaiming his love to random hookups over and over, but he was still ... open. With his friends. With almost anyone. He never hid how he was feeling, good or bad, even when people wanted him to.

Spencer shrugged. "Dunno. Only way I know how to be."

"Doesn't it hurt?"

"Oh yeah." Spencer nodded. "But feelings get hurt either way, don't they? Whether you bottle them up or not." He reached into his chip bag, then paused, giving Chase an incredulous look. "Dude, are you looking to *me* for relationship advice? Please tell me you're not. I'll call Noah in. He's, like, normal about this shit."

Against all odds, Chase found himself smiling. "I love you, Spencer."

He didn't know why he could say it to a friend and not to ... other people. Didn't know what held him back, other than a fear so bone-deep it hardly registered in his brain. Like it was so much a part of him—this anxiety over what would happen if they named things that had been unspoken until now—that Chase hadn't even known it was there.

And he'd fucked everything up because of it.

Spencer looked positively moony. "Aww, I love you too."

"My parents don't, I don't think." Chase took a deep breath. Let it out. Let the truth out. "They don't love me. They never have."

Chase hadn't spoken to his father since that night. He'd left his number blocked, and he'd blocked his mother's while he was at it. It was novel, being the one doing the ignoring. He probably wouldn't be able to keep it up forever, but it was working for him for now.

Spencer's response was instantaneous, without an ounce of hesitation. "Then they're selfish, shitty assholes who don't deserve you."

They were only words, but they loosened something in Chase. Something Killian had already wiggled free with his tenderness and care and protection. A tightness Chase had been living with all his life.

He let his eyes fall shut, let himself breathe easily as he admitted, "I don't know how to just ... be loved by someone. I don't know why it's so scary."

Spencer scoffed. "You've been loved. *We* love you."

"It's different. You don't have any ... expectations."

"And does this professor expect you to be something you're not?" Spencer sounded pissed off by his own question, like if the answer was yes he'd jump up and go hunt Killian down for putting too much pressure on Chase.

His anger almost had Chase smiling. "No. But when I picture him with someone long-term, it's someone ... put together. Someone who knows who they are and what they want." Chase opened his eyes, raising his brows at his friend. "I don't even know what I want to be when I grow up."

Spencer waved a hand. "Who the fuck says you have to? You can grow together and shit. That's what those relationship things are supposed to be for." He suddenly grinned, his eyes full of mischief. "Plus, I already know what you should be."

"You do?"

Spencer set his bag of chips down, dusting his hands. He leaned forward, the picture of solemnity. "You should be a therapist," he said, each word deliberate.

"What?"

Chase honestly couldn't tell if Spencer was joking. Except for the fact that it was almost always clear when Spencer was joking.

So he was serious.

"You listen," Spencer told him, frank and open. "You *always* listen to me, no matter how much I gripe. And you're like that with everyone. You have this way—you're present without being pushy. You put people at ease."

To some extent, they were words Chase had heard before—he'd been told he was a good listener lots of times, actually, by various people—but something about the blunt compliment made it one of the nicest things anyone had ever said to Chase.

Still ... a therapist?

Chase nibbled at his lower lip, considering. "But ... I have my own issues. Like, a lot of them."

"Oh yeah." Spencer nodded. "You definitely need therapy, Chasey. But everybody does. My school counselor once told me every therapist has a therapist, and that if they don't, you should find a different therapist. Plus, betas do really well in that field. Not as susceptible to wonky pheromones."

Chase could only blink at him. It sounded ... really fucking tempting, actually. Or at the very least, a direction he could look into. He hadn't even had that much before now.

Spencer started laughing, punching a hand into the air. "Damn, I am *killing* it at advice today! I should be a fucking life-style guru or something." He danced in place for a moment, contorting his torso this way and that while staying seated, and generally looking so ridiculous Chase couldn't help grinning at him. Then Spencer grimaced. "Can we get off your bathroom floor now? My ass is getting numb."

"Yeah, man." Chase stood and held out a hand, pulling Spencer to standing.

It was clear neither of them felt up for video games or a movie or any sort of distraction yet. They ended up on Chase's bed, both of them on their backs with their hands folded on their stomachs, staring at the ceiling.

After a few minutes, Noah entered the room, took one look at them, and crawled onto the bed with them. He shuffled close to Chase, nuzzling his head on Chase's shoulder to scent mark him wordlessly.

"No Eli tonight?" Chase asked. He'd thought after his last refusal to go partying, Noah might have decided to stay with his omega.

Noah folded his hands on his stomach, mirroring Chase's and Spencer's positions. "Thought it might be better to stay home tonight."

He and Spencer had both been doing that since Chase had come back from Killian's, too numb and shell-shocked to share with them what had happened. They'd been sticking close and supporting him without prying. Waiting for him to open up. Just like Killian had apparently been waiting.

Chase let out a long breath, letting his body relax and sink into the mattress. In some ways he felt lighter than he had all week—it was weird the release a few truths spoken out loud could provide —but he wasn't exactly floating on air.

He was surrounded by the scents of spiced tea and ocean air, and they were comforting, but they weren't leather and cherry. They weren't the pheromones Chase had come to associate with everything good in the world.

Chase missed his alpha.

The missing hurt, like an ache he couldn't get rid of. Even when he slept, he felt it—he'd wake up in the middle of the night in pain and unable to figure out why, until he was alert enough to remember what had happened. The way he'd left Killian looking so devastated.

Chase knew it was on him to fix it. He just had to … say things. Admit things. Ask for things.

It should have been easy, but it wasn't. But that was how it was, and maybe beating himself up about it wasn't helping anything. Maybe he just needed to admit it was hard and admit he was a little broken and do it anyway.

"What are you thinking?" Spencer asked. "Dreaming about your stalker professor?"

"I'm thinking that it was easier with you guys. Letting you in."

Noah snorted a laugh. "Yeah, but we also kind of just … latched onto you after orientation. And there wasn't any pressure for declarations or any of that, so we had time to worm our way in without you noticing. Your professor's too lovesick for that. Poor guy."

"How would you know?" Chase asked. "Did you have a chat with him too?"

"Eli told me," Noah said easily. "They had a meeting. Apparently it was super pathetic, and now Eli's given his full approval."

"And that's his official diagnosis?" Chase asked. "Lovesick?"

Just saying it out loud made the ache in Chase's chest worse. Or maybe better?

"Oh yeah," Spencer chimed in. "Lovesick for sure. Guy almost bit my head off when I called you handsome." He cackled. "He's gonna be fun to tease."

Chase smiled at the thought—Spencer and Killian in a room together. Noah too. All the people Chase cared about. Meeting. Getting to know each other.

Chase could have that. He could have everything he was too afraid to say he wanted, if he could just admit it to the one person who needed to hear it most.

But maybe it wouldn't hurt to practice a little first.

"I like him," Chase said, directing his words to the ceiling. "I really, really like him. Maybe even more than like."

It was definitely more than like, but Chase was allowing himself a few baby steps here.

Spencer rested his head on Chase's other shoulder, and Noah patted at Chase's chest. "We know, bud. We know."

23

Killian

It was late, but Killian was still awake. Wide awake.

Sleep hadn't been kind to him this past week, not unless he was willing to down an unhealthy amount of whiskey. There were too many empty spaces in his house, spaces that should have held Chase within them. And of course, that empty pit in Killian's stomach where the usual warm sense of rightness lay.

And since Killian wasn't in any hurry to make himself into a maudlin alcoholic, he was both sober and, as he'd already established, wide awake.

He had ten minutes of Friday left. The first Friday in months that Chase Adler hadn't been in his bed.

All because Killian had been a pushy asshole, demanding promises from someone who'd just been yelled at by his dick of a father.

Killian should have held his tongue. He should have been

more patient. He *definitely* shouldn't have stalked the boy today, let himself be seen by—

There was a knock on Killian's door, so quiet he almost missed it.

Killian set down the book he'd been staring at blankly and rose from the couch, his heart pounding hard enough to escape from his chest. Because while theoretically it could have been Devon or Prince knocking, both of them would have texted first. There was no one else who would come over unannounced. No one except maybe ...

Killian opened the door, locking his knees to keep from sagging into the wall.

"Chase."

There was Killian's beta, painfully handsome as ever, wearing a baseball cap and soft, worn athletic clothes, with a bag slung over his shoulder. The duffel Chase had started bringing over when he'd begun staying the night.

Killian tried not to read too much into that. He failed completely.

Chase smelled like baby alphas, not even an ounce of Killian's pheromones to be found, but for once Killian didn't mind, because he was *here*. On Killian's doorstep.

Chase's expression was smooth and placid, without a hint of what he might be thinking underneath. "Sorry I didn't text first."

"Come in." Killian tried to make it sound like a request, but it came out like a desperate, barking command instead.

Chase's lips quirked up at the corners the slightest bit, and then he stepped inside.

Killian made room and then closed the door, locking it behind them. He was doing his best not to give off the feral energy of an alpha about to kidnap his beta and force him to stay forever. He was no doubt unsuccessful.

Chase set his bag down in the entryway and straightened, looking to the couch. "Can we sit?"

They could do whatever the fuck Chase wanted—stand on their heads and have an upside-down tea party—as long as it meant Chase stayed the night.

Killian inclined his chin. "Of course."

He strode to the couch and sat down, feeling an odd sense of role reversal: Killian obeying Chase's orders for once, even if they'd been expressed as requests. And despite that request, Chase remained standing. He glanced down at the book Killian had been failing to read, brows lifted.

"Any good?"

Killian didn't look away from Chase's face. "I have no fucking idea."

Chase huffed a soft laugh and stepped closer and then closer again, until he was wedged between Killian's spread knees. He took his cap off, setting it carefully on the coffee table.

Killian waited. He didn't push or command or whisper a single one of the endearments crowding his throat. He'd learned his fucking lesson for the moment.

Chase took a deep breath, letting it out slowly. "I'm sorry I didn't text," he said afterward. "Not just tonight. This whole week."

"I told you to take your time."

Chase cocked his head. His green eyes were unbearably soft. "That was hard for you, wasn't it?"

It had been excruciating. Killian cleared his throat. "I wanted you to be sure."

Chase's fingers clenched at the soft material of his pants, then released. "It wasn't about being sure. It was about ... wanting something so badly and having to say it out loud. Having to ask for it and trust that you would—that you would care." His cheeks had gone pink, the color traveling down his neck. "That you would care enough to give it to me."

Killian clenched his own hands into the couch cushions, holding himself back from lunging forward. "I want to give you *everything* you want."

"I know." Chase took another deep breath. He placed one knee on the couch. Then the other. He straddled Killian's lap and held himself there, with his perfect athlete's posture. He cupped Killian's face, his fingers warm against Killian's skin. His expression was still calm, but his eyes were bright and burning. "And I do want it. I want it all. I want to be your boyfriend. I want to live here one day, and that feels like it's too soon to say, but I'm saying it anyway. I want to wake up every morning, and I want you to make me breakfast. I want to come home to you at night, and I want you to break me down and put me back together over and over again. I want to be clingy and needy, and I want you to handle it. I want you to tell me I'm good, and I want you to mean it."

It was everything Killian had been dying to hear, and the relief that flooded through him was so powerful it hurt. He was so fucking proud of his sweet boy for opening up, for telling Killian all his wants and wishes.

"You *are* good," Killian said gruffly. "You're perfect."

Chase shook his head with another of those soft, lovely laughs. "I'm not perfect."

Killian would beg to fucking differ, but he didn't push the point. "I'm not either," he said instead. "I'm pushy. Demanding. Greedy."

Chase grinned, a flash of white teeth that took Killian's breath away. "Yes."

"You don't mind."

"I like that about you. I think I need it. I need you to want me so badly that you make it painfully obvious." Chase shifted forward, his perfect, muscular ass brushing against Killian's cock. "I crave it. I wake up every day craving you. So let's just do the whole thing. Because that's what I want. All of it."

And then he was kissing Killian, and Killian couldn't hold back any longer. He was all tongue and teeth and desperation. He couldn't stop cupping Chase's throat, gripping his shoulders, pressing against him chest to chest. He was so *hungry*. Hungry for Chase. Hungry for more. But just for a moment, this had to be enough, ravenous as he was. Having his beta back in his lap. In his arms.

Or at least Killian tried to let that be enough.

Eventually he couldn't wait another second, and he broke the kiss, nuzzling against Chase's neck. Scent marking him like he'd been dying to do since Chase had walked in that door.

Chase tilted his head to give Killian better access. "I'm surprised you held off this long."

"I was trying to be considerate," Killian grumbled, licking at the warm skin displayed in front of him, just because he could.

"My family—" Chase began.

"*I'm* your fucking family."

Killian said the words too loud. Too mean. More growl than any coherent speech. He took a breath and leaned back, meeting startled green eyes. Did Chase really still not understand what he did to Killian? "I mean, I could be," Killian amended, trying to sound like a more reasonable man. "If you'll let me."

Chase kissed him again, sucking on Killian's tongue sweetly like the good fucking boy he was. It was a long time before he broke away again. "I've kept them blocked, but I'm going to undo it soon," he told Killian breathlessly. "I'm going to try and have a conversation. And—and I'm going to start therapy."

"Good." This was important information, and Killian was not going to be distracted by Chase's erection rubbing against his through their clothes. "Therapy. Very healthy."

He couldn't stop kissing Chase's neck. Had he said kissing was enough? It wasn't enough. Nothing was enough.

Luckily for Killian's sanity, Chase seemed to agree. He lifted his arms so Killian could get rid of his soft, worn shirt. And then they maneuvered awkwardly, attempting to take off the rest of their clothes with Chase remaining in Killian's arms as much as possible, stealing kisses from each other after every lost item.

And then Chase was naked on Killian's lap, rubbing on him like he was just as hungry as Killian was, sliding their hard cocks together, hot skin against hot skin.

Killian couldn't stop fucking kissing him. Chase tasted minty and fresh, like he'd brushed his teeth right before coming over— which he probably had, polite and conscientious to the end.

Killian cupped Chase's bare ass, greedy fingers exploring.

He paused at what he found: Chase ready for him, hot, wet, and slick.

"Oh, sweet boy," Killian sighed into the beta's mouth. "You came prepared."

Chase pulled back to smile at him with glazed eyes. "I missed it." He pushed back, silently urging Killian for more. "I missed you."

Killian pressed a thick finger into that prepped channel, groaning at the tight squeeze. "You need me to fuck you, baby?"

Chase nodded frantically, already rocking against the intruding digit. "Yes. *Yes.*"

Killian added another finger, sliding them in and out again, over and over, just for the pleasure in being allowed. "You're going to come with my cock inside you," he promised. "And then my mouth on you. Because I've fucking missed the way you taste. And then I'm taking you to my bed and doing it all over again."

"Yes, yes, yes."

Killian gripped his rigid, aching cock at the base, holding it steady. "Come here," he ordered.

Chase rose onto his knees until he was hovering over Killian's cock, then slowly lowered. Each inch was torturously won, and he pressed his forehead against Killian's, each of them panting into the other's mouth.

Killian rubbed soothingly at Chase's hips as he bottomed out. Or he tried to be soothing, but it was probably more like a mindless pawing. It just felt so fucking good inside him, Chase squeezing Killian so tightly as he shifted and panted and whimpered. It had only been a week—why did it feel like months since Killian had been inside his beta?

Chase rose again, right to the tip, then slammed himself down, groaning loudly. "Oh god, Alpha. You feel good. You feel so good."

Killian couldn't help but kiss him again, wet and raw. And bless those fucking athlete's thighs, as Chase bounced on his cock like he was made for it, whining into Killian's mouth.

But Killian's sweet beta wasn't satisfied. His whines took on a plaintive tone as he fucked himself on Killian's cock. "Alpha."

"I know, baby." Killian soothed him with another kiss. Or maybe he soothed himself, taking a detour and sucking on Chase's neck so hard the hickey would be unmistakable in the morning.

Killian tackled Chase onto his back on the couch, withdrawing from that perfect warmth just long enough to flip him over onto his hands and knees.

Chase scrambled up, gripping onto the arms of the couch for dear life. Killian set one knee behind him, one foot on the floor for leverage, and then drove back into him like a desperate man.

"Oh *fuck!*" Chase cried.

Killian let go completely, let the beast inside him take over, pounding into his beta. His boyfriend. His future fucking mate.

"You're going to come like this," Killian told Chase, rough and low. "Filled by my cock. Don't you dare touch that pretty dick, Chase Adler."

Chase keened with the next thrust, maybe in acknowledgment or maybe not. Either way, he was good for Killian. He didn't touch that pretty dick.

And still, he erupted mere minutes later, spurting all over Killian's expensive Italian leather couch.

Good fucking boy. Killian told him so, biting at his shoulder to get the message across more fully.

He braced a hand on the couch arm, putting his whole weight into fucking Chase through his orgasm, drinking in every whimper and cry until the pressure building within him became too much, Killian's balls high and tight and fit to burst.

Killian bit down on Chase's shoulder again as he came, filling his beta with his cum, his ears buzzing so loudly he could barely hear Chase chanting, "Oh god. Oh god. Oh god," over and over.

When his hips had stopped their stuttered, determined press against Chase's ass, Killian removed his teeth from Chase's skin, licking at the indents he'd left. He slowly and carefully dragged Chase's limp form down from the couch arm, until Chase was on his back again, one leg behind Killian and one on his lap.

Killian massaged those muscled thighs, brushing at the coarse hair there. He stroked the soft skin along Chase's creases. And then slowly—deliberately—he brushed his fingers along Chase's soft cock.

Chase whimpered, automatically covering himself with one hand. "No," he whined, his eyes still closed as he recovered from his orgasm. "I can't. Not so soon."

Killian hummed sympathetically as he knocked Chase's hand away. "Color?"

"Fuck." Chase threw the hand over his eyes instead, shoulders shuddering with his sigh. "Green."

Killian could choose to be merciful right now. He could throw Chase's thighs back and eat his lovely ass, give that poor cock a break as he worked his sweet boy up to another orgasm.

But Killian didn't feel like being merciful or even particularly kind. They'd already established he was a pushy fuck, and he felt like pushing now. Felt like reminding Chase that Killian knew what was best for this delectable fucking body. Felt like reminding him how perfectly Killian could drive Chase to his limits and beyond them.

So Killian stroked that pretty, soft cock. Petting its length, thumbing at the head (Chase *really* whimpered with that move), praising it in soft, low murmurs.

And then he shuffled back on the couch, leaning forward to take Chase's limp cock into his mouth, sucking at the perfect, salty flesh.

Fucking delicious.

Chase let out a long, pained moan. Poor baby. So oversensitive.

Killian kept at it, sucking and licking as Chase whimpered his feeble protests. He sucked until Chase's moans took on a different cant. Until his hips started twitching up in encouragement, and his cock thickened in Killian's mouth.

It was Killian's turn to moan, hollowing his cheeks as he grabbed Chase's hips, encouraging him to lift up and fuck into his mouth.

Chase followed his lead, one arm still thrown over his eyes as he gave in to instinct and rocked up again and again, giving Killian exactly what he wanted.

It took long enough that Killian's jaw began to ache, but eventually Chase's back arched, his cry echoing in the quiet room as he shot into Killian's mouth.

Killian drank it down, licking and swallowing until Chase was pushing frantically at his head, "Please. Fuck. No more."

Killian chuckled lowly, wiping his mouth as he let Chase be.

Chase collapsed back onto the couch, his body still trembling with the aftershocks. "Shit."

"Come, sweet boy," Killian crooned. "Time for bed."

24

Chase

It was late. So late that it had become early, no longer Friday night but Saturday morning.

And yet neither Chase nor Killian was any closer to closing his eyes. They lay on their sides, facing each other, in Killian's bed, their legs tangled together.

Killian was petting Chase's body, his fingers warm and rough against Chase's naked skin. It was soothing, relaxing any bit of tension Chase still held, and yet Chase couldn't let his eyes fall shut. Even with his body wrung out and hung to dry from multiple orgasms.

Chase wanted to keep looking at his alpha.

The week had been tough on Killian, Chase could tell, which made Chase feel a little better about what a fucking zombie he'd been himself.

Killian looked fucking edible as always—especially with his dark hair in disarray and his blue eyes all sleepy and satisfied—but there were dark circles under his eyes, and he'd let his facial hair grow longer than he usually did.

Chase brushed his fingertips against the stubble. "Scruffy," he commented mildly.

"The better to terrify my undergrads with, my dear," Killian said, baring his teeth in some dorky approximation of a wolf.

Chase arched a brow. "Like Spencer?"

Killian's fierce expression shifted into a rueful smile. "He told you about my ... visit?"

"Of course." Honestly, if Killian had thought Spencer could keep that a secret, he hadn't been listening closely enough about Chase's friends. Or maybe he'd been giving in to wishful thinking. "But he also helped me process."

Killian let out a sigh, though the smile stayed on his lips. "Then I suppose I owe him a beer."

Chase owed Spencer way more than a beer. A six-pack at the very least. Or possibly a full weekend with all three roommates at the house, which they hadn't had nearly enough of lately. At least not without Chase nearly catatonic from despair.

Killian would hate that, Chase leaving his side for so long after they'd just been reunited. But he wouldn't stop him, not if it was something Chase really wanted..

Although, maybe Chase would get spanked again.

Speaking of ...

"Am I going to be punished?" Chase asked.

Killian's fingers paused the patterns they'd been tracing on Chase's hip. He grasped him in a gentle grip instead. "No, sweet boy. Not for that. Not for needing time and space."

Chase hadn't thought so. But maybe he'd just needed to hear it out loud, that Killian wasn't angry with him.

The alpha certainly didn't *look* angry, and his pheromones weren't heavy at all. They were light and cherry-stained, maybe from relief or lust or ... affection.

The thing was, Chase had felt kind of ridiculous after his talk with Spencer, that he'd had such a hard time making things official when he and Killian had basically been seriously dating already, according to everyone but him.

But it *did* feel different, here and now in this bed with Killian, the two of them so soft and content. So maybe it was everyone else who'd been silly.

Chase had always felt safe with Killian; that much hadn't changed. He'd always known he could let his defenses down and trust his alpha to hold him up no matter what. But with them lying here in bed, unable to stop touching each other, unable to keep these goofy little grins off their faces, it all felt ... open, in a way it hadn't before. Like things were brighter and lighter and yet sturdier than before. Like Chase was giddy but also grounded. Floating and rooted in the dirt at the same time.

Maybe that was the fatigue talking. Or maybe not. And either way, Chase still didn't want to close his eyes. "I'm going to unblock my parents in the morning. This morning," he corrected, stealing a look at the time.

Killian frowned but nodded, his fingers tracing their patterns again. Maybe he wasn't surprised that Chase didn't have it in himself to keep them out of his life forever. He seemed to know Chase better than Chase knew himself sometimes.

"I was thinking I should maybe ... refuse their money?" The words came out as a question. Chase hadn't had the heart to really come to any decision about it while he'd been missing Killian like a lost limb, so really he was spitballing here.

"To make a point?" Killian asked, his voice carefully neutral.

Chase shrugged as best he could in his awkward position.

"It's your decision. And I'm here for whatever you need, financial or otherwise. But I'm also a practical man. I would say take every opportunity you can while you can. Let them fund the rest of your schooling, at least—you have plenty of time for independence later."

Chase mentally skipped over the part where Killian had basically just offered to bankroll him if needed. He couldn't process being a sugar baby this late—or early. "I could get a part-time job. Noah and Spencer both have them."

Killian's fingers paused again. "I could make you my TA."

"That's a terrible idea."

"Oh, I think it's a great idea." There was a dangerous gleam in Killian's eyes now, and Chase could literally see the alpha's cock stiffening as he spoke. "You'd work so hard to please me, wouldn't you? And when you'd done a good job, I could just bend you right over the desk and—"

Someone had to be the voice of reason here, right? Chase interrupted the pervy vision Killian was painting. "It would make this thing between us a real issue to the university, in a way it's not right now."

Killian scoffed, pulling Chase closer on the bed, until his erection was brushing Chase's stomach. "They won't fire me," he said, nuzzling Chase's hairline. "And if they do, I'll supplement with lecture appearances until I figure out my next steps."

It was weird, the way it hit Chase just then. He'd known Killian had been upset when Chase had suggested denying their relationship; that much had been obvious. And he'd had an inkling that Killian parking outside his house like a creep had maybe meant the alpha wasn't handling the separation all that well. That he'd missed Chase possibly even more than Chase had missed him.

But it was *this* moment—Killian daydreaming in all seriousness about jeopardizing his career for a chance to have Chase on his knees for him at work—that really drove it home.

"You're kind of obsessed with me, aren't you?"

The dreamy look left Killian's eyes, and for a moment, they widened with shock. And then he was vibrating, the bed shaking with the force of it, and it took Chase a minute to realize it wasn't with anger.

It was with deep, belly-shaking laughter. The kind that took a moment to sound like anything at all, stuck in the person's throat until it erupted in guffaws.

It lasted a really long time too.

Chase furrowed his brow as he watched Killian completely lose it.

Like, it wasn't *that* funny, was it? Maybe Chase needed to put Killian to bed for real now.

"Oh, Christ." Killian wiped at his eyes once when he'd calmed down. "Don't tell me you're just realizing this *now*?"

Chase stared at him in bemusement. "Should I have realized it sooner?"

The look Killian gave Chase was unbearably tender. "I guess I'd be in trouble if you had." He rolled over, forcing Chase onto his back, laying his considerable weight on top of him. It was nice. Warm and secure. Chase wiggled underneath him, just to revel in how trapped he was.

Killian cupped Chase's cheeks with his broad hands. There was no trace of mirth in his expression anymore. "Obsessed doesn't begin to cover it. You have me by the balls, sweet boy."

"How romantic."

Killian only grinned, nuzzling Chase's cheekbone with his nose. And then he was whispering in Chase's ear, like it was a secret too precious for even the empty room to hear. "I'm going to claim you one day, Chase Adler. You're going to have my ring on your finger and my mark on your neck."

The words traveled through Chase's body like liquid fire.

It turned out it was still painful, in its way, to be wanted this much. Like it was forcing muscles Chase had never used before to awaken after a lifetime of atrophy. But it was a welcome kind of pain. A growing pain, maybe.

Killian was somehow still hard, his cock resting heavily on Chase's hip. Chase widened his legs in invitation. "You said you'd do it all again after taking me to bed," he reminded Killian.

Even after what they'd done in the living room, Chase craved it. He craved the reassurance of it, his alpha's cock and his alpha's praise.

Killian hummed his pleasure, grabbing a pillow and tucking it under Chase's hips without losing any of their skin-to-skin contact. "What a good fucking boy you are, Chase Adler."

———

CHASE SAT at the kitchen table, his phone in front of him. Looming. Or as much as a small rectangle could loom while placed horizontal on a table.

A glass of orange juice appeared next to it, and Chase gave Killian a brief, tired smile. "Thank you."

Killian remained standing behind him, his warm, possessive hand resting on the nape of Chase's neck. "I'm going to start breakfast, but I'll be right here."

"I know."

Chase had originally suggested making the call outside, but one look at Killian's face and he'd recanted immediately. Apparently his alpha was feeling protective, and Chase was feeling vulnerable enough to allow it.

Neither of them had really slept long enough considering how late they'd been up the night before, and their fatigue was showing. Killian was already on his third cup of coffee in almost as many minutes, and no doubt he'd be bullying Chase into a nap later in the afternoon.

That sounded fucking perfect, actually. Chase's eyelids were heavier than they should have been, and for the first time, he envied Killian his caffeine addiction.

But before breakfast or naps or any of the rest of it, Chase needed to take care of this. He didn't want the mess with his parents lingering at the back of his mind, distracting him from getting resettled with the man he'd just decided to commit to a future with.

Chase picked up his phone, quickly unblocking his parents' contacts. Whatever messages they might have sent him while he'd had them blocked were lost forever. And there was always the strong possibility they'd hadn't tried to contact him at all.

Maybe it was better not knowing.

Chase hit his mother's number, not sure if he was surprised or not when she picked up quickly. It wasn't like she'd ever refused his calls. She just hadn't made many herself.

"Chase," his mother greeted calmly, no hint of emotion in her voice that might point to how she'd been feeling about not being able to reach her son for a week. "Your father's quite upset."

"I know. So am I."

His mother's sigh was genteel enough to sound calculated. "I understand he spoke with you in anger, but really, we're both quite concerned."

Concerned? That was a funny choice of word. They'd never seemed concerned with very much when it came to him before. When he'd been a child crying over a scraped knee, it had always been the nanny who'd come to put the Band-Aid on over the wound.

And then there were more recent events.

Chase followed a drop of condensation on his juice glass with his finger. "Last year, I quit a sport I'd played all my life without any notice, giving up a scholarship I'd worked really hard for. You weren't concerned then."

"Well, we've always trusted you to—"

"Do my own thing?" Chase cut in. "Know my own mind? Live my life without any affection or support?"

His interruption was followed by silence. Chase didn't know

whether she was really considering his words or only processing his rudeness.

He wasn't sure it mattered much either way.

"I'm dating a man named Killian Burke," Chase told her, a little more calmly. "He's a professor with a prestigious reputation, if that kind of thing is what you're most worried about. We're very happy."

Killian had been mixing something in a bowl, giving Chase the illusion of privacy while remaining close for support, but now he came over and pressed a hand to Chase's shoulder again. Chase leaned into it shamelessly.

His mother cleared her throat. "I'm not sure if your father and I can continue to fund—"

Chase interrupted again. He was really on a roll acting like a brat. Killian would never let this kind of sass fly normally. "That's fine if you cut me off. Killian has already offered to support me financially." That felt like a half-truth, since he and Killian had never formally discussed it, but Chase already knew in his bones that Killian would do it if he asked. "And if I run into any of dad's business partners here in Phoenix, I'm sure they'd be delighted to know I'm a kept sugar baby."

There was a quiet huff of surprised laughter behind him, right in time with his mother's harsh puff of breath. "Well, of course we'd never cut off funds for your schooling, Chase." His mother let out a mirthless laugh. "We're not *monsters*, darling."

No, they weren't. But they were cold and distant and more concerned with their reputation than his happiness, and that had done its own damage.

Chase had gotten what he'd needed, and he'd had enough for now. "I'll see you at Christmas. I'll be bringing my boyfriend, if he's available."

His mother made a noise of assent—or possibly of horror,

Chase wasn't listening closely enough to tell—and Chase hung up the phone.

He stared at the blank screen for a moment. Killian was still gripping Chase's shoulder, massaging the tense muscles there. For once, his pheromones were under tight control—Chase couldn't read into them at all.

Chase sighed, placing the phone face down. "That was pointless, wasn't it?"

"It wasn't," Killian told him firmly. "You said your piece, and now you know you have financial support." He must have been able to hear Chase's mother through the phone, or maybe he'd picked up enough from context cues. "You're not ready to cut them off entirely. That's not a flaw."

Killian sat down in the chair next to Chase, turning to the side to face him completely. Chase could smell bacon in the oven, and Killian had a dusting of flour on his wrist. His dark-blue gaze bore into Chase's, his expression as unreadable as his pheromones.

Eventually Killian spoke, "I'm not particularly close to my parents."

"So you've said."

"But we're not at odds, either, and I already know they'll adore you. You've a sweetness about you, underneath that poised exterior of yours. You'll let them coddle you like I never would. We can go to them for Thanksgiving next year. My mother will try to feed you to death, and my father will give you all the boring, pointless life advice you don't need."

There was that ache again, the dull pain of Killian giving Chase something so deeply needed it hurt to receive it. "That sounds really nice," Chase told him, the only response he could come up with. He meant every word.

"I thought it might." Killian's fingers circled Chase's wrist, and he tugged until Chase rose from his own seat and ended up in

Killian's lap, Killian's arm around his waist. "Drink your orange juice. Your hands are shaking."

Chase grabbed his glass and chugged it down, suddenly unbearably thirsty. He sucked in a breath when he was done, sinking back against Killian's broad chest. "I love you, you know. Have I told you that yet?"

The ensuing wave of Killian's pheromones was so overwhelming it knocked the air out of Chase's lungs, but somehow Killian's voice was steady above him. "You haven't." There was a pause. "Will it scare you off if I tell you I love you too?"

Chase rested his head on Killian's shoulder. "No. It hurts a little, but it's a good hurt." Chase let his eyes fall closed as he asked, "You want to meet my friends? Officially?"

Killian's answer was immediate. "Yes."

"There's going to be an end-of-year pool party at Eli's. To celebrate making it through finals."

"Ah," Killian said mildly.

"Your pheromones are really intense right now."

Killian cleared his throat. "I'd be ... pleased to attend."

He'd really hated Chase going without him that one time, hadn't he?

"Obsessed," Chase said, nuzzling a little into Killian's neck.

"Horribly so. Let me finish our breakfast."

But Killian didn't loosen his grip on Chase's waist, and neither of them made any move to get up. They sat there together in the kitchen. Very tired. A little raw. And apparently in love.

25

Killian

Killian had never been in such a good mood during finals week. He was practically smug with it, all the usual annoyances rolling off his back like the inconsequential nonsense they were.

He was responding via email to a student who, in this very last week of class, was requesting extra assignments to make up a grade they'd been allowing to languish for months—ignoring all the generous opportunities for extra credit Killian had already provided—and Killian was doing it with a smile.

Not that he was actually allowing any extra assignments—the student would have to live with the grade he'd earned—but still, Killian wasn't growling at his computer.

The lasts of his tests had already been administered, all assignments were either turned in or past the acceptance deadline, and Killian was finally free. And sure, he had two weeks of grading and pointless, obnoxious staff meetings before it was officially summer break for him, but Killian still had his first summer event tonight. Friday night.

A pool party at Eli's.

The baby alphas had apparently been unable to wait for the weekend, too eager to celebrate being done with all their exams. And it was hot enough already that it would be a relief to start things off in the late afternoon and continue well into the night, avoiding the crushing heat of the peak afternoon sun.

And as it was now 3:59 p.m., Killian gathered his laptop and placed it in his briefcase, standing to leave.

He would stop at home quickly to change, and then he'd meet Chase at Eli Miller's house. Apparently Chase had heard Eli was stressing over getting ready for guests and also tying up the loose ends of what had been a hectic semester, and Killian's responsible beta had offered to go over early with Noah and get everything set up, as neither of them had any Friday exams to stress over.

Killian didn't begrudge Chase the task. Because unlike Chase's awful fucking family, Chase's friends knew how to appreciate how good and thoughtful he was. At least as much as young men in their early twenties were capable of appreciating such things.

And because while they may not have been arriving together, he and Chase would still *be* there together. As a couple. Officially and publicly and in front of the few other humans to whom Chase had already given his heart.

Killian found himself grinning as he exited his building into the arid desert heat of the afternoon. He was distracted enough that he was caught by surprise when a floppy-hatted omega torpedo barreled into him and away again without so much as a word, completely oblivious to Killian's gut-punched, "Oomph," at the impact.

Killian rubbed at his side as he watched Professor Thomas hurry along down the path, completely unaware that he'd almost knocked Killian into the pathway shrubbery.

"Don't take it personal," a deep voice drawled. "He never notices anyone."

Killian looked to the left to see an unfamiliar alpha seated on the edge of one of the university's planters. He was an intimidating specimen, tall and broad, with sandy blond hair and tattoos up to his chin. He was wearing worn jeans and work boots and a tee that was faded enough to rival one of Chase's.

In short, he looked like a ruffian, and he smelled like motor oil and ozone. Judging from the splotches on his jeans, he came by the former honestly. The latter must have been his pheromones, which maybe rivaled Killian's in intensity.

"I'm aware," Killian said shortly, his hackles up in some instinctual standoff against another potentially dominant alpha. "I know Professor Thomas already."

The omega scientist occasionally consulted with Killian whenever he came across a tricky bit of statistics in his research, his questions and explanations often arriving uninvited and at great length.

Killian had learned more about lizard mating practices in his tenure here than he'd ever wished to, thanks to that man.

Killian didn't mind as much as he might have, mainly because Professor Thomas was never offended when Killian reached his limit and walked away without a word.

The strange alpha was still watching Professor Thomas rush down the path. "Even blasted him with my pheromones once, just to see," he murmured, quietly enough that Killian wasn't sure if the words were meant for him or not. "Not even a twitch."

That was ... inappropriate, to say the least. The pheromone version of catcalling, and this guy had done it to a respected, tenured professor.

Killian took a closer look at the stranger. He was older than the usual students, definitely mid- to late thirties, maybe even early forties. And he wasn't a professor; Killian knew that much.

Killian let his own pheromones unfurl enough to make a statement, leather brushing up against electrical currents. His voice was cold as ice when he asked, letting the words drip with disdain, "Excuse me, but are you *employed* here?"

Killian doubted it—the man wasn't wearing a uniform or a name tag—but if he was, he should probably be looked into.

But the alpha only flashed Killian an amused grin and stood lazily, wandering down the path in the same direction as Professor Thomas without sparing Killian another glance.

Ah, fuck. Was this something Killian had to deal with?

But no, it was none of his business. Besides, Professor Thomas had been rushing in the direction of the biosciences building. And while the man was petite and scatter-brained perhaps to a fault, he had an extraordinarily devoted group of grad students who studied under him. Killian had been subjected to their offended glares more than once when he'd failed to afford Professor Thomas the proper respect (not that Thomas had noticed). If they thought this alpha was up to no good, they'd have campus security called within seconds.

Killian let the incident drop from his mind as inconsequential and strode in the opposite direction.

He had a social engagement to prepare for.

———

THE NEIGHBORHOOD ELI lived in was closer to campus than Killian's—the kind where every house had stucco walls around its property, and presumably its own pool to match.

Killian hummed thoughtfully as he took stock. When he'd bought his home, he'd preferred having a little distance between himself and campus, despite the annoyance of a commute. But maybe Chase would like his own pool?

Although, Killian *could* add one to his own backyard. There was room.

But it was equally likely Chase might need to relocate for grad school—Killian had done his research, and becoming a licensed therapist required a master's—so perhaps Killian should table any real estate purchases or major home renovations until Chase had decided on where he might like to go.

Killian was arriving later than he'd planned, thanks to an unwelcome phone call from a colleague asking his advice on managing a tricky situation with a student. There were a few cars outside Eli's house already, and it seemed likely everyone had arrived before him.

Eli answered the door when Killian rang the bell, and it was vaguely unsettling seeing the tidy omega professor in swim trunks and a T-shirt. Judging by the way Eli blinked up at Killian, he might have felt the same about seeing Killian in swim trunks and an unbuttoned short-sleeve shirt that bared his chest.

But then Eli broke into a smile, a little shy but nonetheless welcoming. "Professor Burke. I hear congratulations are in order."

Killian arched a brow. "You know we have to be on a first-name basis now."

The baby alpha Killian hadn't officially met yet came in behind Eli, all broad shoulders and loose blond curls. He slung an arm around Eli, grinning at Killian like they were old friends. "Hi. I'm Noah."

Maybe it should have looked strange, this younger alpha draped over an older omega Killian had only ever seen act professionally before. But there was nothing but ease and affection between the two of them, and their pheromones mingled pleasantly.

Killian had the sudden, overwhelming urge to see his beta.

"Is Chase inside already?"

Killian already knew he was, and maybe he was being rude, but Noah's grin only widened. "In the kitchen."

He and Eli stepped back in unison to let Killian through.

The single-story house's floor plan wasn't complex, and Killian made his way directly to the kitchen.

And there was Chase, standing at the counter next to Spencer. He was in front of a cutting board. Holding a knife.

Killian couldn't help but tease. "Are you actually cooking?"

Chase looked up from his task, breaking into a smile so relaxed and pleased that it made Killian's chest ache. "I'm cutting fruit for a fruit salad. Does that count?"

Killian smirked at him. "And here I was fearing it would be all Jell-O shots and overcooked hamburgers."

Spencer cackled. "I'm telling Eli you thought he was serving Jell-O shots to his esteemed guests."

Chase just kept smiling. He was shirtless, his shoulders already a little darker than earlier from whatever sun he'd gotten.

Killian wanted to kiss him. Aggressively so. But Spencer was giving him an obnoxiously knowing look, so Killian made do with walking over and pressing a chaste peck to Chase's cheek. "I've brought corn for the grill. And extra beer. As instructed."

"Thank you." Chase turned his head, pressing a kiss to Killian's lips after all, completely ignoring Spencer's delighted hoot. He tossed the watermelon he'd been chopping into a large bowl and took it off the counter, grabbing Killian's hand. "Come on. The cooler and everyone else are already out back."

Everyone else turned out to be Noah's younger brother and his surly, tattooed friend, as well as Eli's alpha sister and her omega wife. Eli and Noah had already joined the others, sitting on the steps at the shallow end of the pool, which was small and already crowded with floaties that Killian could only imagine the younger contingent had brought with them.

Chase deposited Killian's offerings into a large cooler and then led Killian to a lounger in the shade. Killian shrugged his shirt off the rest of the way, pleased with the undeniable flush that rose on Chase's cheeks with the move.

"Whoa," Spencer's voice cut in, closer than he'd been a second before. "I've never seen Chase, like, lust after someone before." He came up behind Chase, fighting to wrap a hand over Chase's face while Chase tried to duck the intrusion. "Cover your eyes, Chasey!"

The altercation ended with them both in the deep end of the pool, each fighting to get the other underwater. And somehow that quickly morphed into Noah and his younger brother Ash joining them, breaking into teams for chicken fights while the surly friend followed it all with an intense gaze.

So not Jell-O and dry hamburgers, but definite elements of youth.

Killian sat back on the lounger and watched, occasionally sharing amused glances with Eli. Killian would make an effort to socialize more in depth after a beer or two, but no one was pressuring him at the moment, and he was content watching Chase enjoy himself.

Any jealousy Killian had once held toward Chase's friends was long gone. They were official now. Chase was *his*, and Killian had no doubts about his beta's loyalty.

But while Killian had felt like he knew the boy inside and out, this was a side to him Killian hadn't had the pleasure to witness before today: the way Chase fit with his chosen family.

And he *did* fit; that was easy to see. Spencer may have been louder, and Noah was maybe more naturally magnetic—one of those golden alphas people gravitated toward without thinking—but Chase was a fixed point the other two kept returning to, coming to him for backup or affirmation over and over, drawn to his steady warmth like flowers to sunlight.

Killian couldn't help considering his own two closest friends, and how they might fit if Chase wanted to host a gathering. Killian thought they might actually fit quite nicely.

Devon and Prince had begged to come tonight, but Killian had refused. He wasn't letting them get up to any mischief on Killian's first official meeting with Chase's friends. They'd get their turn in time, after Killian had already established himself as a suitable partner.

Was Killian overthinking it? Possibly. But overthinking was better than underthinking—it meant he wouldn't fuck it up.

Eventually Chase tired of roughhousing and—wet and dripping—came over to Killian's lounger. "Make room?"

Killian shook his head. Instead, he grabbed Chase's wrist, drawing him down to lie between Killian's legs as they did at home. Chase melted into him immediately, setting his head on Killian's chest, his acquiescence soothing any leftover nerves Killian might have held. They murmured together while everyone else pretended not to watch them, some (Noah) having more success with the subterfuge than others (Spencer).

"Did I leave you alone for too long?" Chase asked quietly.

"I was enjoying the show," Killian told him, tracing his fingers over Chase's cool, damp shoulder. "And you? Are you content, sweet boy?"

"Yeah." Chase let out a happy sigh. "I wished you were here last time. And now you are."

That was so unexpectedly sweet that Killian could only press a kiss to Chase's wet hair, words escaping him for once.

There was a loud, yodeling yell, and a splash from the pool. Spencer had tackled the surly one into the water, and Ash was hollering his approval.

Chase rose just high enough to whisper in Killian's ear, "Also, you were right. Spencer and Ash hid Jell-O shots in the back of the fridge."

Killian startled himself with the loudness of his laughter. He buried his face in Chase's neck to muffle it, then reluctantly pulled them both to standing. "All right. Where's this grill? We're going to need to feed you all if we want to make it out of this night alive."

26

Chase

After only a moment of hesitation, Chase entered Killian's office without knocking.

It felt oddly wrong to ignore the proprieties on campus, but Killian already knew Chase was coming. And the semester was over, so it wasn't like there were any students looking for office hours.

And they were boyfriends, goddamn it. Chase was allowed to not knock.

The building had been quiet when he'd walked through—Chase hadn't seen a single other person. But Killian seemed to have an aversion to working from home, even when his presence wasn't required on campus, so he was finishing the last of his grading in his office.

Killian barely glanced up at Chase's arrival, although his lips twitched into a small smile. Oddly enough, that lack of reaction warmed Chase's chest. It felt significant, that they were so sure of their continued presences in each other's lives that they could stand to be distracted every now and again. And yet Chase never felt ignored. If he needed Killian to pay attention, his alpha would. Immediately.

"Just about done," Killian told him after a moment, still typing away.

Chase came up behind his desk. Killian was entering his grades in the system. He was done with the worst of it, then.

And since he was right there, Chase began massaging Killian's neck, gratified by Killian's soft, pleased moan. Chase didn't do this very often—it was always Killian stroking or petting Chase, not the other way around—but it kind of felt good to dig his hands into those solid muscles.

Maybe Chase should insist upon it more. Or ask Killian to insist.

Chase could imagine that perfectly: Killian stripping naked and sprawling on the bed, ordering Chase to service him. To knead his muscles and massage that muscular ass. Maybe he'd even tell Chase to put his mouth to work, to tongue Killian's hole while his body was loose and pliant from Chase's dutiful ministrations.

Fuck. Chase was getting himself hard.

He cleared his throat, digging his thumbs into the base of Killian's neck.

Killian let out an amused noise as he tapped away. "What are you thinking about back there, sweet boy?"

Jesus. Did Killian really know how to distinguish Chase's horny throat clearings from the rest of them? It wasn't like Chase had pheromones to give himself away.

"How was grading?" Chase asked.

"Tedious." Killian hit a few final keys with obvious satisfaction, then grabbed Chase's wrist and pulled him around and into his lap, scooting his chair back from the desk to make room.

And he was apparently not fooled by the change of subject,

because he immediately cupped Chase's hard cock through his joggers, nuzzling his nose into Chase's neck. "Mm. Did you come here to distract me?"

It was a ridiculous question. Killian had told him to come. "We're supposed to go to lunch," Chase reminded him.

"Fuck lunch." Killian's other hand wandered to Chase's lower back, dipping under his waistband to cup his ass. "I'm hungry for something else."

The words were cheesy as hell, and yet they had heat pooling in Chase's belly. Or maybe that was the rough warmth of Killian's palm on his ass. "Killian, we're at school."

Killian paused his groping, though he didn't remove his hand entirely. He leaned back far enough to look Chase in the eyes. "Do you know how rare it is for you to say my name?"

Chase kind of did, since Killian hadn't known he'd been referring to him as Burke for the entire beginning of their relationship. But did Killian mind?

"Should I say it more often?" Chase asked.

"No. I like the rarity." Something hard rubbed up against Chase's ass as Killian shifted his hips, revealing just how much the alpha liked it. "Goes straight to my cock." His hands began their teasing again as he nuzzled Chase's ear and murmured, "But I'm about to fuck you open, so you should probably call me Alpha, shouldn't you, baby boy?"

Chase looked back to the door, which he definitely hadn't locked. He was squirming for real now, trying to escape Killian's determined clutches. Or maybe to sink into them further. Chase wasn't exactly sure. "Not here."

Killian clucked his tongue in false sympathy. "Oh, sweet boy. It wasn't a request." He lifted Chase by the hips, moving him to his feet. "Hands on the desk."

And of course Chase's dumb, horny body moved before his brain could reason with it. He had his hands on the desk in an instant, his ass pushed out in a way he definitely hadn't given it permission to do.

And Killian took immediate advantage, tugging Chase's joggers and underwear down to his knees, pushing Chase's legs open as wide as the fabric would allow.

Chase couldn't help glancing at the door again.

"Would you feel better if I locked it?" Killian asked.

Chase nodded with relief. "Yes."

Killian's hand snaked around to fondle Chase's cock, still completely hard, the traitor. "Too bad. Color?"

"Oh fuck." Chase thought it over. He could say yellow, take a pause and lock the door before they started up again. Killian would never be angry or disappointed with him for something like that. But the risk was doing something to Chase, that heavy heat warming him from the inside out. And he trusted Killian not to let anything bad happen to him.

Even an obsessive, horny-as-fuck Killian would always protect him.

"Green."

Killian let out a low hum of approval, and then he pulled one of his desk drawers open, grabbing something from it. Two seconds later, slicked-up fingers were at Chase's ass.

Chase shook his head. "You do *not* have lube in your desk drawer. What a perv."

He was rewarded with the sharp sting of Killian's palm smacking his ass. "Such sass today."

And then he was opening Chase up, his fingers steady and sure, although his pheromones had deepened, and Chase could feel that massive erection at his hip. Killian certainly wasn't unaffected by what was going on.

"You know," Killian said, his tone almost conversational as he twisted two fingers inside Chase. "I've always liked a bit of kink, but I never really considered myself a pervert. Not until you."

"So it's my— *Ungh.*" Chase swallowed a moan as Killian added a third finger. He wasn't used to keeping his sounds contained, not when Killian always ate them the fuck up. "My fault?"

Killian didn't bother answering him at first, too busy notching that cockhead to Chase's entrance, sliding into him with a satisfied grunt. His voice was lower and rougher when he finally spoke, his girth stretching Chase's inner walls. "The things I want to do to you. I'd have you sitting on my lap, stuffed full of my cock while I held office hours, if I thought I could bear someone else seeing you without losing my mind."

And of course the only answer Chase could give was a slutty moan he only barely kept down to a decent level.

Killian covered Chase's hands with his own, and then he was driving into him, fast and deep. There was no slow build or teasing. Maybe he was more conscious of the unlocked door than he let on.

Fuck, it felt good. Chase was biting his lip so hard it was going to bleed, trying to keep himself from keening at the fullness.

Killian kissed his shoulder, mouthing at the bit of skin revealed by Chase's loose neckline. "So tense, sweet boy. Relax. The building's deserted."

"I'm not—" A whimper escaped Chase's lips, and he had to swallow hard before he could speak again. "Not very good at keeping quiet."

Killian's laugh was downright mean. "I know. That's what makes this fun."

Chase would have liked to beg to differ, but he didn't really have a leg to stand on, did he? Not when his cock was a rod of fucking steel, the discomfort bubbling together with the arousal in his belly to make everything all the more heightened.

Killian's weight was heavy enough against him that it was a struggle for Chase to keep his hands in place—not like they were doing anything to hold him up, anyway. But his alpha had said hands on the desk, so Chase's hands stayed on the desk.

Chase was overly conscious of every sensation. The harsh brush of Killian's leg hair. The low grunts sounding from behind him. The hard press of the desk against his hips. It was all in sharp focus, even as everything else in Chase's brain grew fuzzier.

"You're doing so well, baby," Killian crooned. "Taking me like you always do. Like you were made for it. I love it. Love the way you submit to me. And I'm going to love leaving here with my cum in your ass. And that's what's going to happen, isn't it? You're going to milk me dry because you're fucking perfect."

It was too much. Chase was always weak for Killian's praise. And when Killian was driving into him, that thick cock of his hitting Chase's sweet spot with every thrust?

Chase shuddered, his moan louder than it should have been as his cock erupted over Killian's desk.

Fuck. Good thing Killian had moved his laptop. When had he even done that?

Killian growled, biting into Chase's shoulder as he pounded into him, his hips stuttering and that hot warmth filling Chase before his own tremors had ceased.

Chase stayed with his hands on the desk, trying to catch his breath. He managed not to whine as Killian withdrew his softening cock, and Killian planted a trail of kisses down his spine afterward.

There was a swipe from a tissue, and then Killian was tugging Chase's clothes back up. In less than a minute he was back in his chair, pulling Chase onto his lap again.

Fuck. Chase should probably avoid this building when school was in session. Killian was going to get them both arrested for public indecency at this point.

Killian pressed a warm kiss to Chase's neck. "You should come by the office more often."

"I was just thinking I should stay away." Chase tilted his head to give his alpha better access. "Aren't we trying to stay discreet next year?"

"I'm not particularly hopeful of managing on that front." Killian paused. "Unless you're worried about scrutiny from other students? Or even your professors? I can contain myself if need be."

Chase gave it some thought. He was trying to be more mindful these days of actually processing what he wanted when someone asked a question like that, instead of saying things were fine or that he didn't care one way or another.

But it didn't take long for him to reach his answer this time. "No, I don't really care."

Chase had good, solid friendships that mattered more than what some random students thought of him. And he was a polite, punctual student—professors could hate him, but they wouldn't have any good excuse to fuck with him.

He leaned back to catch Killian's gaze, trying not to be distracted by how fuckable the alpha looked, his hair tousled and his face glowing with the exertion of fucking Chase into the desk. "But for the sake of your job, I'd like to put in at least a little effort. Like, bare minimum, no one catching us fucking in your office." Chase arched his brows. "Just as an example."

Killian had the gall to let out a disappointed huff. "And you won't be moving in until after you graduate. This is all very taxing." But he was teasing. Chase could tell by his tone.

Still. "How did you know?"

Chase had been waiting for the right time to bring it up, the whole living situation thing. Noah had already told him he wanted to finish out school living with his friends, and Chase wouldn't have wanted to leave Spencer all on his lonesome either way.

"I assumed," Killian said lightly. "You've been with those two from the beginning."

"We'll still have plenty of sleepovers," Chase reassured him, even though Killian didn't seem to need it.

"I know. I'll be staying over tonight, if that's all right." Killian nodded to the corner, where there was a bag on the floor Chase had missed before. It was nicer than his own duffel—some sort of expensive leather—but it was still unmistakably an overnight bag.

"You're okay sleeping over at my place?" Chase didn't know why he was so surprised, other than it broke their usual pattern.

"Of course." Killian's brow furrowed. "Why wouldn't I be?"

Chase thought of Killian in his bed, thought of his sheets and pillows smelling of leather and cherry. He thought of Killian at the breakfast table with Spencer, eating cereal because that was all Chase ever had in the mornings, unless Noah was cooking. Or maybe Killian would insist on feeding them all something more substantial, or Spencer would whine at him or Noah until they conceded. Maybe Noah would have Eli over and they'd *all* be at the breakfast table, Chase's friends and their people and his boyfriend.

Killian could have never offered, and Chase wouldn't have pushed. Killian had a nice house, and he liked his solitude, and Chase understood that well enough that he would have let it be.

But Killian *was* offering. Because it would make Chase happy, and that was something Killian considered. He'd been considering it when he left the house that morning, packing a bag just on the off chance Chase would agree.

Chase cupped Killian's cheeks, rubbing his thumbs against the light stubble there, meeting those dark-blue eyes. "I really, really love you."

Killian's smile was as wide as Chase had ever seen it. "Now I'm definitely fucking you in my office more often." He ignored Chase's eye roll, pushing them both to standing. "Okay, sweet boy, who I love more than anything or anyone else, let's get you fed. Do sandwiches sound good? It's too hot for hot food."

It all sounded good. Every bit of it. Especially that "who I love more than anything or anyone else" part.

Killian gathered his belongings and led them through the door, and Chase walked through the empty halls, hand in hand with his alpha.

He thought almost idly that missing that statistics exam was the best thing he'd ever done. Because if Chase hadn't had that makeup test in Killian's office, saturated in Killian's pheromones, he'd never have gotten his first real taste of something he'd really, really wanted. Something he'd wanted so badly he hadn't even been able to recognize it as want. Chase had classified it as fascination instead, a feeling that had been intense but still safe.

Or at least he'd thought.

And if that hadn't happened—Chase's missed exam, his makeup test, his confusing fixation on an alluring professor— Chase might not be here now, loved so thoroughly and so well that it made him dizzy. The good kind of dizzy. The kind that hit a person like a fresh hit of leather and cherries.

Chase's favorite scent in the whole world. A scent he loved more than anything or anyone else.

The scent of his alpha.

EPILOGUE

Killian

The room the venue had given the newlyweds for their private time after the ceremony was small but well appointed, with a tray holding two glasses of champagne and a small selection of canapés to choose from.

Killian would have offered Chase some, but his poor husband was a little occupied.

Instead, Killian hummed his pleasure, the sound only barely rising above the sweet sounds of Chase choking as Killian tightened his hold on his hair. "Pinch my thigh if you need to."

But though Chase's hands were already resting on Killian's thighs, he kept his fingers oh so carefully straight, as if fearful Killian would interpret the slightest bend as an attempted pinch.

Chase took a frantic, messy breath through his nose, and then he relaxed the way Killian needed, letting Killian's thick cockhead slide into his throat.

Fuck, that felt amazing.

"My sweet, precious slut. You need my cock more than you

need to breathe, don't you?" Killian loosened his grip, just enough to stroke those wonderfully soft strands. "And you're sucking it so well. Your throat feels perfect, sweet boy. Swallow for me."

Chase obeyed immediately, swallowing around the head. Killian groaned at the tight constriction. Fucking. Amazing.

Killian pulled Chase back by the hair. His gorgeous beta's face was covered with tear tracks and spit, and he had that perfect, dazed look in his eyes. "Almost there, sweet boy," Killian crooned.

And then he drove back into that perfect, hot, wet mouth. Killian was too worked up at this point, could only manage small, aborted thrusts. He didn't fight it when his balls drew up tight. They were short on time. "Swallow again," he ordered. "We can't have you making a mess."

Chase let out a whimper, thrusting his hips up into the air as he swallowed desperately. Killian erupted down his throat, groaning at the relief, holding Chase's head in place until every last drop was gone.

Killian finally released his beta. Chase's suit pants were unzipped, and his erection was tenting his underwear. But he'd been a good boy and kept his hands at his sides. He looked fucking gorgeous in his disarray.

Killian tsked, eyeing the evidence of Chase's arousal. "We can't have you going out like that. What will our guests think?"

He grabbed Chase's hand and tugged him off the floor, then deftly pulled Chase's pants and underwear down and dropped to his own knees.

He wrapped his lips around Chase's cock and swallowed him down.

"Oh fuck! Fucking god!" Chase cried. And then—perfect boy that he was—he came almost immediately, barely allowing Killian to hollow his cheeks before his cum was filling Killian's mouth.

Chase chanted continual blasphemy at the ceiling as Killian swallowed every drop—he wasn't a hypocrite—and then tucked

Chase carefully back into his pants, straightening his own clothes afterward.

Chase stared down at him, his chest still heaving. "Oh fuck. You're right. How are we supposed to go back out there?"

Killian petted soothing strokes down Chase's thighs. "Relax, sweet boy. I'll get us sorted out. Here." He handed Chase a champagne glass.

When drawing up the day's schedule with the wedding planner, Killian had insisted on twenty minutes after the ceremony wherein he and Chase wouldn't be disturbed, while the rest of the guests were enjoying cocktail hour. He'd known Chase would need somewhere private and quiet to settle after the intensity of exchanging vows.

And there was one way Killian knew how to settle Chase best.

Killian wasn't sure what couples usually used this private time for. It probably wasn't meant to be a space for one groom to throat-fuck the other, but spending these allotted moments doing other-wise was wasting precious time and resources, in Killian's opinion.

It had taken him approximately thirty seconds to get his new husband on his knees.

Killian grabbed the wet wipes he'd stashed earlier and wiped Chase's face down in between sips of champagne. He then straightened his beta's hair—not that it needed much help to fall perfectly. Then lastly it was only a few more adjustments to each of their tuxes.

And voila. All done. A respectable pair of newlyweds.

Chase's eyes were perhaps a little red still, but some tears were expected on his wedding day. And his lips were—well, his lips were always delectable. Who was to say they were any more so than usual?

And they still had—Killian checked his phone—five minutes left.

Maybe he shouldn't be proud of how quickly he'd come down

his beta's throat, but so be it. It was Killian's wedding day. He was allowed to be emotional.

Killian took a seat, then set Chase on his lap. He grabbed a second glass of champagne for himself.

"I'm sorry," Chase said quietly, resting his head on Killian's shoulder.

"Whatever for?"

"I stumbled on the vows."

Killian laughed. "Because you were fighting back tears. I was too. You had me gutted, sweet boy."

Chase let out a little sigh, and Killian knew he was letting it go.

His beta had come a long way when it came to expressing himself. He was coming on three years of therapy now, though the frequency of his sessions had decreased. But Chase still often ached for reassurances, and Killian had no problem giving them to him as often as he needed.

Killian rubbed his thumb over the distinctive bite mark on Chase's neck. It was still relatively fresh, as Killian's rut had fallen close to the wedding.

He'd had the patience of a saint, waiting to bite his intended mate. But Chase's therapist had strongly suggested Chase might benefit from time—to heal and grow and pursue his path to become a therapist himself—so that he might feel on more equal footing before they bonded somewhat irrevocably.

It had been ... sensible, Killian hated to admit. And the goal had been to avoid harm to Chase, so Killian had supported the idea, ignoring his own baser instincts that would have had him biting Chase that very first rut they'd shared.

But Killian's time had finally come. Chase had finished his master's and was beginning his supervised clinical hours in a few months. They'd ended up staying in Phoenix, at least for now. Chase had chosen an online program, and his internships had been organized by his program at approved locations in the area.

And now—a ring on his finger and a bite on his neck—Chase was Killian's, even more than he had been before. And Killian belonged to him in turn. By bond and by marriage.

Killian wrapped his arm tighter around his beta's waist. "I'm so fucking proud of you."

Chase gave him a cheeky grin. "For marrying you?"

"For everything."

Instead of Chase shying away from the compliment, his grin softened. "Thank you. I'm proud of myself." And because he was still the sweetest fucking boy around, he added, "And I'm proud to be yours."

Killian couldn't resist pressing a kiss to his forehead. Chase glanced at the door. "We should probably get back out there, huh? You swear I look okay? You couldn't have waited to get me on my knees until after the professional photos were taken?"

Killian didn't dignify that last question with an answer. "There are no words for how you look. Prince has been lamenting all evening over not finding you first."

Chase rose to standing, setting his glass on the tray. "He's just messing with you. Besides, you didn't find me. *I* found *you*."

Killian couldn't argue with that. So he didn't. He followed his husband out the door to join their guests.

THE WEDDING GUESTS were milling about the garden, drinking their cocktails. Killian could hear the bright cackle of Spencer's laughter above the polite conversation of everyone else.

Killian would have loved to grab one of those cocktails himself, but they had photos to take first.

Family photos.

And the family in question might have been part of the reason Killian had needed to get a bit of ... alpha aggression out.

A reason besides Chase looking so immensely fuckable in his tux.

Chase's parents were here.

Killian had known they would be, and he'd even understood that Chase needed to invite them. Chase didn't expect much from them these days—he'd worked with his therapist quite a bit on that—but he would most likely never be the kind to cut off contact completely, not unless his parents switched coldness for outright cruelty.

Said parents were standing off to the side by the veranda, looking distinctly uncomfortable in their bubble of two.

Chase smiled at them as he and Killian approached, and Killian worked to turn his expression into something that wasn't a grimace. "Mom. Dad. Are you ready?"

Chase's mother gave him a tight twist of lips that was perhaps supposed to be a smile of her own. "We are."

Killian wrapped a hand around the back of Chase's neck, stroking the bite mark there. The father's gaze darted to the motion, and Killian bared his teeth in what could have passed for the semblance of a smile.

That's right. He's mine now.

Killian squeezed Chase's nape. "Will you let the photographer know we're ready? He's probably with the catering lead."

Chase didn't quite roll his eyes, but it was a close thing. "The photographer whose name is Terrance? And the catering lead, Amanda?"

Killian shrugged, and Chase whirled away, but not quickly enough to hide his fond grin.

It was nice when one's husband appreciated one's quirks. Killian never had to learn names anymore—not that he'd ever bothered to before—because Chase was always getting everyone's life stories left and right.

And then Killian was left with two people he detested.

"Lovely location," Chase's mother drawled.

But Killian had no interest in small talk, and there wasn't time for it anyway. He tucked his hands into his suit pockets. "If I had my way, you wouldn't be here right now."

Chase's father blustered. "I beg your—"

"But you are." Killian raised his voice to be heard over the interruption, and the father immediately backed down. Of course he did. He was a complete coward when it came to his reputation, and he wouldn't be caught arguing with his son's groom at his son's wedding. "Because the two of you somehow raised, without a scrap of care or affection, a wonderful, dutiful son, who only ever aims to please, and he wanted you here. So this is how it's going to go. You are going to pose for photos. You are going to look goddamn *delighted* in every single one. You are going to hug your son afterward and ask him no fewer than three personal questions: about his honeymoon plans, his impending clinical hours, take your fucking pick. And you are going to bow out politely after dinner so we can enjoy the rest of the evening without a reminder of the people who failed Chase so horribly. Does that sound like a plan?"

It was the mother who spoke this time. "I—"

"The question was rhetorical."

Chase reappeared before either of them could attempt to speak their minds, and Killian wrapped an arm around his husband's waist. "Your mother was just commenting on the loveliness of the venue."

Chase beamed. "Isn't it great? Devon found it for us."

Killian doubted Chase's parents remembered who the hell Devon was, but they were wise enough not to reveal it.

"Terrance said groom and groom are first," Chase told him.

"Perfect." And Killian led Chase away from the parents without another word. He'd said his piece, at least for the moment.

And the two of them knew by now that Killian had money and connections of his own in this town—they'd behave.

And Killian's own parents were waiting on the other side of the veranda, arms already open to embrace Chase, who they loved like ... well, like a much more lovable son.

And after photos and dinner and speeches, the family part of the evening would be over, and it would be time to dance and revel with their devoted friends, who had never once let either of them down.

And none of that fucking mattered anyway, because the most important person of all was already at Killian's side, where he would stay for the remainder of the wedding celebration. Loved, coveted, and protected.

Killian grinned, bright and fierce and proud, as Chase leaned into him, trusting Killian to guide them where they needed to go.

Secure in Killian's arms.

Just as he would be for the rest of the night.

Just as he would be for the rest of their lives.

THE END.

AUTHOR'S NOTE

Thank you so much for reading Hot for Teacher! I'm grateful to you all for joining me on this omegaverse journey.

I'm usually incapable of picking favorites when it comes to my couples—they all give me joy and frustration in equal measure—but I can admit to having a major soft spot for Chase and Killian. Their dynamic unfolded so easily, and so clearly, and it gave me such pleasure to write. I love them both an absurd amount, and I love them together even more.

A big thank you to Charity and my early Patreon readers for hyping these two up. Your comments and enthusiasm added so much joy to the process!

What's Next?

Spencer is getting his HEA! I'm so excited to give this hot mess everything he doesn't know he wants and needs. His book will be

MMM (with a certain codependent undergrad duo) because honestly, it takes more than one boyfriend to handle him.

If you're too impatient to wait, you can read WIP chapters as I write them on Patreon.

If you want to stay in the know, you can sign up for my newsletter for updates and news on upcoming releases. And I can always be reached by email if you just want to say howdy. I love, love, love hearing from my readers!

graebryanauthor@gmail.com

ALSO BY GRAE BRYAN

Vampire's Mate Series

Roman (Book One) – Danny and Roman

Soren (Book Two) – Gabe and Soren

Lucien (Book Three) – Jamie and Lucien

Johann (Book Four) – Alexei and Jay

Wolfgang (Book Five) – Eric and Wolfe

Colin (Book Six) — Colin, Fox, and Dane

Cassian (A Vampire's Mate Novella) – Blake and Cass

Demon Bound Series

Wreaking Havoc (Book One) — Sascha and Kai

Inviting Bedlam (Book Two) — Ivan and Nix

Calling Chaos (Book Three) — Cooper and Chaos

Unleashing Mayhem (Book Four) — Matty and Nightmare

Novellas

An Unwitting Bargain - Benny and Helio

Contemporary Omegaverse

Overeager (Extra Credit, Book One) - Noah and Eli

Hot for Teacher (Extra Credit, Book Two) - Chase and Killian

ABOUT THE AUTHOR

Grae Bryan has been reading romance since she was far too young to know any better. Her love for love stories spans all genres, and there's nothing she finds more exciting than all the fictional worlds she has yet to explore.

She lives in Arizona with her family, who graciously share space with all the imaginary men in her head. When not writing or daydreaming or parenting wild children, she can generally be found reading more than is healthy, walking her monster-dog, or cuddling her demon-cat. She loves all things gothic, cozy, lovely, or strange.

Find her online: graebryan.com
    Patreon: patreon.com/GraeBryan
    Facebook: @GraeBryanAuthor
    Instagram: @authorgraebryan
    Sign up for her newsletter: graebryan.com/contact
    Join her Facebook reader group: Grae Bryan's Reader Den

www.ingramcontent.com/pod-product-compliance
Lightning Source LLC
Chambersburg PA
CBHW020636260626
47157CB00008B/2766